1

The rope creaked as it swung with the barely perceptible motion of the boat. There wasn't much swell in the marina, despite the winds of the past two days. Down below in the main saloon of the luxury cruiser, the light might even have been called cosy. Someone had decided to go with traditional materials, overlaying the hi-tech which was undoubtedly there under every surface, so there was the subtle gleam of bronze at the portholes and the lushness of dark red leather and upholstered cushions on the soft-looking bench seats. There was even enough headroom for all three of us, although the shoes of the man hanging from the ringbolt in the deckhead cleared the carpet by no more than a few centimetres.

A few centimetres were all it had needed. He was the burden which stretched the new white rope taut.

I don't like death. I'd left Midway three weeks ago because I'd had enough of it. I didn't want to be here, staring at the livid face of a man I'd never seen alive while one I'd never wanted to see again watched me.

"Suicide?"

That made it five times now that Morgan Vinci had spoken directly to me. If he was asking, not just thinking aloud. There was a note on the chart table. Hand-written: old-fashioned. The bench seat was only a long step away from the dangling feet. The rest of the cabin was neat. Ordered. Nothing out of place. *He put his household in order, and hanged himself.* "How would I know?"

2

How would I know anything? Twenty-four hours before, I had been at sea expecting my next landfall to be somewhere with a French or Spanish accent, plenty of sun and a good supply of wine. My only problem had been trying to ignore the nagging guilt left by a message from home I'd chosen to ignore. Now, thanks to bad weather and a damaged drive, I was back in Midway. I had limped in last night, just before the August light failed, sneaking through the marina lock behind a hi-powered racer which was more flash than stamina and just ahead of a very new cruiser whose owner looked almost as new. He was clearly worried that every touch on the wheel might prove catastrophic. For such sailors are pontoon edges made to be yielding. No need to alienate the paying customer.

I wasn't paying. Free berthing and water rights for my barge were the only good things to come out of my recent clash with the Vincis, the Family who owned the Port along with large slices of the rest of the world which I didn't want to know anything about. Where you have Families – which is what the great corporations that run EuroGov these days like to call themselves – you have power, and corruption. Experience hasn't done anything to change my mind on that.

If I could have afforded it, I would have chosen any port but Midway, the port on the fiercely tidal river creeping into the middle of the sprawl which was the megacity formed by Sutton and Pompey. Unfortunately, not only was the price right but it was also the nearest downwind harbour for *The Flying Pig* after the night's blow and

A Thankless Child

Penny Deacon

CREME DE LA CRIME

First published in 2005
by Crème de la Crime.
Crème de la Crime Ltd, PO Box 523, Chesterfield,
Derbyshire S40 9AT

Typesetting by Yvette Warren
Cover design by Yvette Warren
Front cover photography by Zefa Visual Media UK
www.zefaimages.com

Printed and bound in England by Biddles Ltd, www.biddles.co.uk

ISBN 0-9547634-8-3

A CIP catalogue reference for this book is available from the
British Library

www.cremedelacrime.com

About the author

Penny Deacon was born in Scotland, christened in Dorset
and partly educated in Sri Lanka. She spent ten years living
on a yacht, and has taught sailing for a living. Her first
published novels were romance, but she finds crime more
rewarding. Humility, she promises, will return.

Thanks to Douglas Hill, the best kind of editor.

an ill-advised jibe had left me with a barely functioning drive, a torn mainsail, and a lot of broken crockery. Including my favourite mug. The fact that I had fled Midway swearing not to come back this year – if ever – was just one more annoyance to add to the list. I'd meant to moor, then crash. Look at the damage tomorrow. The *Pig* was safe. She wasn't going to sink under me and I wasn't going to drown, or be rescued and homeless. None of the Bad Things which had been running through my mind like a horror holo without an off-switch was going to happen. I could deal with minor details, like the lack of credit for repairs, in the morning.

Like all my plans lately, this one didn't work out. I'd no sooner finished coiling the end of the last mooring warp on my bedraggled decks than I was hailed from the opposite pontoon.

"Barge, ahoy!" Words like *ahoy* make me grit my teeth. I looked up, not quite snarling. The voice had come from the cruiser which had docked just after me. The owner of the voice wore the sort of expression which goes with relief at having accomplished something he'd feared would end in disaster. "Come and have a drink!" Sounded like he intended to celebrate the fact that his boat's auto-drive and park had lived up to its builder's claims.

I could have said no. Instead, I tried to remember I had to live alongside these people for the next couple of weeks. Besides, he wasn't the only one who'd earned his drink. I waved back.

"Thanks. Be along in twenty."

Long enough for a quick shower and a change into clothes which weren't rank and stiff with salt water.

The cruiser was called *The Happy Family*. It almost made me change my mind, but I hadn't seen any sign of children and it would be rude or cowardly, or both, to back out now, so I stepped on board.

She had all the modern aids to easy sailing which always broke down when I approached. Everything automated. And, from what I had seen earlier, in working order. I didn't have a chance to explore as the guy who'd called me over was on the afterdeck. It was big enough for two small round tables and several soft chairs.

"Hi. I'm Stephen." He was middle height, brownish hair, paleish skin. His smile was open and friendly. "This is Amanda."

She was altogether more focused. Same pale skin but sharper features: good bones or good sculpting. Hard to tell. Her smile was cooler, but she gestured to a cabinet which looked as though it dispensed every drink a guest could dream up.

"Hi. What would you like?"

My dreams don't go much beyond red wine.

"Thanks. Red wine if you have it." As if they wouldn't. "I'm Humility."

The pause I'd got used to was barely detectable. The name says I'm one of those weird people from a Puritan Community somewhere in the primitive west country. The questions about what I was doing on a barge in one of the most expensive marina developments on the south coast had to be swallowed before normal good manners and respect for privacy could continue. It wasn't the first time I'd been glad of the privacy conventions: the answers were either too complicated or too personal. And I was still asking myself what, storm damage apart, I was doing here.

With all that the cabinet had to offer, she was drinking water. He had beer. Nice, normal drinks that didn't fizz or offer kaleidoscope colours or promise mildly erotic hallucinations. I could be social. We made small talk about boats – theirs was as new as I'd guessed. They'd come all the way round – at least five miles – from Pompey and the cruiser had coped well with the rough weather. I smiled supportively and admitted that my barge had come a little further. "As you can tell from the state she's in."

They looked across in the fading light and probably couldn't see much. I wondered if they could tell damage from the usual wear and tear of a passage in full daylight.

"You're here for the Opening," Amanda assumed.

The Opening was exactly what I'd planned to avoid: Morgan Vinci's celebration of his new Port development. Corporate entertainment on a grand scale with several eyes on the media and publicity and scoring points over the other Families. I felt my smile become fixed.

"Looks like it." Gestured around the marina which was filling up nicely. "You know many people here?"

"Not yet." Amanda's attitude suggested that the festivities might be a good place to start some profitable networking. "There's just Andy, over there."

I looked towards the boat moored down from them. Smaller, equally new.

"Andy's our partner," Stephen explained. "You'll like him. He's usually good fun to have around but he didn't enjoy the rough trip here so he said he'd spend the evening alone. I'm sure you'll meet him soon."

It sounded as though I wouldn't be allowed to escape. Although perhaps, when they realised I wasn't linked to any network which could benefit them, their hospitable enthusiasm would relent.

"I'm sure I will," I agreed. "You're in business together?" They'd given me the opening, I might as well take it.

"Yes. We're all three directors of a ferry company. Ardco. Just started up less than a year ago." He smiled. The proud parent.

"Brave of you – up against the big two." Both Family-run and dominating the business. They'd wipe the upstart at the first sign of inroads into their profit margins. But small ferry companies could survive for a while. Very profitably. Although the profits were seldom made on the goods declared on the manifest.

Amanda's smile was unworried by the thought of competition. "We're not big enough to upset anyone yet. Ardco's just a small firm, dealing in perishables and fragile cargoes. Mostly stuff the big companies wouldn't find profitable. We're getting by."

Judging by their boat, they certainly were.

I smiled and talked and admired their boat and their enthusiasm. We had little in common but it had been kind of them to call me over. Besides, their wine was excellent. They asked a little about the *Pig*, were as baffled as most people at the thought of living on board, and agreed to visit sometime soon.

I went home and crashed with a sense of having been rewarded for behaving myself with an evening that had been more enjoyable than I'd expected.

The sleep of a labouring man is sweet.

3

Unfortunately I wasn't allowed nearly long enough to enjoy my sweet sleep.

Somewhere too soon after dawn the curtsey of the *Pig*'s hull and the sound of swearing from above had me up and out. Fast. If whoever had just tried to come aboard was persistent, he or she was about to find themselves in the water – and my visitor just might be someone I didn't want to immerse. My half-asleep instincts were unusually good. Stephen was standing on the pontoon shaking a wrist which was probably numb from the shock it had received. "Stephen?" I palmed the alarms off. I wasn't going to apologise. He might be new to boats but he must have guessed that every vessel in the marina was armed. Perhaps he'd assumed the *Pig*'s system would be as primitive as my background.

He grimaced. "I'm sorry. I didn't mean… I wasn't sure what we…"

I took my first real look at him. He was shaking, and it wasn't just the shock from my barge. "What's wrong?"

He took a breath. Steadied. "I'm sorry," he repeated but he managed to hang on for a complete sentence this time. "I, *we*, didn't know what to do. You're the only person we know here and you said you knew the Port well. We thought you might know who we could talk to."

"About what?" I gestured for him to come on board, but he shook his head.

"It's Andy. Or we think it is." The friend I hadn't met; I nodded to show I remembered. Even if he still wasn't making sense. He swallowed. "Look, could you come over to his boat? Just let us know what you think?"

It didn't seem much to ask. "Let me grab some clothes and I'm with you."

He blinked. I wondered if he'd even noticed I was wearing nothing but a ratty-looking robe. "OK."

Amanda was standing by their friend's boat. *Felicity.* I hoped it was a good omen. Amanda's lack of expression and the way her knuckles whitened on the hands clasped in front of her were not encouraging.

"What's wrong?" I still didn't know whether this was about something catastrophic or one of the automated plug-ins had developed a glitch and they'd run out of hot water. I was hoping for the latter.

"We don't know," she admitted. "We could be crazy, but we haven't seen Andy since he said goodbye yesterday evening. He said he felt rough and we laughed, because we thought he was seasick and he's the one who's always saying how much fun sailing's going to be." A smile flickered on her face.

"And now?" I prompted.

"He's not answering his phone and he's locked himself in. The screen says he's not taking calls." That was Stephen. "Andy *never* cuts off the screen."

"You think he might really be sick?" I interrupted. "You don't have his codes?"

Both shook their heads. Which meant they couldn't easily break in – not without risking damage to themselves. I thought they were probably fussing too much over someone who didn't want to be woken before he'd slept off the embarrassment of being seasick, but they clearly weren't willing to leave it. And he was their friend, after all.

Two choices. Contact Gus, the Harbour Master, or go one higher. I had good reasons not to want to do either.

Gus and I had history: he disapproved of someone he thought of as a water-gypsy who lowered the tone of his Port, and who had, by some underhand means which no one had thought to explain to him, managed to persuade the owners to grant me rights which I didn't know how to appreciate. One higher than him was the Port Officer, in overall immediate charge of the whole complex. Six weeks ago that had been Daisy, my closest friend in Sutton. Since her death I had no wish at all to get to know whoever had been pulled in to do her work.

But I knew which one would get the job done.

"You'll have to call the Port Officer," I told them. "He can authorise a break-in. If Andy's lodged his codes with the Port it should be easy." All residents were meant to lodge their codes. I never did. Confidential means keeping things to myself. But new boat owners like Andy and his friends just might be more willing to follow the rules.

4

It took a call and a long wait until someone appeared. There were stirrings on one or two other boats, and I hadn't yet had my first caf of the day. I watched the lanky man walking towards us without much enthusiasm. Watched his companion with even less.

Gus was half-trotting to keep up with his tall companion's long strides. When he saw me the expression of professional concern on his face gave way to scorn.

"I saw you were back. Should have known you'd find trouble – if your craft can't meet Port standards…" He focused on the couple beside me, managed to restore the concern. "I'm sorry if this person's given you trouble, she – "

"But she hasn't." Stephen, protesting. "She's been a real help. It's our friend we're worried about." He indicated Andy's boat while Gus's expression faded into doubt. He glanced at the man who'd come with him, who was waiting with an only slightly exaggerated assumption of patience.

He was somewhere in his mid-fifties, I guessed. Not much to look at with his grey-brown hair and faded eyes. Credit for not bothering with enhancements. The Company had obviously brought in someone with experience. He ignored Gus and looked at the three of us; a grimace creased tired eyes.

"I'm Lloyd, the Port Officer here." He was speaking to Amanda and Stephen. His eyes had sort of met mine and slid over me before they focused on the others. I wondered what he'd heard. What Gus had managed to pour out on the way down here. "I gather you have a problem?" Polite. Not bored, but not buying into anything dramatic, either. Just the right tone to make any passer-by shrug and move on. Not bad.

I listened to Amanda explaining about Andy again. Heard the touch of panic in Stephen's voice as he explained that I'd come to help. Saw Lloyd make the decision which would probably have Andy swearing at him but would stop these two clients from demanding that someone, anyone, do something. Unwritten policy rule one: always take the option which will cause least disturbance.

At least Andy had been civic-minded and notified his codes. We watched Lloyd punch them in and heard the alarms click off. Amanda moved forward but he stopped her. "I'm sorry, ma'am. I must respect your friend's privacy. I'll check with him and let him know your concern." He shut the door on her protest.

Gus took up a guard position.

Lloyd was gone too long. I found myself thinking it as the minutes passed. When he appeared his face was unreadable. He locked the door behind him. Held up a hand to stop whatever Amanda was going to say – a stormy hint in her expression said she didn't like being cut off. Twice. If he cared, Lloyd was hiding it.

"Thank you for contacting me. I'm afraid there's been an accident. I must seal the boat until we've had a chance to look further into this." Formality made his voice stilted.

"Are you saying that Andy's…?" Somehow people always wanted to avoid the word which made it real.

Gus had paled. Lloyd was nodding. "I'm afraid so. And there's no doubt. He seems to have been dead some hours. I'm very sorry for your loss, but you must let Port procedures take over now. I'll let you know as soon as we can give you more details or release your friend to his next of kin."

"That's us." Stephen's voice was raw. "He was our business partner as well as our friend. He doesn't have any relatives."

"I'm sorry. This is terribly distressing for you. I'll alert the Port Counsellor and you should contact her at any time for information or if you feel you need to talk more about this. Now, if you'll excuse me, I must contact the people who can deal with this."

I let him go. Watched Gus gobbling in his wake. Stephen and Amanda said they just wanted time alone, to take it in. To talk and grieve. I felt sick. I'd left the Port to get away from death and it had sneaked in again. I hadn't known the guy, but his friends were holding on to each other, shaken and wretched. They didn't need me around.

I walked back to the *Pig*. Pity for a couple whose week of fun and networking had been destroyed mixed with the growing need for as much caf as I could brew. I didn't want to hear the shrilling of my own screen as I stepped into the deckhouse.

5

Lloyd's face was on the screen. He couldn't have been back in his office for more than a few minutes. The sense of dread which had been growing in me since I saw his face as he came out of *Felicity*'s cabin began to solidify.

"Humility. Sorry to trouble you. Could you come up to the Port Office in the next half hour?"

It was barely a question. I wasn't sure how much he knew about the last time I'd been here, but it sounded like he wanted to involve me and I didn't feel like being involved. I was about to say I was busy when he took a step back so the screen display widened. Showed someone else in the Port Office. Morgan Vinci.

I still didn't know how I felt about Morgan. Or how he felt about me. We'd met when I was trying find out who'd killed a friend of mine and I had nearly been killed while doing so. The fact that the murderer had been Morgan's brother made things complicated. He owed me because his Family had nearly got me killed – hence the free mooring – but that didn't alter the fact that I was responsible for his brother's death. Since he also owned Midway Port, I didn't think refusal of his invitation was an option. Even though it could only mean trouble.

As I headed for the gangway leading ashore, I saw they were already having the *Felicity* towed away from the marina towards the dock by the sheds. Gus was supervising. Amanda and Stephen were staring after the boat, looking lost.

I walked over to the harbour offices and was nodded through security without having to say anything at all.

Suited me. I was in no mood for small talk. I'd known I'd have to tread this path again soon – walk though the doorway that had been staffed by a hired killer and step into the office which had been my friend's territory – but I'd thought the timing would be my choice.

Morgan nodded as I walked in. "Humility."

"Morgan."

"Something's come up. You might be able to help."

Me? Help him? I didn't actually say it aloud but he must have known what I was thinking. Morgan wasn't subtle, but he wasn't stupid.

"How?" Gratitude for a free berth wasn't going to make me stupid either. Besides, I'd earned that berth. And I did have some idea what this could be about. The word *No* was already trying to get out.

Morgan didn't let me say it. Stood. Said, "I'd like you to come with me." Not quite an order. Lloyd straightened. Without looking in his direction or altering the flat tone of his voice, Morgan added, "No. Just me and her. I don't want to turn this into a spectacle if I don't have to."

And someone spotting me and Morgan Vinci together wouldn't ask questions?

He wasn't going to answer any. Didn't need to. I turned and left the grey room. Morgan followed.

6

I hadn't expected them to have left the body there. Which was why no one had mentioned it. Morgan would have known I wouldn't have stepped on to the boat's deck if I'd known what was below.

Staring at the dead man didn't help. Nor did the faecal smell. Hanging is not a pretty death. I looked around. Focused on the fittings, the charts, the note. Anything but the body. Then I faced Morgan.

"Why are you involving me in this?" He hadn't dragged me down here just to see if I'd be sick. "Why me? Last time everyone did their best to stop me."

His mouth twisted. It might even have been a smile of sorts. "And they didn't succeed, did they? The Port Opening is days away and I have to know if this is aimed at disrupting things, if the Family's a target. If someone wants to generate unfriendly media coverage and sink the Opening. Or…" He gestured but did not look at the thing dangling from the deckhead. His voice was just a little softer. "…if it's just what it looks like. And I need to know fast."

I didn't have to ask what he'd do if he learned it was aimed at him. I know Family well enough to understand that they don't like threats, especially not to something they valued. Being paranoid may also go with the territory. But he still hadn't answered my question.

"Why me?" I repeated. "You can call on the best investigator in EuroGov."

He looked as though he'd bitten something sour. "I called on him. He's finishing up some job for another

Family."

"Byron." It wasn't a question.

Morgan nodded. "He suggested you. When I told him you'd been there when Lloyd found the body he said you'd be the right person to take it on further. Said you had a nose for it."

He studied me, balancing his faith in Byron against what he saw standing in front of him: a medium-height woman with red hair and poorly styled clothes. A grey-market wine shipper whose only experience with investigation had been at his Family's expense. I could see him deciding. Reluctantly trusting Byron. As far as he trusted anyone. "So will you look into it?" I drew breath but he went on before I could answer. "For a fee that will get your barge repaired and give you credit in hand."

That stopped the words I'd been going to say. I had some idea of the credit it was going to take to have the *Pig* hauled and repaired, and no idea at all where it would come from. I couldn't afford the satisfaction of sending a message to Byron about what he could do with his ideas.

"Give me a couple of hours to think about it."

He stood back to let me get to the companionway. "Tell Lloyd when you've decided if you'll help."

7

I'd been through this before and I didn't want to do it again.   Except now I'd seen the body. A slight figure with a grotesquely swollen face, in a painfully neat cabin which looked as though he'd wanted to leave as little mess as he could. He deserved to be treated as more than a potential nuisance at a Family party. His grieving friends needed to know what had happened to him.

And I needed the credit.

Caf didn't improve my mood as much as I'd hoped. The mechanical jobs of deck-clearing and scrubbing, sail-mending and stowage only allowed me to put off a decision which was already made. But there was one thing I could do before I called Lloyd and gave him the message for Morgan.

I called Byron.

Not every lo-tech drone has a major technocrat on easy access. It wasn't a call I'd thought I'd be making. If Byron Cody had an opposite, it was me. He didn't like to get his high-maintenance shoes wet and he thought in systems I couldn't even imagine. The only thing that irritated him was human error. And I suspected that the only thing that baffled him was human emotion

The knowledge that someone I'd just described as the best independent investigator around had even suggested me to Morgan could mean a number of things. None of them good. Some of them probably had something to do with the fact that I'd beaten him to the solution of the question of who was stealing ID implants during our last encounter. I'd always thought he was competitive. Now I wondered if he held grudges.

I didn't doubt he'd take the call.

"Humility." The face on the screen was bland as ever. He wasn't surprised because he'd have factored in this call as soon as he'd mentioned my name to Morgan. I didn't recognise wherever he was. It looked more like personal space than the office I'd have expected. Some soft touches, a couple of holos whose details I couldn't make out, as well as the expected dark grey of systems waiting to serve him. Then I remembered he was working for someone else. I didn't even want to know where. "You've seen the data?" he prompted.

I decided he meant the note and whatever information Morgan had access to. Did him the credit of not thinking he meant the body. Not out of any humanity. For Byron, a corpse was so much waste: a pathologist might find it informative, but for him it was a deleted file. No backup.

"Not yet. Seen the body. What's it to me?" A sadness.

"Interest. I remember you tend to be curious. Can't see you watching things happen right by you and not get tied in. It reads like self-termination but, after what happened with Milo, Morgan's cautious."

As far as I knew, Morgan had been born cautious. "I should have known the free mooring would have a price."

"Not unless you want it to. He asked you to look at it, didn't he? No threats?"

"No." Not even an unspoken hint. *That* was unexpected and I should have noticed. "He said he'd pay." Byron looked at me. For someone who didn't read people and claimed my mind's lack of logic was enough to send his own circuits into overload, his silence was too knowing. "OK. Say I take a look. What do I charge him?"

The idea of presenting a bill to a Family member was

just bizarre enough to appeal.

"Think what you might get out of him. What you need for repairs and what you've lost in trade. Double it."

I blinked. Byron didn't joke – he had a sort of sense of humour but this wasn't it. I did some mental math. "You think he'll go for it?"

"Might negotiate. You could always settle in the middle. He might not think it's worth haggling."

He might not think *me* worth haggling with. It sounded easier than trading with Tom Lee for my wine shipment. That was almost reassuring – in a disturbing sort of way.

And Byron was right. I couldn't just walk away now. I'd been hooked from the moment I saw the hanged man.

I called Lloyd.

8

The conversation with Morgan – once Lloyd had connected me – went almost too easily. He didn't haggle, which left me wondering what he really considered the job worth. He just agreed to send me whatever information he had on Andy and his boat, and cut the connection. But now at least I could afford the *Pig*'s repairs. Even though I was told I'd have to join the queue and wait until 'all this fuss' was over.

While I argued about just how long that would take and where was I in the queue, I waited for the screen to deliver the details I'd been promised. I didn't want to go and look at the boat. I'd told Morgan I wanted to see the rope but I couldn't find any good reason to see what had dangled from it again. The medics could deal with that. I wouldn't recognise a drug that could make someone suicidal if it turned up in my own drink.

When the call came through, I assumed it was the one I'd been waiting for. I'd forgotten the one I hadn't answered days ago.

I knew why it had taken so long for the call to be repeated. There was only one person in the Wessex New Puritan Community who would deliberately contact me and she would have to call when there was no risk of being overheard - at the single, *communal*, terminal. It was almost impossible to move in the Community without someone asking or knowing your business, and calls out to the world were unusual enough to require explanations. Calling your heretic daughter might be the sort of explanation which was worth a beating. Or at least an hour-long sermon from a panel of Elders. Myself, I'd take the beating any day.

"Mother?" It was always hard to keep my voice steady when I spoke to her. It came out harder than I meant.

"Humility. We need your help."

Whatever I might have expected – renewed demands for my return, rebukes for my selfishness and ingratitude, disapproval of my immorality – this would never even have made the long list. Her face stared back at me, impassive. She wouldn't beg. I noticed for the first time that the hair which had once been as bright and red as my own, and an embarrassment to my father so that he preferred her to keep it covered, was dulled and threaded with white. Her eyes were still the same cool grey as mine.

"What sort of help? And who is *we*?" There were plenty in the Community I would have been glad not to help. And she knew it. "If there's rebellion in the Community, you know whose side I'm on."

"Daughter! Please."

I hated her power to make me feel ashamed. Even with my screen's poor definition I could feel the weight of that patient rebuke which had burdened all my childhood's misdeeds. Sometimes I would have preferred open anger.

"So tell me what's wrong."

"Your brother's child…"

"My brother's child is my brother's problem. You aren't going to tell me he knows you're calling?"

Something which might have been shame made her look down, but when she looked at me again there was no relenting in her expression. I hoped she wasn't going to talk about being his keeper. She didn't. She did at least know me that well.

"It is a child. It is your kin."

21

The first had more meaning than the second. Neither meant much to me.

"So?"

"She has left us for the city. For Sutton, we believe."

I could see the foul taste left in her mouth by the city's name.

"A girl of sense." What did she expect me to say? Leaving the Community was the best decision I ever made. That I had ended up in Sutton had been chance, but I didn't regret it. Despite all I'd seen since I'd arrived as little more than a naïve child with a protector who even I had known couldn't be trusted to look after himself.

Mother's stare stayed level. "A *child*," she repeated. "She is thirteen."

And alone.

"What do you want me to do?" As if I didn't know.

"You must find her. Persuade her to come home."

Must. Mother knew just how to make me want to do the opposite of what she asked. "Will the Community take her back?"

"Of course. If she…"

If she repents. The sentence didn't need completing. The repenting sinner would provide the Community with food for an orgy of self-congratulation which would last for days. I couldn't imagine trying to persuade anyone to become the centrepiece of such a feast. But thirteen *was* uncomfortably young. I knew better than my mother just what traps the city set for the unprotected.

I sighed. "You'd better tell me the rest of it."

"There is no time now. I have made up a parcel and will send it. It will tell you what you need to know."

"Send it how?" If she was going to trust it to general post I could consider it lost. Besides, the discovery that it was

22

being used to send the ID implants of murder victims to the man who wanted to copy them had left me with a deep distaste for the system.

"Through this terminal. We are not quite as primitive as you think, child."

No one of my age likes being called child. Nor did I like the tolerant scorn for my ignorance which looked too much like my own response to others' reactions to the Community. "I'll look at it."

Awkward silence, unfilled by all the other questions: How are you? Are you safe? Do you have friends? They remained unasked as they had done for fifteen years and, as I have done for fifteen years, I told myself it didn't hurt. She looked at me, not knowing any more than I did how to break the connection. Then she glanced away and I saw movement behind her.

"I must go. God with you."

The screen blanked before I could respond. I stared at its greyness for a long moment before I went back on deck and made an unnecessary check on the mooring's security.

9

Morgan's information awaited me the moment I ended the call with Mother. Andy had bought *Felicity* new. Girls' names were out of fashion at the moment and I wondered if he'd been thinking of happiness instead. Naming the thing in the hope of getting it?

As Stephen and Amanda had told me, Andy had been a director and one of the senior vice presidents of Ardco. I thought about ferry companies. I don't know much about business but I could predict this one's progress. They'd set it up because they thought they'd found a gap waiting to be filled. And because they thought they could use it to import or export discreetly. I'd seen it before. Watched the bright new company disappear when the other two major ferry lines – which were Family-operated – eventually noticed its existence and decided to squeeze a little. Rather like what might happen to a dinghy caught between two tankers which sort of leaned on each other. Nothing violent. Just pressure. And nothing much to show afterwards except a little flotsam on the water. Not a scratch on the tankers. If Stephen and Amanda knew what they were doing, they'd sell out at the top. If not, they'd go down with everyone.

But that wasn't why Andy had died. The company was still good for a while and he must have known its status when he went in. Make a profit while you can with whatever semi-legal freight you can carry.

Everything I saw said he'd killed himself. The knot in the rope was right. The marks on the neck apparently consistent. There was no sign of struggle. The note might have been a model of its type: *I'm sorry. I can't go on. Please forgive me.* He'd left his business and home contacts, named Stephen to deal with his estate. His company shares reverted to his fellow directors. He'd had no partner, no child. No relatives as far as the records went. Looked like only Stephen and Amanda were left to mourn.

I couldn't see that Morgan had anything to worry about. His celebrations could go on undisturbed. From the picture I was getting of him, it was what Andy would have preferred.

Which only left the puzzle of why he had chosen to opt out now. And here.

Considering the amount Morgan had agreed to pay me for smoothing out his concern, I owed it to him to look a little further before I told him I'd done all I could. I had no image in my head of this new ferry business, hadn't come across its carriers. I wanted to see it for myself. See whether anything in its appearance contradicted what the balance sheet had to say.

Time for a trip ashore.

10

Building sites are all alike. Months of chaos and confusion with anonymous heaps of junk growing and diminishing and reappearing elsewhere. Mud. Spoil heaps and broken ends of unidentifiable garbage. Turn your back for a couple of weeks and someone tosses the whole mess into the air and it falls back finished.

When I'd last been here the mall beside the marina had been little more than a shell, an inverted ark, hollow on the inside with only the occasional haphazardly placed partition or removable screen or holo to suggest a completed design. Now it was finished. That it still looked as though it had been put together by a land-bound designer told to think boats and hyped up on a cocktail which would probably be illegal even today was less surprising than the progress which had been made. I didn't want to go right inside but even more I didn't want to turn and look behind me across the river to the far bank. I'd been not looking at the river's east bank since I brought the *Pig* into harbour.

I turned.

Beautiful. Trees shielded the distant view and, in the foreground, the park was smooth turf with flowerbeds scattered with careless art on its immaculate green. If I had a better sense of smell, and if the wind was in the right quarter, I had no doubt I would be receiving the benefit of scents selected to put me in harmony with myself and my surroundings. The stench of death was just my memory playing tricks. I thought of the man who'd salvaged a body there when it had been heaps of muddy spoil, and his prediction that they'd have to replant every night if they wanted anything to bloom in that soil. I wondered if he'd been right.

I had to stop thinking about the past. It was gone. I'd done what I had and it was too late to question whether I'd been right or wrong to interfere. I had new problems now. Two of them. I thanked fate that at least one looked straightforward.

If you believe that you'd better give up playing cards.

I have given up. And I don't gamble.

Not with cards.

Jack still haunted me. Jack who'd rescued a teenage runaway who'd been trying to scavenge a living on the edges of Midway and given her a berth on his barge. Who'd put his unquenchable faith in one forlorn hope after another and died of a worn-out heart and left me feeling orphaned. It's bad enough hearing a ghost's voice but it's worse when a born loser tries to give you advice from beyond the grave. I shook my head at my own imaginings, turned my back on the charnel house transformed into parkland and went into the Ark.

It was busy. People scurried all around, not looking at me – not after the first assessing glance which weighed and dismissed my importance. The porter drones swerving out of my path, burdened with fabrics and fittings, were more aware of my existence. I walked past clothing outlets whose styles seemed to have no basis in what I thought of as the primary function of clothes, didn't pause at the frontage whose opaqued window swirled in a range of pastels and where those who found the idea of a day at sea too stressful could find solace. My step did break when I glanced across at something which called itself The Chandlery. The shelves offered items whose relationships to sailing even I could see – items spaced carefully lest a customer should think these things were anything but exclusive – and the holo of waves which cascaded over them, revealing first one and then another, was beguiling. At least, I assumed it was a holo. An illusion. Just like the apparent practicality of the goods on display: chameleon canvas for sails which would shift colours with their background, the latest mini sat-nav systems gleaming and whispering – more intelligent than their owners would ever be. No one who *worked* on boats would ever buy anything here. Strictly playground trade. Rich playground.

Souvenirs were next door. Antiques. These I did like. One or two would even have been at home on the *Pig* once the gloss had worn off the bronze deadlights and I'd dented the mounting of the magnetic compass. Brass bells and wooden wheels and paper charts were artfully displayed. I peered at the charts. My well-used collection might be more valuable than I'd realised.

Despite all the activity, the mall wasn't crowded. It never would be. Designers went to a lot of trouble to make sure that luxury space – space is always a luxury – never held anything as vulgar as a crowd. Clear plex walkways arched smoothly over the main concourse while tunnels and teasing corners coaxed clients to explore tantalising glimpses of even more expensive outlets. I ignored the diversions and took the direct path to the central plaza where they'd sited the main food concessions.

The guy I'd hoped to see wasn't there.

"Shit."

"Eloquent as ever, Humility."

I turned. The woman was leaning against a pillar, watching me. She wore something that glittered and shifted in pale yellows, high in the neck and long in the

28

body with something else that draped at the back. Too much for a morning which had got off to a bad start, but she'd always had a preference for disguise over surgery. What she couldn't disguise, she flaunted.

"Millie! Don't tell me fairies are going to be in this month. Please."

She grinned as she straightened and gave a quick twirl. "Why not? Fantasy always sells."

"Because reality sucks?" But I couldn't suppress a grin. Millie had that effect on me. She's put in at least twenty more years than I have and it shows in the wrinkles and the hoarse edge to her voice, but the light in her eyes says she's good for another fifty. At least. We'd met when she'd been changing careers, going into profiling and event design and had the idea she could sell the Puritan look. A few sessions with me soon made it clear that her version of the image was a whole lot more marketable than the reality, but we'd stayed friends. Her *Puritan* range had made her more credit than I'd earn in several lifetimes, and it still made me laugh when I saw old vids where an opulent house and its inhabitants were outfitted in the sort of expensive simplicity and subtle earth tones you don't get by using real mud. The floating robes wouldn't have lasted long in the Community, either.

Millie tucked her arm in mine, pulling me close. I eased free a little and she let me go, grimacing.

"Puritan. I forgot."

Like hell. But I didn't mind. And if Millie was involved with the mall she would probably know even more about what was going on than the man I'd been hoping to find.

"I was looking for Steve – guy working on the food set-up," I explained.

"He's off doing construction somewhere else." Millie

grinned. "Knew how to have a good time, he did." Millie took good times where she found them. "What did you want with him – unless it was the obvious?"

Something hopeful in the question but she didn't seem surprised when I shook my head. "It wasn't really him. I just wanted to know if Tom Lee had decided to take up one of the food concessions."

She shook her head. "We need a drink. Just when I think I've got you sorted, I remember you keep really weird company."

Tom Lee might run the best caf-house in Sutton but that wasn't where his credit came from. He controlled the largest territory in the city: if it was illegal, or even marginally illicit, you dealt with Tom Lee or went out of business. Terminally. He'd been considering opening a branch in the new development. It might even have been legit – mostly.

Millie had dragged me towards a small table and conjured a serving drone from somewhere.

"Drones?" I wondered, sidetracked. "I thought this place was going to be classy."

She passed me the caf I'd ordered and took a sip from a tall glass filled with swirling colours. Sighed with pleasure. "That's better. Real staff come in for the Opening. Until then, drones are more efficient. And they don't drink. Cheers."

I lifted my cup. Not bad.

Millie laughed. "Don't tell me. You make better on that rust heap you call home."

True. "Come and sample it some time."

"I might, now that you've got a decent berth. You *are* going to tell me how you managed that, aren't you?"

"Probably not. But you're still welcome. What about

Tom Lee?"

"Not here, sweetie." She'd work on getting the story of my marina berth out of me later. "New PO wouldn't deal."

I'd have to get used to reminders that Daisy wasn't Port Officer, or anything else, any more. "His loss."

Everything shimmered as Millie shrugged. "Some might call it sense. Why the hunt for Tom Lee? You got a cargo for him?"

Between shady deals and exceptional cookery, Tom Lee occasionally found time to buy a cargo of wine from me. Yesterday's blow, however, had brought the *Pig* back with mostly empty holds.

"No. I wanted information." If anyone in the city knew what was going on in the transport business – and where to start looking for a vagrant child – he would.

Millie stared. "You're planning to ask him a favour and you have nothing to trade?"

She wasn't saying anything I hadn't already thought. I wasn't naïve enough to expect free advice from Tom Lee. Millie, however, was full of it.

"You're mad. What's so special you need to go to him? And why are you back here, anyway? I'd have thought you'd want to keep clear until all the fuss of the Opening had faded. And – " she emphasised with a gesture big enough to encompass the whole mall – "if it's left to me it won't fade quietly."

It was going to be as bad as I'd feared. Why wasn't I safe in France sampling liqueurs brewed by monks Mother would call emissaries of Satan? Or worse. I groaned and Millie's grin widened. Shark-like.

"Have another drink and tell Millie all."

Too many blurred evenings had begun that way, but I was safe enough before lunch. And sticking to caf. I stared down into its blackness. Decided I could tell her my half of it, leave Morgan's problems out. Took a breath and met Millie's expectant gaze.

"I've been asked to look out for a runaway. New to the city. A kid."

A soft hiss of breath drawn in. She heard what I wasn't saying. "From your background?"

"Yes."

"How old?"

"Thirteen. A girl."

Her glass was empty again. I was still watching the ripples in my cup. She filled time with a gesture at the waiting drone and tapped gold nails on the table's slick surface. Her face was set in more serious lines than usual. "You think the kid'll end up in Tom Lee's territory?"

My turn to shrug. "Likely. She'd have no place to go, no connections, no credit. Street's the only place. And most streets in Sutton belong to him."

"She know you? Contact you?"

I shook my head. "Not likely. I'd gone before she was born. My name won't be spoken anywhere she'd be likely to hear."

"Unless she chose Sutton because of you. And don't tell me the kids in your Community don't gossip. They're human, aren't they?" I'd already thought of that and hadn't liked it, but Millie was more pragmatic. "It would make it easier, wouldn't it? If she just arrived at your door? Sorry, your hatch."

"And what would I do then? Take her in? Send her back?"

Millie winced. She knew there was no room on the *Pig* or in my life for a child. She also knew I wouldn't force anyone back to the life I'd run from.

"Look for her first. Sort out what to do after."

It wasn't very constructive but it was the conclusion I'd come to as well. "So where do I start if not with Tom Lee?"

Millie didn't involve herself with other people's problems. Buying me a drink and demanding my news had put her in a corner she was going to have to slide out of. It took several sips of gaudy cocktail before she came up with something.

"What about Town Hall?"

I laughed. Everyone laughs at the idea of anything useful coming out of the Town Hall bureaucrats. Millie waited. In theory, Town Hall had records of everyone who used credit in Sutton, everyone on the housing list, everyone with criminal records and everyone who tried to register for aid. Only the very naïve saw any point in applying to the aid lists but this girl would be more naïve than any cit. More than the average incomer. I stopped laughing.

"At least Town Hall's legit," I acknowledged.

Millie couldn't hide her relief. "Good. Call them. Tomorrow. Now have a real drink."

I shook my head. Duty before pleasure.

11

Her name was Charity. The thin file of papers which had arrived at my terminal told me that, gave me details of her height and weight and told me she was the fourth child of my eldest brother's wife. The second daughter. I thought about that: not much welcome for another mouth too young to help with children yet to come, and not another precious son to work the land. At thirteen she would have had a clear sight of her future in the Community and I would be the last to blame her if she hadn't liked it.

I flipped over the pages.

She'd been gone six weeks. There had been no note. It was only when another girl, a friend of Charity's, had broken down and told her eldest sister, unable to carry the burden of a secret which had seemed exciting when she'd been given it, that they had had any solid idea where to look. Before that... I had a brief moment of sympathy for the parents as I thought of hours and days of pointless searching, sleepless nights and the dreams which would have been worse than waking. They would have believed her dead. Perhaps now that seemed better than what they had learned: that Charity had talked for months about running away, had spoken of the cities, of Sutton more than the others, had watched every forbidden program she could find about a world she had never seen. She'd probably been beaten more than once for looking at banned shows and vids. I knew better than most how much good beatings did to change a rebellious mind. And they wanted *me* to send her back?

The picture slithered out from between the last two

pages. Not a holo, or a portrait. Nothing as vain as that. This was a simple photo taken to celebrate the end of harvest. Last year, I'd guess. The whole family smiling in front of the overflowing barn. I counted them. Three adults. Seven children. I read the caption, identifying them all with an odd sort of pain.

My brother was in the centre, standing foursquare. One hand held a pitchfork, the other was on his hip. I'd thought the unsmiling figure was my father until I remembered time's passage and knew him. His wife was beside him, smiling slightly, looking meekly down as was proper. The children were around them, sons nearest the centre, daughters at the edges. The hired man stood behind them. The caption gave me names. Charity was second from the right, her hand in the hand of a girlchild who looked as though she had not long learned to walk. I wondered what work they'd found for her in the harvest. Then I looked at the girl they wanted me to find.

She was staring defiantly ahead of her. Plump, dark, awkward-looking. As unsmiling as her father. For all the Community's professed contempt for vanity, she'd have been better off taking after her mother like the pretty girl on the other side of the group who must be her elder sister. Something twisted my gut. I tried to blame an overdose of caf, but couldn't. I recognised her. Oh, I'd never seen her but I knew her in a way I doubted her family ever would. Knew why she'd run.

Knew I couldn't force her to go back.

Knew, too, that I couldn't leave her survival to luck. If she was in Sutton I was going to have to find her.

"Hell!"

I was angry. With my mother for asking for something like this. With myself for letting her do it. With Charity for not having the patience to hold out for another year or two, for not making better plans. For not waiting until I was out of the country – preferably with an unplugged screen.

If the Community wanted her back, why couldn't they have gone to a professional? Someone whose business was investigation, not wine? I heard the echo of my questions to Morgan and tried to find it funny.

But I knew the answer this time. The Community did not want her; my brother probably didn't want to have to receive an erring daughter back into his home. Only my mother cared enough to ask the one person who might help. And what her motives were I couldn't begin to guess. I wasn't willing to examine my own. All I knew was that I couldn't ignore the sullen face staring at me from my chart table.

I swore again and grabbed my sack and headed for the dock gate. I was in no mood for talking to anyone on vid and I might as well take out my temper directly on the transport system and Town Hall.

12

Town Hall is a warren. Or perhaps it's a bunker. Its employees spend a lot of time ducking missiles – not always or exclusively verbal – lobbed by cits driven by impotence and evasion to attempt violence. There are forcefields and security guards but someone always seems willing to try to break through.

Official places have their own smell. Dust and the faint ozone-scent of a hundred terminals combined with the lingering taint of hopeless people: unwashed, anxious, afraid. In a place they don't want to be, asking questions which won't be answered. The smell of stale information left to moulder. Perhaps it had been built with some sort of civic pride but generations of defeat in the war against the city's real governors – usually criminal and frequently lethal – had worn it down. The open entrance hall with its grand staircase and marble floor had been divided and subdivided into mean cubicles whose occupants' only purpose was to redirect anyone foolish enough to come making enquiries to another cubicle and then another until finally they were driven away in despair. The floor was scuffed and chipped. I imagined bored feet kicking until stone itself gave way, and tried not to think what might have caused the stains smeared into the cracks and darkening every corner.

It wasn't crowded. To deal direct when there's always a terminal nearby would be absurd. The bureaucrats in their cubicles spoke mainly into screens or let their hands tap out messages of discouragement and delay. The few clients loitering round the fringes of the hall had the look of people with no other place to go. Little hope of finding any comfort here; unless they began to shout they were ignored. Occasionally there was a shout. Or sobs, which went unheard until they faded into embarrassed silence. Even the ceaselessly roving surveillance vids were indifferent.There is a word my father liked to use, letting it hiss from his mouth to pool on the Meeting House floor when he reminded the Community of its sins. *Accidie.* I hadn't really understood its meaning until I came here.

My first visit had been years ago, trying to deal with the details of Jack's death at sea. They knew he was dead. They could have known before I did if anyone had been interested in watching the records: the ID implanted in your head hours after you're born stops sending when brain function ceases. I'd gone on swearing at him and refusing to accept for more than an hour that a heart which was emotionally functional, sometimes *too* functional, had gone beyond any physiological help. The place hadn't improved since then.

At least I'd learned not to bother with the ground floor.

The stairway was, of course, barred. I headed for the barrier.

"You can't go up there!"

I turned to look at the man who had shouted. Not one of the security guards, I guessed. One of the form-fillers. He was thin and would be tall if he ever stood upright, but his shoulders were hunched and his protest held the plaintive echo of a thousand daily excuses. *He multiplieth words without knowledge.* He blinked repeatedly.

"Stop me."

He couldn't. There were no *procedures.* Already he was regretting the impulse which had made him raise his voice, draw attention to himself. His head pulled closer into the shelter of his shoulders. He retreated to his cubicle. A security guard turned in my direction.

I took the first stair. The barrier was across the third. It needed a pass I didn't possess before it would lift but it hadn't been programmed to react to someone willing to climb over it. Unused to the pressure of being stood on, it made a squashed sound echoed by the man who had protested. Behind me the security guard shouted something I ignored. Nothing else happened.

The primitive corridor upstairs, lacking even a one-speed walkway, was lined with doorless offices. No indicators to say in which the Accommodations Unit was housed. I took a small and worthless coin from a pocket and watched its spin. Heads. I walked through the first doorway on my right.

The room held two desks. A figure at each of them. The one behind the larger desk had her back to the opaqued window, rejecting the contamination of the outside world. She sat very straight, fair hair almost colourless around a face with the dead pallor of someone on one of the cheaper antisol drugs. It gave her a look of a china doll I had once seen in a museum. Polished. Brittle. There was nothing doll-like in her expression. She was glaring at me with irritation but no surprise. The guard downstairs hadn't done nothing: he'd called up a warning.

"You have no business here." An emotionless voice, as impersonal as the figures flickering across the desk in front of her. Designed to intimidate.

"How do you know?"

She hadn't expected a challenge. Usually those who found themselves in front of her were already too cowed to do anything but mumble excuses or pleas before they fled.

"This level is not open to the public." She might have been reading from an official document.

"Rote, not reason. You don't know why I'm here." It's so much easier to be rude to someone who's never going to like you.

I still hadn't seen the face of the woman at the second desk, only the cropped black hair of a small head balanced on a thin neck. A pulse jumped there as though an impulse to turn had been felt and suppressed. Her fingers continued to move on the touch surface in front of her.

The woman by the window went on glaring. Then, unwilling to ask but unable to find any other response, "Why are you here?"

"I want to find a girl who's new-arrived in the city."

Her smile was as thin and cold as her voice. "Enquiries are dealt with downstairs."

"Enquiries are smothered downstairs. This one is more complicated than most so I've come to someone who can deal with difficult cases." I was willing to flatter if it got me the access I wanted. She looked unimpressed but let me go on. "She's underage. From the Wessex New Puritan Community."

It caught her, as I knew it would. It also tasted sour: I was deliberately using the usual curiosity about the Communities, but I didn't have to like it.

"Name?" She sounded bored but was interested enough to key in a code.

"Charity."

Small creases bracketed her mouth. Amusement. Her fingers moved on the desk's patterns.

"Your authority?" The next question on the official list.

"She's my niece." Two steps to the desk to offer an ID read. Her hands stilled.

"Your ward."

"No."

"You have her consent, or her legal guardian's, for a search." That's what the rule book demanded.

"I wouldn't be trying to find her if I knew how to contact her for consent, would I?"

I didn't bother imagining how my brother would react to any request from me for access. If he had wanted to retrieve his daughter, my mother wouldn't have had to face a Council contempt citation by calling me.

Thin fingers retreated to the woman's lap.

"You have no authority. A child's Privacy Rights are as non-violable as those of an adult. This office cannot help you." Satisfaction in the smile. Her first real pleasure.

"Even if the girl's at risk?"

"You have no evidence. And no authority."

If she said it again, I'd do something violent. I tried to sound calmer than I felt. "What evidence do you want? Her corpse? A report from her pimp or a bodydealer?"

The words slid off her façade. Meant nothing. "It's outside our reference. You should contact the guardian and request their input. There are public terminals downstairs for your use. My Sec will show you out."

The careful emphasis told me that a human Sec was her prized status marker. It was her own humanity I wondered about. She had shut down. If she'd been a screen the blankness couldn't have been more complete. I hesitated. Shrugged. I'd blown it before I arrived. I'd hoped to find a rule-bender up here, away from the regulations desks and codes downstairs; instead I'd found their prototype. I turned as the other woman swung her chair away from her desk and stood. ﹅

She was young. Olive skin with the dark hair. Small

features dominated by straight brows. Probably in her first job. A step towards security, perhaps even opportunities to leave Sutton and find work on a private Estate if she had the skills. Knew the right people. She looked nervous. Hoped I wasn't going to refuse to leave. At ten centimetres shorter and several kilos lighter than me, it was understandable. Besides, I doubted if she'd overcome the inhibitions against physical contact which most cits grow up with.

Then again, I couldn't see what defences she carried and I had to assume the office wasn't unprotected. The woman by the window was clearly untroubled by any thought that I might refuse to leave. She had erased me from her agenda and was dealing with Something More Important. I was her Sec's problem now.

The anger which had brought me here without any real plan, and stopped me thinking out a less aggressive approach which might have served me better, drained away. I had never expected anything useful to come out of Town Hall; why was I fighting? I gave the Sec a smile she didn't find reassuring and walked ahead of her through the doorway.

"No need to keep me company. I can find the stairs."

"I'll go with you."

Her voice was breathy, as nervous as her face. I stopped what I'd been going to say. I didn't think it would help.

We were away from the office, almost at the stairhead, when she spoke again.

"Do you really think she's in danger? That pimps might...?"

I stopped. Her hands were twisting together in front of her.

"Charity?" She nodded. "How would you have managed

if you'd come to Sutton for the first time at thirteen, from a no-tech background, with nowhere to stay, no one you knew?"

Her hands stilled. Gripped each other hard enough to whiten her knuckles. "Yes. You're right, of course. I…"

Something in her voice. The humanity missing from her employer. She looked over her shoulder at the empty corridor.

"You'll help?" I urged.

It took her another half-minute but when she spoke it was in a rush as though she had to download the information before it was wiped.

"I had a look. While you were talking to my supervisor. She isn't…"

"Wait a moment. Which *she*? Charity or your android supervisor? And what do you mean, you *looked*?"

Something which might have been a smile, quickly smothered, flickered over her face. "I meant the girl. Charity." Her voice softened on the name.

"You checked the records?" I stared. Remembered the anonymous fingers flying over keys while I confronted the woman by the window. I'd been as bad as her supervisor: treating her like a machine, forgetting she could hear what was being said. She was nodding. Guilty. Did she expect me to run back to the office and denounce her? I reached out. Gripped her shoulders. Frightened her. Let go. "Sorry. *Thank you*. What did you find out?"

She shook her head. Regret clear in a face which seemed unable to hide any emotion. Perhaps I'd been wrong about her: perhaps she'd joined Town Hall because she thought she might be able to do some good. Perhaps she would. I wished I believed it. Wished I didn't have to hear what she was saying.

"There's no trace. I found her ID registration and she's still listed at the Community. She's not Missing."

Which only meant she was alive and she hadn't yet been Shunned. "Nothing else?"

"I'm sorry. No. She hasn't applied for anything from the City: aid or accommodation or even information. I wish …"

"So do I. But thanks for trying. She probably doesn't even know there's any aid on offer or how to access it. I'll have to look elsewhere."

"But where *can* you look? The streets…" A shudder completed her opinion of the streets.

"You can survive the streets. If you know the rules. If you're lucky." Charity wouldn't know there were any rules. I hoped she was lucky. The girl's face was disbelieving. Not sure why it mattered, I tried again. "I know one or two people."

There was a faint buzz. The girl flinched and shook her wrist. She was being recalled. She hesitated, uncertain.

"You'd better get back. No need to watch me go: I promise not to upset anyone else as I leave."

A faint smile. The hint of mischief. "I don't mind. Work's not often this interesting. I hope you find her."

"I'll try."

She left, steps neat and quick on the floor. I watched. Saw her falter before she reached the office, turn. Defiant. "I'll keep checking."

13

Tom Lee's wasn't far. I could walk over there. Soothe myself with the best caf in town. Indulge a sweet tooth. Put out more feelers for Charity. But Charity wasn't my only problem. There was Andy. And Morgan, who was offering real credit for answers. Add to that the fact that Tom Lee would know I'd come in with empty holds, and we'd had some dealings lately which had been more in the nature of favours traded. It wasn't a currency he liked. Besides, while I wasn't in a mood to be tactful I had just enough control left to recognise that saying the wrong thing to him would be a bad move.

Which left me the choice of looking at my other problem. Andy. I kept circling back to *why* he'd killed himself. I could get Byron to run a deep check on his background, but the one thing I knew for certain about him was that his life had been tied up with his work. The ferry company. I wanted to see if I could picture him there, find out what they traded in, how he and his friends were making enough money for two new boats and berths at Midway during the Opening. Find out if anything on show didn't match the data I'd seen.

I took the bus to the docks. It jerked and swayed along its programmed route, slowing at corners for passengers to swing aboard. No point in competing for public transport if you're hesitant or crippled.

"Watch who you're shoving!"

A harsh voice. The bus's motion had pushed me too hard against the man standing next to me. I smelled sour sweat and looked sidelong: he was heavy – not all of it fat

– wearing clothes which had once belonged to someone a size smaller, split at the seams. Waiting for me to mutter something, look down, ease back. Not worth a fight I'd likely lose. Lose face was better. Except I'd left the Town Hall in no mood to be pushed around.

"Shove off!"

In a narrow space with hardly room for another passenger to swing on board there was suddenly air around me. Everyone had breathed in a little, edged back a few millis. Except the man beside me. The bus jolted on. A couple of people got off. A woman waiting at the road-side decided to wait for the next bus. Sensitive antennae. The man hesitated. He wasn't used to this, hadn't expected me to do anything but back off. Hell, *I* hadn't expected me to do anything else. Now neither of us was certain what would happen next.

We were past the old walls, among narrow streets which widen out into the straight road running by the dock gates. Behind the force-fences and the brick barricades the ferry company logos flapped in the sluggish wind. The man beside me breathed heavily through his mouth. My own mouth was dry.

Don't take on anyone bigger than you. Don't accept a challenge.

Remember it's not your territory.

Jack had always given better advice than he'd taken. I owed him a hearing. Swallowed. The bus was slowing. I took a step back, felt passengers give me room. The man didn't follow, kept breathing hard. The smell was deterrent enough. I left.

Jarred my knees. It was my own fault. I *did* know better than to cross the privacy of someone bigger, tougher than me. Knowing made me no happier. I was angry and embarrassed and wouldn't have got back on that bus if it had stopped and waited for me. Nothing to do with Bad Breath, not really: I just wouldn't be able to face the crowd who'd seen me back down.

Childish, I know. But that didn't improve my mood.

I glared around. No one looked back. Cits are careful not to see anything that isn't profit or threat. Drab coveralls and a battered sack said my credit wasn't worth much but I didn't look as if I'd roll easily. And I obviously wasn't a threat to anyone. Especially not to fat thugs on buses. Ignore. Mental screens flashed the signal without their owners even being aware of the program they'd initiated. Walkers passed me by without pause. Unseeing.

I wasn't far from where I'd meant to be.

It's an odd part of Sutton. Busy and dead together. Trucks in and out most of the time, usually drone-driven or auto flatbeds with container loads. Sometimes a human driver. The two main ferry companies deal mostly in freight – no one who has any credit crosses the Channel in anything but a flitter or a luxicruise. I'd heard about the cruisers. Some were rumoured to have off-limit possibilities which were still illegal onshore. I don't have the sort of imagination to work out what they might be but I do know of one Family type who takes a luxi roundtrip every few months and never bothers to get off at any port of call. Out of my league. Light years from Sutton docks. Any passenger on vessels from here travels that way because there isn't a cheaper way to cross. Or they don't want to bother the Revenue.

Revenue checks on the baggage of the wealthy are inconspicuous but thorough. At freight docks they scan the seals and inventory markings on the containers but shrug off whatever might be in the pockets of anyone who walks ashore. If they do get bored and pull you over it doesn't cost much to get away clean. If you can't afford that sort of tithe you shouldn't be travelling – even Revenue officers have to live.

A truck powered past me, the backdraught nearly blowing me over. Its autopilot knew I'd been in no danger so it hadn't slowed. I waited while my heart rate accepted the same message a bit more slowly. *I* don't have automated judgement and I hadn't heard the truck. Fusion has its disadvantages: at least the old fossil-fuel engines make enough noise and stink to let you know they're coming.

The truck turned in at gates which swung wide to admit it then began to close. The movement as much as anything else drew my attention to the logo flaunted on gates and banners. Bright red new paint. A scarlet triangle in a white circle.

I'd seen it before. On notepaper with a company name – and a farewell message. Ardco.

The gates were almost shut when the girl slid through behind the truck. Could have been a boy except that the glimpse I had of her pale face was defiantly female. The entry was a practised move. One she knew the sensors wouldn't pick up – knew because she'd done it a thousand times before. I looked around. No one else showed any sign of having seen anything. It was wiser to see nothing. Other people's business was best avoided.

Only this just might be my business.

Getting in to Ardco was simple and didn't involve slipping in behind anything. Required only a strong thumb for a bell and a stubborn streak a metre wide. I have both.

The screen beside the gate flickered in to life. "Yes?" The

48

face was on the sort of head which becomes a neck with no evident alteration in girth. I guessed he carried his belly in his lap. If my interruption had brightened a dull day spent watching drones perform tasks with depressing efficiency, it didn't show.

"Hi. Name's Humility. Connection of one of your directors – Andy?"

"Not here."

"Can I come through?"

Difficult question. Andy's name helped him make a decision. "Through the lock."

A small door cycled open beside the main gate.

The sooner surveillance finds a better way of scanning visitors than trapping them in an airlock while it does so, the happier I'll be. I *hate* the things. A part of me which I prefer not to think about whimpers at the idea of being shut in a small space and refuses to let experience convince it that the door at the far end will eventually open to let it out. I have spent subjective years in such places and this one added another couple of centuries to the tally.

He must have decided I was harbouring nothing either lethal or compromising because the end of the passage did cycle open at last to let me out into the same murky daylight I'd left an ice-age earlier.

The truck that hadn't hit me was just disappearing up the ramp into the backside of a ferry stern-on to the dock. No sign of the girl who'd followed it in. The rest of the place confirmed that this was strictly freight: no passenger facilities, automated loading bays, and a line of drones pushing containers up rails to the ferry's open deck. If the ship carried a human crew, it was nowhere to be seen. A constant low mechanical throbbing and the intermittent clatter of colliding metals interrupted by the occasional admonitory bleep were the only noises. My guess was that the two humans required by regs would turn up at the last second and would be ignored by the drones which, after all, would do all the work.

"That's far enough."

The man was watching me through a plex window. He was sitting in a box-like structure just inside the gate.

I walked over. Tried a smile. "Hi. Slick operation you've got here." The smile didn't work.

"What you want?" Simple. Direct. No frills. He'd spent too long watching drones. "Told you Andy's not here."

"The others? Stephen? Amanda?" Headshake to both, but I was hoping the name-dropping might gain me cred. "Sorry about that. Question. Can I get a tour of the place?" I can be direct, too.

"Why?" He wasn't quite ready to throw me out but I could see where his preference lay.

Time to lie. Sort of. "Told you I knew your directors. Met them on their boat. This sounded like an interesting venture. Company really going places."

Throwing management names around made him pause fractionally. He didn't actually smile but he made the sort of effort that went with thought. Blinked. Decided he couldn't decide and wanted to pass it on. "Got to make an appointment."

"That's great. When?"

Another blink. "Not my job. Call up the office. Or the people you say you know. They'll fix something. Perhaps." Low marks for human relations. Perhaps he didn't have any. He looked at me, frowned. I probably didn't seem like someone who had dealings with management, or who might be something important in media, but he wasn't going to chance it.

"Thanks." I gestured behind me. "Looks good."

Most of the rigs were still new and the ferry whose hold doors were swinging shut had the shine of new paint on it. There was an almost uncomfortable sense of order about the place. I was used to docks where debris had accumulated just outside the well-travelled tracks of the loaders and where every cable and chain was heavy with that mixture of grease and rust beaded with salt water peculiar to shipyards. Ardco looked new and prosperous, but not quite busy enough.

"Mind if I look around?"

Of course he minded, but I'd walked away before he could find a way to tell me to get out. I gave no sign of hearing the shout which followed me.

"Keep clear of the ferry! And don't try to get under the security scan!"

I looked up at the flimsy gantry, high enough for loaded trucks to pass under, and noted the bulbous growths along its length. Lasers? Hostile to life-forms larger than rats, I guessed, and wondered how high they'd set the charge. Something humanitarian, like *stun*? Unlikely.

Nearer the moored ferry and beside the tracks leading towards its doors, I saw the now-familiar logo repeated again and again and, under it, *Ardco*. I moved off, away from the forbidden area towards the far side of the yard. Beyond Thick-neck's line of sight.

Here was the mess I'd missed. A wasteland where no machines ran and whatever scrubby grasses could survive on sump oil and seawater warred with each other for the thin soil under the cracked concrete. Heaps of rusting, amorphous metals lay abandoned, anonymous. Only the occasional coil of cable or loop of chain or angled corner of engine-casing could be distinguished. On the far side, where the mirage shimmer of a force-fence marked the edge of Ardco's territory, was a crazy apartment block of ruined containers piled together like toy bricks abandoned by some giant's child. They'd been discarded, I guessed, by a previous bankrupt entrepreneur, not worth the cost to Ardco of clearing them.

Dockyard scrap keeps the *Pig* afloat. I didn't have room for much in my sack but I never waste a chance to scavenge. At least I might salvage something from a wasted day.

I must have crossed an unseen border. I didn't feel any shock or hear an alarm and one patch of cracked paving was no different from the next, but the words were clear enough: "No further."

The girl was standing ten paces away and there was more authority in two words from her than the fat man would achieve in his lifetime. And she didn't need an alarm: the warning was clear enough. I stopped.

She was the one who'd slipped in behind the truck. She wore black, fitted defiantly tight to a figure sexlessly thin. The streets didn't encourage spare flesh but there was nothing fragile in the way she stood, balanced on spread feet. Nor in the way she held the spiked chain looped between her hands. She might be as much as ten years younger than me but those dark, unblinking eyes sunk in the white face had seen more than I ever wanted to.

I'd waited too long. I didn't see her give a signal but three other girls stepped out of the containers' shadows and stood silent behind her. They were thin, too, wearing black, but different: followers. Their eyes flickered restlessly from their leader to me. She didn't turn but she knew they were there, waiting for orders. I knew better than to try for conversation. Raised a hand. Stepped back. Didn't turn till I was well clear and back on the too-tidy ground of Ardco's territory. Then I left. Walk, don't run. Not with that dead black gaze following me.

I'm not sure I drew breath until I was back out in the road.

14

"So you were run off from Town Hall?"

Not how I liked to think about it but Millie had a point. And she was buying the drinks. "I prefer to think I made a strategic withdrawal."

She grinned. "Bullshit."

"That too." I stretched my legs and the mall chair fitted itself more comfortably to my demands. I'd been back in Midway about ten minutes before Millie had spotted me and called me over, taking time only to pat a passing drone on its head. She'd bribed me with drink and I'd given her an edited version of my visit to the Town Hall and the docks.

She considered. Nodded. "You've done what you could. Now you can forget it and concentrate on more important things."

It tripped my caution circuits. And Millie's agendas can get complicated. Sometimes she's just being maternal/friendly. Other times... I stay wary.

"Like what?"

"Like the fest that's going to get under way with this Opening. It starts officially in two days but my guess is those who aren't panicking over last-minute details will be ready to party tomorrow."

"And which will you be doing?"

"Sweetie, have you ever known me to panic?"

I grinned, then re-ran what she'd said. "What do you mean, the Opening *starts* in two days? How long's it going on for?"

"The rest of the week. At least. Family's down, I hear."

I hadn't told her I'd already talked to Morgan. It hadn't been a festive sort of discussion. She was smiling at me and it didn't bode well. "I don't think I can bear it. What's the program?"

"A lot of speeches. Some spectacular holo displays, lots of music and entertainments. Think circus crossed with VR epic. Word has it they've got a licence for some real fireworks."

"Hope they've cleared all the glitches from the fire-fighting system by then." And that she wasn't thinking Roman circus.

"You're all enthusiasm, aren't you?"

I tried not to smile but couldn't subdue a flicker of interest in the fireworks. They hadn't been legal in my lifetime: someone in the Family had swung a lot of weight – and credit – to get a licence. Holo displays were one thing; this might be something else.

Millie caught the interest. "That's better. Now tell me what else you got up to in this pest hole they call a city." I thought about it. Gave her an edited version of the docks visit: let her think it had been part of the search for Charity. She didn't need to know about Andy. Made a joke of the lout I'd barged on the bus. She didn't approve. "You'll get yourself wiped if you're not careful. Didn't Jack warn you…?"

"All the time. Never kept him out of trouble, either."

"True. But why you couldn't use a cab, I don't know."

"Credit, mainly." Plus I hadn't thought of it. I looked at the sneer on her face. "Don't tell me you've never been on a bus?"

"Not in ten years, sweetie."

15

Back on the *Pig* I went on with the deck-clearing and cleaning. There were frayed halyards to sort out, some major sail-mending to be done, and the winch that had jammed on me and started all the trouble to take to pieces and clean. I left that to one side and did the general clear-up first. At least the *Pig* could look seaworthy, even if we both knew she wasn't going anywhere till I'd had her hauled out and taken a really good look at the rudder.

There was something calming about the mechanical tasks. My hands knew what to do as I coiled and stowed lines and opened up every ventilator and porthole to get some fresh air in to clear out the stuffiness left by two days of being battened down against the sea. I was so absorbed in the work that I didn't even hear the couple approach.

"You're busy."

The jib I was trying to stow with something approaching tidiness slithered from my hands. Stephen and Amanda. Well-groomed, dressed for fashionable sailing, good ads for sculpting. Would have looked a whole lot better if they hadn't worn matching expressions of uncertainty that contradicted the positive approach and polite smiles.

I straightened, gestured at the heap of sail. "Hi. It looks worse than it is." I hoped. "You OK?"

The smiles were suddenly fixed, then they faded. "Not really," said the Amanda. She wore bright colours, and the slash of red on her lips was stark against pale skin.

"It's about Andy," Stephen said flatly. His shoulders lifted slightly but his hands stayed in his pockets. His voice was tired, as though emotion was something he'd over-done years ago. Not the genial host, triumphing in his first successful voyage, of last night.

As if his words had broken some sort of barrier, Amanda hurried on. "We saw you with Morgan. Saw you go on board *Felicity* with him. Why you? They haven't told us anything except that Andy's gone. We don't even know why or how – did he fall? We thought you could at least tell us *something*." Half-angry, half-pleading. Desperate to know more; resenting the stranger who'd got to see their friend's body while they'd been shut out.

I'd have traded the experience gladly.

I wasn't quite sure what to tell them. Decided that if Morgan wanted to stop them making a noise or talking to the media, it was better to give them something than to have them pestering Lloyd or Gus. Perhaps I should have referred them to Morgan, but I wanted to know more about Andy and Ardco and this was too good a chance to miss.

"Come on board." I stepped back from the rails. "We can talk inside."

16

They looked curiously round the shabby deck-house. It wasn't what they were used to – not enough gloss and a little too much evidence of recent struggles. I gestured to the bench seat and hitched myself up on to the tall chair by the wheel.

"I can't tell you much because I don't know much myself." There was something comforting about the fact that the truth coincided with what I would have said anyway. "Morgan asked me to go with him this morning because I'd been able to help him with something else earlier this year." Which might have sounded as though it meant something. Considering that I was still not quite convinced I knew exactly what Morgan's motives were, it was the best I could do. "I'm sorry about your friend."

"What happened? Did he slip? Hurt himself?" Amanda seemed to be the leader in their partnership. "He was perfectly all right when we last saw him, wasn't he, Stephen?"

Stephen nodded. Even that gesture was uncertain "Yes, of course. Just tired and a bit seasick. Didn't want the medics. Was that it? Something more serious than sea-sickness?" I could see him remembering teasing Andy. Wishing now he'd been more concerned. Had sent for help. At least I could reassure him.

I shook my head. "There was nothing you could have done. He wasn't sick." At least, that wasn't what had killed him.

"But where is he now? What have they done with…?" She didn't want to say the words. "We're his friends. He doesn't have anyone else and we need to…"

To do all those things you never want to have to do for someone you love. The things you can't leave to anyone else. "I'm sorry," I told her, repeating myself because there was nothing else to say. "I don't know what's happened to him now." I'd been in the little morgue behind the discreetly hidden medical centre once, and had no intention of visiting there again. "You should contact Lloyd about that."

Amanda was barely listening, caught up in memory. "We've known him for five years now." As though that made his death even more impossible.

"Six." Her partner's correction was automatic, as though he had the sort of mind that remembered details, didn't like them to be wrong. "Remember, we met when we all got involved with that warehouse business in Folkestone? Perry's. That was six years ago in September."

Her mouth twisted. "I remember." She glanced at me. "One of those business deals that don't work out quite as planned." A light laugh. "And I gave up medicine for transport!"

I smiled as though I knew all about business deals. I don't think they were talking about the sort of credit that changed hands between me and Tom Lee over a tank of wine.

"But what *happened*?" she insisted. "How could he be dead? I know he wasn't ill because we all had thorough screenings when we signed up as partners in the new business. If there had been something wrong, heart or anything, we'd have sorted it out then."

A quick transplant. Nothing that takes more than the time the tissue engineers need to grow you your own, and there you are, another fifty years of life guaranteed with free replacement if there's any sign of failure before the scheduled renewal date. A pity Jack never had the credit for a nice little package like that. Or even for donor transplant. Hell, he'd have gone with synthetics if he could. He might still be alive.

"So it was an accident?" She was becoming too insistent and I had a decision to make. Pass them over to Morgan or tell them the truth and keep them talking.

No contest. Besides, I knew what he wanted me to prove. "I'm sorry. No, it wasn't an accident." I didn't give them a chance to make the leap to the foul play option. "Your friend took his own life." It seemed to sound better, somehow more peaceful, than 'killed himself' or 'committed suicide' and even I can sometimes be tactful.

Shock. A sort of appalled acceptance. "You're sure? I mean…" She didn't know what she meant.

"Quite sure. He left a note." Somehow that made it true for them. I could see the acceptance overriding the automatic protest that Andy couldn't possibly have killed himself, there had to be some mistake. She looked for a moment as though she wanted to ask how he'd done it but some sort of restraint stopped her. Stephen was more bleached than ever, shadows suddenly dark under his eyes. He didn't want to think about it, never mind ask questions.

Suddenly Amanda covered her face in her hands, as though to shut out reality. "God." Her voice was muffled. "How could he?"

Stephen put an arm round her shoulders. "How does anyone know what really goes on in someone else's head? He must have had his reasons. They must have been important to him."

She looked up. Looked at me, half-eager. "The note. Did you read it? Did it say why he did it?" Needing an answer, something that would reassure her it wasn't her fault. I remembered when Daisy had killed herself, how I'd tried again and again to replay it so that I couldn't have been to blame. One day I might convince myself.

I shook my head. "Sorry. It was just a goodbye. There wasn't anything in your work together that was going wrong?"

Her laugh cut off, as though it was somehow indecent. "No. He'd just bought the boat to celebrate how well things were going. It was the first one he'd owned and he was talking about all the fun he was going to have. Making plans. Andy could make plans for ever and he was really excited about *Felicity*. I said the name was old-fashioned. He told me he liked it and he wasn't going to change it – besides, that would have been unlucky." She stopped, remembering that Andy's luck had run out on board his beloved boat. "I don't believe he did this."

She sounded almost angry. Stephen touched her shoulder again. Spoke to me. "He didn't let us know anything was wrong, and that hurts. You'd think he'd have told us, asked for our help, wouldn't you?"

I knew better than to answer a question like that. I was feeling my way here. Byron could think what he liked about my people skills but I wasn't used to playing social games, especially not with someone who'd just heard their colleague and friend had killed himself. "This has been a shock, I know. Can I get you a drink? Wine? Caf?"

Stephen opted for caf and I joined him. Amanda just wanted water.

When people have drinks in their hands – even water – they feel they can't just walk away; they have to go on talking. Since the only thing we had to talk about was Andy, they seemed willing enough to go on telling me what a wonderful person he was, how much he had left to live for and how exciting the development of Ardco was going to be. Grief takes people in different ways. Their excitement over the ferry business and Andy's new-found enthusiasm for sailing circled each other in a sort of whirlpool from which no understanding seemed likely to emerge.

It was when I put on the deck-house lights that they realised how long they'd spent on board the *Pig*. Stephen put his mug down with a clatter, Amanda's glass followed more quietly.

"I'm so sorry." He sounded as though he meant it. "We've imposed on your privacy and you've been very kind. I'm sure you've told us all you know about this dreadful thing." I thought of the swinging corpse. A dreadful thing. "If you do happen to learn anything else, would you…?"

"Of course." I promised nothing. "But perhaps…"

"Yes?" He was eager to show his gratitude. Keen to help.

"I just wondered whether it might be an idea if I were to go over to Ardco, have a quick look around. It might give me a better idea of things. For when I talk to Morgan again," I explained vaguely.

She brightened as though I'd said something sensible. "Why not? You'll see it can't have been anything to do with the business which drove him to do it. We'll take you round ourselves. Tomorrow morning?"

"I'd like that." Although I'd have preferred to have done without their escort, it would be easier to look around with them than having another go at persuading the man on the gate that I had any reason at all to pay him a second visit.

I waved Stephen and his partner off in the direction of their boat, agreeing that of course I would return the visit, and went back in to my cold caf.

17

They called for me next morning before I'd had more than one dose of caf. I smiled and tried to look more eager and awake than I felt. I wasn't really sure what I felt, or what I was hoping to find out. Everything pointed to suicide so far and that was exactly what Morgan wanted to hear. I wasn't sure he had the sort of curiosity that would want to know *why* someone would hang himself from the deckhead of his brand-new cruiser with no more explanation than an apology for the inconvenience. Unfortunately, that was exactly the sort of curiosity I had. Previous experience, it seemed, wasn't enough to put me off.

The cab ride to the ferry terminal was an improvement over public transport. So was the way the door opened after the briefest security scan. I don't know what code Stephen had input but it certainly gained him priority. The tekkie in the plex box blinked at me, saw who I was with. Said nothing.

There was another man there, waiting to welcome us. He was no one I'd ever seen before and wore a professional smile which said he could hardly have imagined a more enjoyable start to the day than to have an unscheduled visit from two of his company's directors. And their hanger-on.

"Stephen, Amanda!" A widening of the smile included me in his delight. "This is a welcome surprise." He almost sounded as though he meant it.

Amanda smiled. "Simon, it's good to see you. We're in Midway for the Port Opening celebrations and couldn't miss the opportunity to pay you a visit. Especially when our friend Humility here told us she'd heard good reports of Ardco – naturally we want to show the place off." We'd decided in the cab that Andy's death wasn't yet something the rest of the company needed to know. Suicide might be a personal tragedy; there was no need to make it a corporate crisis.

Simon looked as though we'd made his morning. "Of course!" He smiled at me, the source of this unexpected delight. "It's mostly offices and warehousing here – no hi-end passenger facilities or anything like that."

My smile was as sincere as his. "I'd heard you were a specialist freight company. Quite slick and sharp – the big two will have to watch out."

A light laugh. "Not yet. But we do pride ourselves on a quick turnround and reliable handling. Come in and see the inside. Have some caf."

Perhaps he was more my type than I thought. I followed him into the building with more enthusiasm than I'd felt ten minutes ago.

The caf was hot, and that was the best that could be said about it. The stuff I made on the *Pig* was infinitely better, and it would have been an insult even to think of Tom Lee's product at the same time. Whatever went into the Ardco brand, it was a long way removed from the original bean. Amanda's decision to stay with water began to look intelligent.

The offices were like offices everywhere: lots of screens and cabinets, coded stream chasing itself off quietly humming monitors, stark lighting that did the eyes no favours and the occasional red light flashing its demand for attention. As far as I could see, the outside vids gave coverage of the whole active area, the docking bays and the street entrance. Wherever the girl gang was hiding must be somewhere off-screen. I wondered just who in the company knew of their presence. Decided not to ask.

Simon took a quiet revenge for the morning's interruptions by showing us everything he could. There were several offices and a warehouse about a third full of boxed stuff and a couple of containers and no clue at all to what was in any of them. They were numbered but not marked with their shipping destination or source as far as I could tell.

"You said you were specialist," I said to show I'd been paying attention. "What sort of goods do you deal with?"

Another chance for Simon to download more information than I needed. "Fragile and perishable items get high-grade care – it's not something the big companies can always guarantee and it gives us a chance to raise our margins." High cost for careful treatment. Made sense. But Simon had more to tell me. "At the moment we're only concentrating on the Euro market, especially France. It's sometimes a bit chaotic, but the goods are individual and we have some very..." He hesitated. "Some very *particular* customers who are willing to pay for our services. Of course, client confidentiality..." Of course. Amanda and Stephen smiled approval and understanding of his lack of detail.

I knew exactly what he meant about the chaos of France. It was why I could trade in the sort of wine which would once have been allowed out of its chateau only after a lot of loving care and some on-site bottling. I always apologised to it for the treatment it got from me, and relied on its quality to survive the trauma of being bulk-shipped on a barge. I hoped Ardco wasn't thinking of overlapping into that trade. Said nothing. Accepted the glossy and expensive paperwork which Simon enjoyed heaping into my arms.

One of the monitors showed a ferry unloading. It looked as new as the one I'd seen yesterday. Not the same one, though. Slightly higher superstructure and wider cargo bay.

"Is it possible to look round one of your vessels?" I could be polite, too.

Naturally it was possible. Nothing was too much trouble for Stephen and Amanda and their friend.

The ferry was standard. Load areas for trucks and other vehicles. Bay for containers. Limited accommodation and supplies for drivers and the occasional foot passengers, a standard-looking bridge. All fairly new.

Simon glanced at the chrono mounted over a wheel which was probably largely ornamental. "I'm afraid this boat's on a tight schedule. Unless there's anything else in particular you'd like to see…"

"No. I'm sorry." Amanda was happy to end the tour. "We wouldn't dream of compromising your schedule – after all, that's where the profit lies, isn't it?"

I nodded to show that I'd understood this lesson, too, and accompanied the others back down to the dockyard. If there had been the flicker of a shadow moving round the discarded containers in that remote corner of the yard, it was too fleeting for me to be certain.

18

Back at Midway I waved Amanda and Stephen to their cruiser, accepted a vague invitation to come over for a drink and a look around 'sometime soon' and walked over to the Port Office.

Lloyd was in and free to see me. "See you've made some new friends." He kept as sharp an eye on his monitors as Daisy had done.

"Yes. I told them *Felicity*'s owner was dead, didn't give them any details. Has the boat been hauled out?"

"Over at the back of the yard sheds, under a tarpaulin. If you want a look round I can clear you. Morgan said to let you wander free."

I wondered just how much Lloyd knew about what had gone on here a few weeks ago, and about my role in it. He didn't seem the type to let someone off the leash if he thought she might make trouble for him.

"Thanks. I'll take you up on that. The owner isn't…"

A sudden shark's grin of white teeth. "No. He's not aboard any more. But if you want access, I'm sure I can arrange it."

"No." Someone had told him I'd thrown up over the morgue floor when I'd seen a body there. Since I couldn't guarantee I wouldn't do the same again, I had no intention of risking it. "But I wouldn't mind a look at the medic's report, if there is one."

"There certainly is. Morgan's making sure no one can say he tried to bury this one."

It sounded as though a bit of gossip had leaked out about the 'accidents' that had happened here before.

Morgan wasn't the type to allow anything to taint his glossy new project if there was something he could do to stop it. And since it didn't look as though anyone else in his Family was involved this time, there was plenty he could do about it.

"I'll send the details to your screen."

Oh good. More reading material. "Thanks. Is there a chance of seeing Morgan? I can update him online but I'd rather meet in person."

Lloyd probably thought I was being security-conscious. Or that I just liked having Family access. Truth is, I don't much like screen-talk. Faces don't tell you nearly as much as body language.

"I'll call him."

I didn't have Morgan's code. And it made sense to keep Lloyd in the frame if I was poking round his dockyard when it was full of media and Family.

"You going to be on your boat?" he asked.

I should have been. There was plenty of work to do there, but I was still juggling two problems and I also needed to get rid of the taste of Ardco's caf. I'd accepted the ride back from town partly because Stephen and Amanda had assumed I would, partly because I hadn't wanted them to know my plans. I was about to head right back in to the city – to treat myself to the best caf available, and to see if I could tap into the one or two sources I had left for info on street life.

"No. Going back into town. I'll be at Tom Lee's for an hour or two. After that, I'm not sure." And if Tom Lee didn't feel like talking, I wouldn't be there any longer than it took to down one cup of his caf. I couldn't afford two.

If Lloyd knew Tom Lee was the biggest fence in Sutton as well as the owner of the best caf-house, he didn't comment. "I'll pass that on. Call you when I've made contact."

"Thanks."

19

Buses had become things I didn't care for. The cab was still around so I negotiated a deal that was a lot less than Stephen and Amanda had paid and let myself be driven to central Sutton.

Tom Lee's was packed. Just gone midday and everyone wanted to eat or drink or be seen. The tables out front were spilling over the pavement beyond the shade of the awning: there were always a few lunatics willing to risk an hour or two's sun even at noon just to be seen here. Inside, the tables were packed so that customers were squeezed into a false intimacy they'd never have tolerated in a place less fashionable. At least they knew they were secure. Someone like Tom Lee hadn't built the power base he had without security screens which were as near impenetrable as you can get. And the petty thief who tried to lift a bag or credit bracelet here would be deleted before he left the building.

But it wasn't security I was interested in. I barged and oozed my way to the stainless counter and managed to order caf. I waited till it arrived and stopped the server before she turned away in that choreographed dance which looks effortless and which gets around tables faster than any drone could manage.

"If Tom Lee has five, will he talk to Humility?"

A flicker of something combining surprise and curiosity disturbed the professional smile for a second. "I'll pass it on." Then she was weaving her way to the next customer, leaving me to preserve my space with my elbows and enjoy the caf without much expectation of a deal.

20

Two things happened next. Cause and effect. Morgan walked in and Tom Lee materialised in the space which had somehow appeared around me.

"Humility."

"Tom Lee," I acknowledged. He was as elegant and unreadable as ever. Thin and dressed in black, white silk at his throat. Face drawn into a skull by the hair slicked back into a tight pigtail. Fastidious, you might say. Then you saw the blackened nails and wondered. Even when we did business, he could make my flesh creep with a barely perceptible shift of expression.

He nodded at the man beside me. "Vinci. A table?"

I'd have sworn there were no tables free and probably a queue logged in for the rest of the week, or even the year, for this time. Apparently not an issue if you were Family.

"For three." Morgan's reply was curt, taking the service for granted. I wondered who the third was. Tom Lee? Unlikely. But he might talk later now he'd seen the company I was keeping.

The table materialised with no obvious effort and no apparent ill-feeling among the other diners. Impressive.

Morgan ordered caf and a salad. Didn't show much interest in it when it arrived. Looked at me without much expression. The beard might not have been meant to make him enigmatic, but it helped. My own guilt about his brother's death – even though his brother had tried his best to kill me – distorted my reading of him. At least, that's what I think the problem was. Perhaps I just didn't care enough.

"You wanted to talk," he reminded me. "This seemed a better idea than Midway."

On all sorts of levels. The food tasted a lot better and the chance of gossip spreading were far less.

"Yes. I wanted to talk about Andy, the guy who hanged himself." Just in case he'd forgotten who I meant.

"That's the point. Did he? Hang himself?" He hadn't forgotten. Of course.

I shrugged slightly. "Early days, but as far as I can see there's no evidence to say he didn't – or none that I've found yet. I've met two of his colleagues – " His nod showed he knew just who I was talking about – "and they seem appropriately shocked. Went round the ferry business this morning."

"Anything off there?" Meaning, more than you'd expect.

"Not obvious. I'd like to know a bit more, though."

"I was warned about that." He looked beyond my right shoulder to the main entrance. "That's why I asked Byron to join us."

The third party. He was as expressionless as always. Tailored clothes. Shoes that shone. Naked dark head gleaming. The map-like pattern that had been there last time we met had gone. Some exotic symbol there now. As meaningless or profound as the map. For others to decipher. Byron specialised in inscrutability and hi-tech. He was every technocrat embodied and he didn't do social or small talk.

"Byron."

"Humility," he acknowledged as he took the spare seat.

Morgan wasn't being sociable. "So you think suicide's the right answer?"

I hesitated. Almost said: Morally or practically? And: Depends what you mean by right. Or do you just want an explanation for poor hanged Andy? Knew the answer and still hesitated.

"Like I said. Looks like suicide. So far. Doesn't make much sense, though."

Morgan frowned. Not what he wanted to hear. "How not?"

"No motive – guy leaves a note, you'd think he'd explain as well as apologise. Besides, would you hang yourself so that you could almost touch the ground if you stretched your toes out a bit?" That had bothered me from the start. Seemed too much like adding masochism to a death wish.

Morgan winced at the thought, but persisted. "But there's no evidence for anything except self-termination?" He wanted a definite answer. I wasn't going to give one.

"None I've found. I've only had twenty-four hours. Leave it with me a couple more days. Perhaps I can find a why to make sense of the how." Looked over at Byron. "With a little tech help."

A nod. "Of course." Byron didn't rate my tech skills. He didn't have a scale that went that low. He was probably faintly surprised I was even capable of accessing the *Pig*'s systems. Which were archaic. But since he was the one who'd involved me in this in the first place, he must have known I'd call on him at some point. He was many things, most of them annoying, but he wasn't a fool. "What do you need?"

"Ardco's background. The scale of Andy's involvement – and the tie-in with Amanda and Stephen," I added as an afterthought.

"I'll send the details to your screen." They'd probably be there before I was. "That all?"

It was clearly too petty for a man of his skills. "If you can work out what they're trading in off the books, that might help. And check out Andy's system? See if there's anything there that might have been a trigger?"

Illegal. The sort of privacy-snooping that really annoyed the limited law enforcement system. Morgan's frown twitched again but Byron nodded. "Logical." Praise indeed.

"Is this necessary? You say you've seen nothing to suggest it wasn't suicide. We don't need to dissect the man's life."

That was where we were different. That was exactly what I wanted to do. Andy alive meant nothing to me. Dead, he was a puzzle, someone who was a victim – possibly just of life's burdens, perhaps of something more calculated – and I tend to side with victims. If Morgan hadn't wanted me to become involved, he shouldn't have dragged me off to look at a dead man. "I don't want to leave it like this."

I saw Byron nod, as though I'd confirmed something. He'd come across my persistence – he'd had other terms for it – before. No End Program key.

Morgan wasn't happy. Not that I'd ever seen him smile much, but this time he was unhappy with me and the fact that I didn't show any signs of worrying what he thought. "All right. You have until the celebrations start. I don't want anything disrupting them."

Two more days. I wondered how Morgan was going to prevent disruptions like rain and decided I didn't want to know. There was probably a back-up plan, plus a well-paid meteorologist keeping him updated with every shift of a low-pressure system. Wished I'd had one last week. Then I wouldn't have been caught out by that gale and I would be moored somewhere in France right now.

And Andy would still be dead.

21

Morgan and Byron hadn't stayed long but I'd waited. At the bar. No one sat alone at a table for three when half the population of Sutton queued for lunch. No one who wasn't Family.

"Tom Lee will see you."

The girl who'd been serving sounded disbelieving but gestured to the mirrored doorway I'd used before.

Another air-lock. Another wait. This one to remind me that I was the petitioner. Had long enough to wonder if he'd have come looking for me otherwise, wanting to know what business Family was trading in. How it might profit him.

"Humility." I released my death-clasp on my sack and walked into the room where he waited, restless eyes moving between screens and scanning data. "You trading?"

He knew I wasn't. What I had in my tanks wasn't enough to trade even if it hadn't been shaken into near-vinegar by the gale. I'd drink it myself or give it to someone I disliked.

"Nothing to trade."

"You sure?"

"Morgan's business is his. Doesn't cross you or yours." That was as much as I was prepared to offer.

"'Kay. Might help."

So I had a glimmer of credit. Not enough, but that hadn't stopped me in the past. "Want to contact Luna. Street kid, blader. You remember her?"

Since he'd taken her on when she'd been beaten up and nearly burned to death, and since Tom Lee never forgot anything that might be useful to him, the question was really whether or not he was willing to admit to it.

"Might. What you need?"

"To talk to her." I hesitated but his stone face didn't alter. I'd known I wouldn't get away without an explanation. "My niece left home. Ran to Sutton, they think. I'm looking for her. No luck so far. She's thirteen with no street sense so she's likely hit trouble. Hoped Luna could keep an ear open or give me some pointers."

Luna thought she owed me. As long as it didn't mean trouble for her with her boss, I'd a good chance of getting what help she could offer. Which was why I'd come direct to Tom Lee.

Who was sitting with his sleek black clothes and filthy fingernails and no expression at all on his face.

"You sure the girl's still alive?"

"Yes." I'd wondered. But that was the one thing they could and would have told me at Town Hall. Her implant wouldn't tell them where she was but they'd have known if it had dropped off the screen. The mess of a few weeks ago had given me a horror of implants and good reason not to trust them, but I had to assume hers was still functioning.

He waited a minute longer. Tom Lee wasn't going to rush into sympathetic platitudes, nor was he going to let me think I could get anything easily. Finally nodded.

"I'll say you want to talk. Up to her to make contact."

"Thanks." As good as I could have hoped. Perhaps the meal with Morgan had gained me more credit than I'd calculated.

22

I'd talked to too many people today. I had two separate problems and both were urgent. Charity had been gone too long not to have found some sort of trouble, and Morgan would only give me another forty-eight hours.

Andy was already dead. If my time with Morgan ran out, I didn't have to stop. I just had to be careful about causing ripples that might reach him. Charity's situation was more immediate. Just waiting for Luna to make contact wasn't an option.

I know Sutton but I'm not street-wise. I've never had to scavenge for food or shelter and learn to detect a predator in time to make an escape. My life with Jack might have been chaotic but it had had its own security: I'd always known I could trust his intentions if not his abilities and though his grand plans invariably ended in disappointment, at least he knew how to dream. Street kids don't indulge in luxuries like dreams. Their eyes are on the gutters and the shadows, and a night without fear or with a full belly is as much as they hope for.

I didn't think it was a world Charity would last long in.

Until Luna decided whether she would help, I was on my own. Almost. There was one person who'd shown some concern. Problem was how to contact her without her dragon overseer stepping in.

A public terminal told me nothing much about Town Hall staff. No surprise. No one who worked there would want their personal details anywhere near the public domain. A glance at my chrono showed me I had an hour before the offices shut. Civil servants keep lazy hours.

Which suited me fine.

A greasy haze veiled the worst of the sunlight and I had UV filters. Even my pale skin wasn't going to burn badly in a short walk across town. Still, early afternoon in summer is not a good time to be out. Tempers fray easily and everyone has just enough energy to fight to keep their own piece of shade. No one moves who doesn't have to. Fumes from the vehicles which manage to find bootleg fossil fuel hang in the air, burning the throat and eyes. No one cares about emission regs. Who's going to enforce them in a place like Sutton? And the bootleggers pay off the cops. No point telling them to change over to fusion drives. They still like noisy cars with lots of power. Just like themselves.

Town Hall shimmered in the heat. The broad steps leading up to the main entrance had once been some sort of white stone. Even now they reflected the glare from their cracked and stained surfaces. The plaza round the building was a desert.

Fortunately, there was an oasis. Just a man with a concession and a frayed awning. Not many people wanted to linger in this area but that suited me. Meant there was space under his awning and I could barter a few old coins for something that he swore was purified water, iced. I wasn't developing Amanda's tastes but I'd gone through too much caf of too many different qualities to try his version. And the water wouldn't kill me. Probably.

So I sat in the shade and waited for an hour.

23

She wasn't the first in the rush for the door. I hadn't expected her to be.

I saw her the moment she emerged, blinking, on to the steps. She was alone. She wasn't looking where she was going and both hands gripped the sack she carried crosswise across her body. Quick neat steps were taking her to some familiar goal and her own privacy shields were as obvious as a solid wall around her.

She didn't see me until I came within a pace of breaching her territory. Then she flinched. Hands tightening on her bag, not knowing whether to throw it at me or to run and try to keep hold of it.

"Hi." I couldn't think of anything else to say which wouldn't scare her silly.

She looked up, stumbled back a pace, panic about to take over. Then her eyes widened. Recognition. Shock.

"I saw you yesterday."

"That's it. I was looking for my niece and you were helpful." Enough to make her remarkable in almost any city context.

"I remember." Her voice was soft, almost apologetic. "Have you found her?"

"Not yet. Did you mean it when you offered to help?"

She hesitated. Wise enough not to commit to something unknown. "If I can, but…"

"I know. You can't risk your job. All I need is for someone to monitor the ID site – let me know if something happens." It's hard to say *if she dies*. "I can give you a contact. All I'd want is a message."

The look on her thin face was relief and embarrassment. "I can do that for you. I wish I could do more."

She couldn't. Just keeping me up to date was a risk. But knowing that someone could access the data for me was a relief. I might have asked Byron to do it, but this woman would care. Enough, I guessed, to look out for anything else which might show on stray kids.

I gave her my contact details. Didn't ask for hers but she told me anyway. "I'm Meera. My site's not secure but I'd get a message if you left it."

Warning me to be careful if I had to make contact. Wanting to know if the story she'd become involved in had any sort of happy ending. I wished I could offer her hope, wished I could feel much myself. I understood the urge to do something about an impossible situation; trouble was that I couldn't think of much useful to do.

What I did know was that I didn't want to talk to my mother until I had something to tell her.

24

I wanted to go home. I wanted to be back on board the *Pig* with no one disturbing me and nothing to worry me except how drinkable my wine supply was. I wanted to avoid the celebrations which were about to start at Midway and I wanted to be able to close my eyes and not see a hanged man or a frightened child.

Because I couldn't, I made myself take a bus ride down to the docks. My mind kept circling back to this new and unusually profitable ferry business which seemed to be the only important thing in Andy's life.

At least this time no one, including myself, was stupid enough to cause trouble. I left the bus just beyond the entrance to Ardco and walked east. If I'd knocked on the door I'd have been let in. Simon, if he was still at work, would have been polite and would have tried his best to offer me even more statistics and paper and unhelpful information.

I didn't want to see Simon again.

I didn't want to see anyone official at Ardco.

I wanted to find a back door. When a business is based on the water, there's usually a back door most people don't bother with. I needed a small boat.

You can find anything in a city if you know where to look or who to ask or have enough credit. I was short on credit and didn't know enough people, but the one area of Sutton I knew well was its waterfront.

There's a place at the east end of the docks, about half a kilometre or a little more from the Ardco site, which is more derelict than most. Around eighty years ago there'd been a ferry landing there for people who wanted to cross that arm of the river to get to work in the main part of the city, but then they'd built the bridge and nothing much had happened to the ferry landing. The asphalt had cracked and the mud had crept in. The few houses and businesses had fallen into decay and collapsed without the little trade the ferry had brought. No one had thought it worth developing.

That didn't mean the place was deserted. I knew that on the opposite shore some unofficial trading went on. People fished the waters for goods and scrap, and the occasional not very appetising fish. There were a few crab pots, struggling to hold their ground against the fierce run of the tide, but I wouldn't eat shellfish from these waters with a gun held to my head. And where there were boats, there were boat builders and repairers and people willing to hire out leaky craft for extortionate sums and no questions. Jack and I had explored down here once, and he'd introduced me to an old man who claimed he preferred to work from this bank because the other "had got too busy." Translation: he'd been driven out.

There was no one visible when I reached the old slipway. I stood around, trying to look unthreatening and possibly solvent without advertising any sort of vulnerability. A hard look to carry off and I doubt if I managed. But it was too hot to start trouble and I can't have looked rich.

After ten minutes I saw movement off to my right. Drifted over in that direction. A kid was digging bait in the mud. I shuddered. It wasn't so long ago that I'd been chased through Solent mud and I knew how it was gritty and slippery at once, letting you slide into it and clinging as it refused to release you. The kid didn't look my way but I felt the movement behind me before I heard the voice.

"Looking for someone?" A woman. Dressed in ragged layers, cloth over her head against the sun. Age indeterminate and voice cracked with shouting or substance abuse or age.

I squinted in her direction. "Solomon. Old guy. Met him here about five years back."

I'd never heard anyone cackle before. "That old sod. The bugger's been gone three years. You owe him?"

A note of hope in the question. I shook my head. "No. Did want to trade, though."

The thought there might be credit to be had kept her there. "Trade what?" Nothing to strangers. "You think we're running a market here?" Her gesture took in the ruins of houses and the filthy ooze at the water's edge.

"Want to hire a boat. Small craft, reliable drive and no major leaks. Use it for the afternoon."

She stared. "And I want fresh running water and credits to spare. That makes two of us who are going to be disappointed."

I liked her. "I might help with a few credits if you have any ideas about the boat."

She whistled. I can't whistle. What she did would have stopped traffic in any street in the city. It even made the mud-smeared child look up. My admiration grew.

"Davy! Get on over here!"

Davy heaved the bait bucket out of the mud, waved one mucky hand and began to trudge towards us.

"Davy's my boy." I'd guessed. "Can't give you a boat. We've nothing to spare and I don't know you to trust you with anything I do have."

"That's fair. What're you offering?" It was going better than I'd hoped.

"Depends where you want to go."

There was no way she wouldn't find out. "Docks. Want a quiet look at one of them."

"There's docks there with security would blow you out the water if you got too close. Wouldn't want to go near them."

"You mean the Family businesses?"

"You know anyone else with credit for that level of protection?"

I was hoping not. "The place I'm looking at probably thinks it's secure. I'm not sure. Wouldn't go in if I thought it was hi-risk."

"So where are you talking about?"

"Ardco. Newish ferry outfit. Lots of clean paint and sparkle."

"I know the place. Security's not bad." It told me something about where her family made most of its living if she knew the status of all the yards. She was exactly the person I needed. She was grinning, showing bad teeth. "Shit-faced guy with a smile full of teeth runs it. Thinks he invented the business and talks more crap than most. You won't get on to one of his ferries if that's what you want."

I shook my head, trying not to laugh at her image of Simon. "No. I just want to get ashore in the yard – not the ferry mooring – for an hour or so."

She looked at me. Considered. Looked at the water. Slack tide.

"Davy, bring round the small boat. See it's fuelled up." Turned to me. "How much you paying?"

In the end the deal was the usual: more than I wanted to pay, less than she asked. Negotiations took slightly longer than it took Davy to come back at the helm of something about three metres long that floated and might have been meant to be some sort of boat. I wasn't about to argue.

I guessed Davy wouldn't be out in it if he thought it was likely to sink in the next few hours.

The boat was aluminium, dented, blunt at both ends with a moulded thwart and water ankle-deep in the bilge. The drive was rusty and the shimmer on the bilge water suggested it leaked fuel. No one would look twice at it, especially not if it was driven by a scrawny boy who couldn't be much more than nine. They just might look twice at his passenger.

Davy was no idiot. He looked at me and the boat and said, "Ma. This lady needs a cover-up. There's that old tarp in the backyard."

"Good thinking." Then, to me. "He's a bright lad. Don't you let him come to no harm."

"I'll try not to." The tarp was stiff with salt water and old paint but once I'd huddled under it no one would think I was out of place on the water.

"I'm going to the Ardco yard," I told Davy. "You know it?"

He frowned. "Place with the flag? Red triangle in a white circle?"

Being illiterate didn't stop you recognising signs. Or logos. I nodded. "That's the one. Can you get me ashore there and pick me up after about an hour without the ferry people spotting me?"

"'Course he can. Just don't stay there once the ebb starts running hard. That drive won't do much against full tide."

I nodded and Davy looked indifferent. It was somehow reassuring.

The drive was too noisy for talk and conversation on water carries further than most people realise. I've heard some tender exchanges, and some hot-blooded accusations, which would have embarrassed the parties involved. Davy might have been young but he knew what

85

he was doing as he eased the leaky vessel along, hugging the shore to avoid what tide there was. There was no dispute over our roles: he drove, I bailed.

25

The trip down the river mouth and west into the Solent, heading up to the docks, lasted just under an hour. Davy took us past the Ardco dockyard and then cut the drive. The tide began to drift the boat back and he controlled our progress by sculling with an oar over the stern. No noise.

He spoke quietly. "There's a place just t'other side of the dock. Don't think the vid scans it 'cause it's got no use: too soft for the drones to work and not enough space to put up another store. You'll get muddy."

Not unusual. "'Kay. Let me off there. You'll be OK out here?"

He sneered. "Know a place to hole up. Might find something useful there." None of my business. "Come back for you when the tide starts to run hard."

I doubted if he had a chrono but he'd know the tides better than any of the pilots on the ferries. Probably better than the mechs.

"I'll watch for you."

I eased myself over the boat's side, shedding the smelly tarpaulin. The mud sucked at my shoes but there was hard standing under it so I didn't sink beyond my ankles. Better than I'd feared. Squelched up to the shore, keeping low.

I wanted to look round one of the ferries without Simon's attention one day, but that would have to wait because there wasn't one docked. Besides, it wasn't anyone in Ardco I was interested in this afternoon. And I was more wary of the person I hoped to meet than I ever would be of Simon.

It was only half a dozen paces to the scrapyard of

discarded chain, half-empty drums of paint and fuel, and rusting heaps of metal. The next step took me over the boundary I'd crossed on my first visit. I stopped and waited.

Nothing at first. Just a sense of being watched which could as easily have been my own imagination and nerves. You don't confront a girl gang if you don't need to. Especially not on their home patch. I had nothing to offer them and they had no reason at all to give me anything but grief. It wasn't just the afternoon sun that had the sweat pooling at the base of my spine.

I waited. Felt the seconds ticking off in my head. Wondered whether the embarrassment of still being standing waiting while nothing happened when Davy returned would be worse than facing the gang.

They came up behind me.

"You're in the wrong place. Again."

I turned slowly, arms slightly out from my body, palms wide to show their emptiness. The same girl who had spoken before had one lieutenant with her. She didn't even need that to take me down.

"I'm where I chose to be. Want to talk."

"Walk, instead." A loaded pause. "While you can."

I swallowed. Most of my life I avoid physical confrontations. This was the second I'd faced in two days and this one was deliberate. I hoped I wouldn't have to back down again; I'd have felt more sure of getting away from the fat guy on the bus than I did with this girl.

Her face was pale. She wasn't wearing any obvious screens but standing in the full sun like that only reinforced her message: she wasn't scared and she wasn't going away. I hadn't expected anything else.

Her hands tightened on the chain she carried. "You're

still here. Got a death wish? Or want to join us?" The last was more sneer than question and the snigger from the girl beside her told me just how unlikely I was as a gang candidate.

"No death wish. Need a favour."

The lieutenant laughed aloud. The girl just stared, but even she couldn't quite hide a flicker of something that had to be astonishment. "You crazy? Or trading? We got all the stuff we need."

She'd have said that if they'd been dying of thirst. Gangs take; they don't trade.

I needed to say my piece before she decided she'd had enough entertainment and called on the others who must be waiting in the shadows behind me. "My niece. Runaway. Don't blame her but want to know she's OK. Safe."

A shrug. "What's safe? And what's she to us? We look after ourselves, that's all."

"She might try to join you. She's from a Community. No street sense. If you see her, can you tell her Humility asked? That she can call on me at Midway if she wants help?"

"Who cares? One more kid don't matter. If she's smart she'll make it. If not..." Another shrug. "We're not a charity."

"That's her name. If she's using it. Will you tell her if you see her?"

Her face remained blank but my persistence was beginning to annoy the lieutenant. Her scowl deepened and she pulled a short iron bar from her belt. "You was told to go and you're still here. You think you can ask all sorts of questions and walk away like some bloody aristo? Let me show her, Sal. Let's see how well she gets back in that boat with a broken leg." She took a step forward, almost up to Sal's shoulder.

I couldn't help my hands clenching, wanting to find a weapon of my own. Knowing I had to get past them both to get to the water where there was no sign at all of Davy. Would he come back? Were he and his ma already laughing over the easy credits they'd earned from a fool who didn't know better? I tried not to think of crawling through that mud with a broken leg to a dinghy which wasn't going to appear. It was as much as I could manage to keep looking at Sal, showing as little emotion as I could. She just waited, weight balanced equally on both feet. She was the real fighter.

The coldest smile I've ever seen touched her mouth and I felt my own blood chill. "Well, *Humility*," she mocked. "Shall I let Annie play with you?"

Annie was still looking all too ready for some light exercise.

"Please don't," I said. "I don't walk well on one leg."

Sal just stared. And then laughed, as though I'd said something that really did amuse her.

"You are truly crazy." She'd get no argument from me. Something indefinable relaxed in her pose, the chain between her hands slackened. "They say it's unlucky to kill the mad, and we need all the luck we can get. So, just this once, I'm going to let you run away." She took a deliberate pace to one side, freeing my path to the water. Annie, after a pause that said she wasn't doing this willingly, copied her.

I felt like a mouse when the cat has raised its paw and let its victim run, just for a few minutes' entertainment. Took a cautious step towards the mud. Hesitated.

"No. Don't say anything else or I might just lose my sense of humour."

Something told me Sal's sense of humour was very fragile. I shut my mouth and walked on down to the water's edge, not even wondering whether I was going to show up on Ardco's vids. Somehow it didn't seem important.

Davy must have been lurking somewhere where he could observe without being seen. I thanked the God I didn't believe in that some people were willing to keep their side of a bargain, and waded to the boat where he reached out a scrawny arm to help me back on board.

His expression suggested that he would have echoed Sal's diagnosis of my mental health. "You really went there to face up to them girls? And they let you go?"

"Seems like. Must think I'm harmless."

He snorted. "They'd have squished you like a bug if they'd thought that. They don't let *no one* come on their ground without being asked."

I huddled under the tarpaulin, chilled despite the sun. "Well, I won't be going back without an invite."

He shook his head and fired up the drive. I wondered whether I'd done anything useful at all, or just taken a stupid chance that should have got me beaten up or worse.

26

The internal chill was only beginning to fade when I got back on board the *Pig*. I wanted to think about what had happened today, whether I'd managed to do anything useful at all and just where I was in relation to both my problems.

I'd done what I could to track Charity, short of walking the streets myself, which was more likely to get me seriously injured than locate a child who didn't want to be found. Meera would let me know if the worst happened; there was a very faint possibility that I'd appealed enough to Sal's sense of humour for her to at least keep a passive watch. And if Tom Lee linked me up with Luna, I might be able to spread a wider net. It didn't seem much but I couldn't think of anything else I could do right now. And, if it involved leaving Midway again today, I didn't want to know about it.

I was less sure I was doing Andy any good. Morgan's patience for what was only a minor inconvenience to him was limited. And I wasn't quite sure what I was looking for. Perhaps nothing. Perhaps a man with some private misery had just chosen this week to opt out. Case closed. Except I wasn't quite convinced and it seemed likely that whatever problems he had were connected with his work. Ardco.

I had little doubt Ardco was smuggling. That was a given. Why else start up a ferry business? That didn't mean the business was driving – or pushing – people to their deaths. Not necessarily. What I had to find out was what they were smuggling, who was running the scam, and did it have anything at all to do with Andy's death? And

Morgan had given me two days.

I hoped the frantic message light on my vid meant that someone was about to come up with something really useful.

27

Amanda and Stephen wanted me to come over for a drink this evening. The medics' report was there. Simon had sent yet more data on Ardco. And Byron had left me enough information to sink the *Pig*. I chose to ignore everything except the medic's report. It was a thorough job: Family requests get special treatment. I tried not to look too hard at the images of Andy and concentrated instead on the colourless tech-speak about asphyxia and rope marks and the lack of signs of struggle.

Something was making me uneasy, but I couldn't pin it down. On the surface it looked straightforward, so why did I have a nagging feeling that it wasn't as simple as it seemed? I went through it again, this time not blocking out the more explicit details or ignoring the images: Andy dangling, feet almost brushing the expensive carpet; Andy on the morgue table, close-ups of neck and face and hands; less disturbing images of the rope, carefully cut to preserve the integrity of the knots.

The knots. I knew about knots. Called for close-ups, looking hard at what he'd tied. Not a hangman's knot: the noose was tied with a slipknot. I winced. Thought of the pain of strangulation on top of the slow suffocation of hanging. Wouldn't he have changed his mind? Fought it? Chosen something easier? There were enough chemicals available, legal as well as street, to float into eternity. Had he needed to punish himself? But if he had I'd have expected him to have needed confession. *To acknowledge and confess our manifold sins and wickedness.* The note had given nothing away.

The more I looked at the medic's report, the less I could see fun-loving Andy stringing himself up and waiting for the end. But there was no hard evidence. Without it, Morgan could as easily decide to go with the obvious and declare it suicide. Make the appropriate sad noises and a generous contribution to funeral expenses. And then get on with the party.

I frowned at the report I'd read half a dozen times. Shoved away from the table and stood up, stretching cramped muscles and rubbing a neck grown stiff with peering at details, trying to make sense of the senseless.

I *hated* the idea of suicide. Rationally I knew it could be an acceptable solution to an intolerable problem, better than ongoing pain or grief or other torment, but I was angry with Andy. He had no right to drop out with no excuse. And if he hadn't done so, I wanted to know who had made that choice for him.

I looked at my chrono. The light was beginning to go outside but I wanted to look at *Felicity*. There was something I needed to check. For perhaps thirty seconds I thought I could leave it till the morning. The promise of a night of dreams haunted by a man's body swinging slowly from a short rope decided me. It wouldn't take long.

28

The tekkie on security duty in the shed didn't want to let me in.

"Call Lloyd," I suggested. "Or Morgan."

He laughed. "Sure. Family's just longing to hear from me." Something in my face made him stop laughing. "'Kay. I'll call the PO."

Whatever Lloyd said didn't please him, but he stepped aside. Gestured at the sheeted boat-shape at the back of the shed. Even put the floods on. "All yours." He walked away with a shrug which told me what he thought of nosy women and a PO who encouraged them to wander all over the place.

Felicity was as sad as most boats out of water. The gloom induced by the covering tarpaulin didn't help. I pulled it back so that I could prop a ladder against the hull and clamber into the cockpit.

Her lights were still working and the saloon looked almost normal. Luxury fittings, nothing too old-fashioned, everything nautical enough to let the happy sailor remember he was afloat but nothing that risked reminding him that life on board might sometimes get rough or uncomfortable. Cruisers like this were for playing around in sheltered waters on calm days, going in little fleets from one marina to another. If you wanted to join your boat in a more exotic location, you hired crew to deliver it – and the saloon was probably out of bounds to them. The ringbolt screwed into a beam in the centre of the deckhead might have had any number of genuine sea-going uses. In the context of this softly furnished comfort it just looked wrong.

I stood on one of the side berths and leaned across to get a better look at it. Whoever had mounted it hadn't bothered to disguise its rawness: the fitting was obviously new. It had been screwed into the beam with no particular regard for the paintwork and no attempt to make it blend in with the rest of the décor.

I looked around the carpet. No sawdust. Had Andy drilled the hole, mounted the bolt, carefully swept away the traces of his handiwork, and then killed himself?

I went through every locker which could conceivably have held tools and several that could not. I learned that Andy was obsessively tidy; liked wearing bright colours; had a surprisingly lurid taste in erotic magazines featuring girls who looked barely legal; drank quite sparingly, and was willing to leave a bottle of wine half-finished; but found absolutely no trace of evidence that he had ever used a tool in his life. The few spanners and screwdrivers and automated tools in his kit had probably come with the boat and never been used.

As far as I could discover, he didn't own a drill.

I wondered just how any of us had decided Andy had killed himself. Had Morgan called me in because he could get rid of the peeps by saying it was under control – and trusted my stupidity or greed would have me saying what he wanted? Or did he somehow trust me to be more thorough than the local peeps who would just want to close the file and take the fee? No matter. What I'd seen here was enough to make me ignore the forty-eight hour limit he'd set. But he didn't need to know that until I'd done a little more research.

29

I decided to accept Amanda and Stephen's invitation.

The Happy Family was twice the size of Andy's cruiser and fitted out to the same high specs. This time I got the full tour, which confirmed everything I'd seen on my earlier visit. None of Andy's gleaming wood and brass for them. Not even a steering wheel. Everything was automated, remote-serviced. Lots of metallic gleam and the opaque darkness of touch screens controlling every activity I could imagine – and probably several I couldn't. The control panel for the drive baffled me completely. It was almost featureless, just a single screen and two dull silver buttons.

"How do you steer?"

Stephen laughed, small boy thrilled to show off his new toy. "I don't. I enter the destination codes – or key in a random plot if we just want to go for a spin round the area – and it does it all itself. Amanda and I both wear over-rides." The matching chunky bracelets began to look less cute and more understandable even if I didn't quite see why they had to wear them in harbour. "It can call up all the boat's functions. It'll even run the bath if you ask it – want to play?" He offered his wrist, his grin engagingly enthusiastic.

I shook my head, wondering about the sort of credits it took to install something so absurdly extravagant of water as a bath. "No thanks." I didn't see the point in boats where you didn't have a chance to do anything remotely connected with sailing. And the fact that he thought of his craft as 'it', not 'she', just reinforced my dislike of all the automation. Didn't help that there was nothing on this tub – including, probably, the bath – that I could fix if it went wrong.

Down below, the saloon wasn't much smaller than one of my cargo holds, and a lot more comfortable. Jack and I had opened up a hold for a memorable party once. My memory suggests we had thirty or forty invited guests and a few who'd come to complain about the noise and just stayed on. There weren't that many people here, probably no more than a dozen, and the atmosphere was a lot more decorous, but it wasn't going to be quite the casual drink I'd expected.

The saloon was furnished in the same hi-tech style as the bridge. Tables and settee berths were slick and glossy, moveable partitions broke up the space and provided display areas for art that was as cutting edge and indecipherable as everything else. I was just wishing Millie could see it when she emerged from behind one of the screens, large glass in one hand and Amanda by her side.

"Humility!" She waved the free hand.

Amanda came over with her. "Did Stephen give you the tour?" she asked.

"He did. I'm impressed. What on earth do you do if anything goes wrong?"

"Backups. Everywhere. And failing that, we call in someone from the port to fix it. But Stephen's the one who knows all about that sort of stuff; I just enjoy it." She gestured and a drone appeared. I accepted a glass of wine that was a lot better than the dregs I was currently carrying, even if it wasn't up to my best standards. "I gather you and Millie know each other?" She managed not to sound surprised.

"Humility and I go back a long way." Millie agreed. "I told you about her wine trade, didn't I?"

"Yes. Sounds impressive." She didn't sound very impressed. She was still on water.

I looked around. Saw a couple of faces from other yachts, no one I knew. "A good party," I suggested.

Her mouth twisted slightly. "Just a few friends. You're probably thinking it's a bit early after Andy…" I hadn't been. If Andy had been the fun-loving type they'd described, perhaps the entertainment wasn't so inappropriate. And I'd long ago stopped being surprised by much in human behaviour. Amanda still seemed to need to explain. "We like an active social life on the boat. At home, of course…" Of course.

You'd be very choosy about who you invited into your real home. But at least I now understood the boat's function. Sailing was just the fashionable thing to be doing; its real purpose was social. When the fashion changed, the boat would be traded in for whatever game replaced sailing. I smiled understandingly, ready to move off, free my hostess.

Hesitated. "About Andy?"

"Yes?" It wasn't the right place to discuss suicidal friends.

"Sorry. Just wondered whether word's got out?"

She understood. Nodded. "Gossip travels. But we haven't discussed details."

Bereavement was one thing, suicide something else entirely.

Millie and I wandered round the room. "So what do you think of the décor?" I gestured.

She was amused. "The hi-tech gloss? Some of the art work's not bad, and the furnishings are straight out of every style promo. Nothing personal. Amanda asked me what I'd do with it –" Her smile was wicked – "but she didn't like the idea of plush furnishings and drapes."

I looked around. Didn't blame Amanda. "Glad I don't have to keep up with trends."

"You wouldn't recognise a trend unless it tried to sink your precious barge."

True.

I circulated as best I could. Exchanged small talk. Wondered when I could leave. And whether there was anything on the boat I hadn't seen that I should have. Stephen had displayed his 'workshop' with pride. All sorts of gadgets. Nothing that looked as simple as a mechanical drill. Plenty of automatics.

The other guests were mostly off yachts in the marina. We exchanged polite details of boats, which confirmed we had nothing in common, and drifted off to have the same conversation with other people. Everyone said how much fun poor Andy had been. Even Simon, who'd had time since we last met to learn of the death of one of his directors. He looked hard at me before the smile reappeared. I wondered whether that was because he'd recently seen a vid of me sneaking into his yard the back way. Hoped not.

Eventually I found myself back with Amanda and Stephen.

"Thanks so much. Great evening," I lied.

"We're glad you enjoyed it." A smile from Stephen.

I wanted to get back to the austerity of the *Pig.* "Thanks for showing me over your boat. I'm impressed."

"Thanks. Andy was the real sailing enthusiast, of course. Such a shame he never really got to enjoy *Felicity.*"

"I went over there this afternoon," I admitted.

"You did?" He was startled.

"Yes. I needed to check something."

"And did it check OK?"

"I found what I was looking for." I accepted a top-up to my glass from an attentive drone as an alternative to explaining.

It took me another twenty minutes to get away, waving to Millie who was still holding court, and a glass.

I walked down the pontoon, enjoying the relative freshness of the summer night after the airlessness below decks on *The Happy Family*. Just who thought of these names? The *Pig* wrapped herself round me and comforted me after a surfeit of polite and meaningless talk. I thought about brewing some caf to clear my head. Amanda's wine was stronger than it tasted.

Then I passed out.

30

I was walking in darkness. Walls closing in and bellying out. A tunnel which curved round so I could see no end. Was there an end? It was getting narrower, pressing down on me. I panicked. Struck out.

Couldn't breathe. Couldn't get my hands to my throat, couldn't free myself from what was smothering me. Something was pushing me down, burying me alive. I screamed and no sound came out.

Drowning. Lungs filling and heart racing. Racing so hard it would burst and I would open my mouth and the sea would flood in and take me. And why was I still struggling?

31

Someone was shaking me. I tried to lift my head. It was too heavy. I was too tired and it hurt.

"Humility! Wake up, girl!"

Tried to prise my eyes open. The light hurt. Shut them again. Got shaken again.

"Wake up!"

Millie. She wouldn't give up.

"Stop it." At least, that was what I meant to say. Even I could hear it come out as not much more than a croak. My belly roiled. If she shook me again, I would...

She did. I did.

She swore. "Damn you. I paid good money for these shoes. Here, drink this."

Water in a mug which probably wouldn't break if I dropped it, which I could hold in two shaking hands and lift unsteadily to my mouth. "Rinse and spit."

A bowl thrust under my chin. I rinsed and spat. Took another sip. Swallowed it this time. Felt it touch something raw all the way down. Wondered whether it would stay there and held myself very still.

Noise behind me. Millie speaking to someone. Not me, so I didn't have to think about replying. Took another sip of water. Fumbled for the bowl as I lost it all again.

"That's revolting." Millie took the bowl away. Returned with another one. Refilled my mug.

Footsteps on the deck. A knock at the deckhouse door. Millie opening it.

"Come in. She's sick."

He could have smelled that. She'd called the medic. If I

thought I could have spoken clearly I'd have protested. Instead I let the medic tilt my head up, shine something into my eyes. Attach something else to my arm and read off something meaningless from a monitor.

"Humility? Can you hear me?" His voice was nice. I tried to tell him so. Heard an undercurrent of laughter. "Come on. Have you got rid of it all? Just how much did you drink?"

"Not a lot." The vowels were round and clumsy in my mouth; my tongue tripped over them.

"Really?" Sceptical.

"She's right." My friend Millie. She'd seen me tonight. Knew I hadn't drunk much. Knew I didn't pass out from drink. "She was sober an hour ago. Mostly. We were at the same do on one of the other boats."

"That's odd. She must have had more when she got back on board. There's a glass on the side there."

I hadn't. I was sure I hadn't had another glass of wine. Remembered something about caf. Not wine. "No."

"Something knocked you out. And we all know what sort of cargo your barge carries."

"Doesn't mean I drink it all." I was feeling slightly better. My guts were on fire and someone had welded a steel band too tightly round my head, but my brain was clearing. Slightly.

Medics were probably trained not to argue with their patients. He looked at his instruments again. Took a pod of pills from his bag and handed one to Millie.

"Dissolve this in water. Get her to take it – slowly, I don't want her to vomit again." Nor did I. He paused. "Perhaps I should take her in. There's space in the infirmary."

"No." I was well enough to make that decision.

"I'll stay with her." Millie. My friend.

He wasn't entirely convinced but he didn't want a fight. "OK. Call me if she passes out again. I'll drop by in the morning."

He gathered his things and left. Millie dissolved the tablet, passed me the opaque mix, sat down heavily and stared at me.

"You're not ill and you're not drunk. What's up?"

"Allergies?" I tried. I didn't want to face what her question meant. Not yet.

She snorted. "We'll talk about it in the morning."

That was far enough off to be acceptable. Then I saw that she was clearing up the mess I'd made. And the bit of my mind that doesn't switch off even when it wants to said, "No. Don't throw that muck out. Not yet."

Startled. "Why... Oh." Millie was no fool. She set the offensive basin aside, covered it. Looked hard at me. "I'll help you to bed."

"I'll stay up here." I didn't want to go to my bunk in the cabin below. Whatever had haunted those dreams was enough to make me want to stay on the berth up here where I could still see the summer sky if I woke in the night.

She looked as though she would protest, then nodded and let me lie back, wrapped me in a blanket and put a pillow under my head.

I remember thinking I needed a shower and then deciding that it could wait till the morning. And then I remember nothing until I woke in the daylight.

32

Millie was dozing at my chart table. When I stirred she opened her eyes and glared at me. "You OK?"

Thought about it. Moved gingerly. Swallowed. Felt spaced-out and frail, uncertain of my own solidity. But not ill. "I'm fine."

"I'm not. You owe me, sweetie. It's a long time since I've sat up all night." She thought about that. A reminiscent grin. "At least not for someone sick." She eased herself upright. Grimaced at joints protesting. "I need caf. I resent feeling my years. I've enjoyed them but they've no business coming back to haunt me."

I focused on the critical word. "Caf?" It came out as a plea.

"I don't know. Isn't caf meant to be a bit hard on weak stomachs?"

That had me pushing the rug aside, ignoring last night's crumpled clothes. "There's nothing wrong with my stomach. Except a lack of caf."

I wasn't as steady on my feet as I'd have liked, but the frightening sense of dissolution which had overwhelmed me last night had gone. The hands holding the hot mug were quite steady. I drank in the rich scent. Sipped cautiously, drank thirstily. The world was coming back to normal.

Millie had been uncharacteristically silent while I tried the brew. Reassured that I wasn't going to be sick or pass out, she straightened. "You going to tell me what's going on? And don't say allergies," she warned when I opened my mouth.

"I wasn't going to. And I don't know what's going on. Either I ate some nibble that I couldn't deal with – in which case I expect our friendly local medic was very busy last night – or I ate or drank something meant for me, and not in a friendly way."

She looked at the covered bowl. "I got that. What I want to know is *why*?"

"I'm not sure." She looked sceptical. "I mean it. You heard about Andy?"

"Sure. Guy killed himself, didn't he?" Her eyes narrowed. "Didn't he?"

Shook my head. "I don't think so. Morgan wanted me to look into it and…"

"And when did you start mixing with Family? And are you going to tell me all about what happened here a few weeks ago? Which no one says anything about but which makes Gus go purple every time your name comes up?"

"He's always going purple."

"Not this shade."

"I don't really want to talk about it. It's tied in with what happened to Daisy and that's just a bit too close still." Sorry, Daisy, you're not just an excuse, but this was the only way I could think to get Millie to back off.

It worked. For the moment. "OK. But you'll tell me some time. Now you need to clean up –" Her nose wrinkled – "and get that mess in the bowl over to the medic who thinks you drink too much."

"A shower." It sounded better by the second. "A good idea."

She stretched. "You sure you're OK now? Not going to pass out again?"

"Sure." I hoped. "Thanks, Millie. I owe you."

"You do. But since there's no way you can afford to do

anything about the shoes I'm going to have to throw out, I'll put it on your tab. Just don't do it again."

I shuddered. "I'll try not to."

She turned to go. Turned back. "You think Amanda or Stephen did this?" A gesture to the covered basin.

That was the easy answer. Not necessarily the right one. "Don't know. Assuming *this* is something deliberate and not allergies, it could be them since it was their boat – but isn't that a bit risky? Besides, there were plenty of other people there who knew Andy. And most people on the marina will have heard I was on his boat before they took it out of the water."

She looked as if she'd tasted something nasty. "Ick. If that means you saw him, I really do not want the details." She wasn't going to get them. "But let me know what the medic says. Come over to the mall this afternoon if you're feeling OK."

"I'll try." No promises. Not if things had moved fast enough to produce attempts to knock me out, if not kill me.

33

I'd managed to clean up before the medic kept his promise and showed up on the pontoon outside the *Pig*.

He was slight and young with the eyes and colouring of someone with at least one parent from China. He smiled at me. I must have looked better than the last time he saw me.

"How are you feeling?"

"OK. Come on board. Caf if you want it. Thanks for the treatment last night – Millie shouldn't have called you."

He stepped on board, looked around curiously. "I don't know. You were a long way out of it and if it wasn't the drink…?" The invitation to confession was gentle. The glance at the glass I hadn't washed up, significant.

"I didn't have anything to drink when I got back here last night." I knew because I hadn't decanted any wine off from my tanks and the dozen bottles of good wine I had left over were still untouched. I'd checked it out before I showered this morning. "Millie told you what I had on the other boat."

He nodded. Didn't argue. "So what brought it on?"

"That's what I wanted to ask you. Your lab's got every gadget going?" A Family medical centre would have facilities to do far more than treat splinters and blisters. Even though the paying public might not normally have access.

"I suppose so." Cautious.

"Then could you look at these?" I indicated the wine glass and, embarrassed, the covered basin. "See whether anything there answers the question."

A raised eyebrow. No extreme reaction or exclamations of denial. As medics went, I liked him. "I could do that. I spoke to Lloyd after I'd seen you last night. He said you had Family access." Didn't sound over-impressed – just neutral, explaining his co-operation.

I grimaced. "Limited. And I'd rather it hadn't happened."

"But if you've got it, you'll use it?"

"Something like that."

He picked up the glass: handle with care. Poured the bowl's contents into a wide-necked flask. Sealed it. "I'll tell you if I find anything." He'd tell Morgan, too. Didn't matter. "And I'll have the caf. Smells good."

Another point in his favour. I passed him a mug. "You know my name. I can't call you Doc."

"True. I'm Mark." It seemed unlikely. But people who don't want to go back to China generally have very good reasons for changing their names. If Mark was what he wanted, then that's what I'd call him. "I like your boat. Not that I know anything about sailing. But this one looks a bit more real than some of the stuff on the marina."

I could really like this man. "Thanks. It's mostly toys round here. Lots of tech but not really meant to go very far. The *Pig* has to work for her living."

"So I'd heard. But you haven't brought in a cargo this time?"

That reminder left a sour taste. "No. Storm damage a few days ago and this was the nearest port. Now I'm stuck till after all the fuss about the Opening."

"Which you don't intend to enjoy." The amusement I'd thought I'd heard in his voice last night was evident.

"That's it." I didn't like feeling I had a reputation as a killjoy. It wasn't how I saw myself. "I don't like corporate fun," I explained.

"You might as well enjoy it while it's on offer. From what I hear, there's going to be no place to hide when it all gets going." I wondered if he'd talked to Millie while I was out of it.

He might be right. I concentrated on caf.

We arranged he'd run the test as soon as he could and he'd get back to me with the results. I wasn't convinced anything would show. I remembered that Andy's tox screen had been clear.

34

I still felt feeble enough to do nothing very active but read some of Byron's reports. They weren't particularly interesting but a couple of things eventually started to stand out. On the surface, Ardco was a prosperous business with a surprisingly good bottom line, considering it ran only two ferries, neither of them maxi-size. Their customer list was limited and gave little away – firms describing their nature as 'general trade' could be, and almost certainly were, doing almost anything.

They seemed to have one major client and a few others who were a lot more transitory. Didn't seem a very solid basis for a business, however good the current credit. I'd get Byron to do a little more digging. There was no clear indication of exactly what traffic Ardco dealt in for its profits. The other thing that seemed odd once I'd been through the material a second time was that the profit seemed to have been there right from the start. No building up a struggling young business.

Bring every work into judgement, with every secret thing, whether it be good, or whether it be evil. Ardco was just beginning to have a faint whiff of something more than routine corruption.

Almost made a suspicious person think the business had been set up because it already had cargo waiting.

Which brought me back to the question I'd asked myself yesterday: Just what were they smuggling?

Got the same answer I'd given myself yesterday.

I coded Byron.

"Yes?" Bland face. He did inscrutable well.

"Got your stuff. Thanks. Looks interesting."

"It does?" Any scepticism was likely more down to doubts about my ability to read a balance sheet than any lack of interest for him.

"I think so. Don't trust firms that are all profit." Something in his smile told me he had similar doubts. "Can you check out a place called Perry's? Seems our friend Andy was involved there, too. Went belly-up, though."

"Better than strung up. I'll look." Something that might have been the start of a frown disturbed his expression. "You OK?"

I must have looked worse than I felt. "Rough night."

The almost-expression disappeared. "Right." The connection blanked.

I did try to read Simon's publicity puffs on the firm, took in a few details about 'special service for valued clients', but some things are destined only for the recycler.

That left one message on the machine. Which hadn't been there last night.

Luna had made contact.

"Heard you wanted a meet." The voice was cautious. Not thready with smoke inhalation and exhaustion as when I'd last heard it, but uncertain, looking for the trap. Luna had been on the streets for years and wasn't much older now than Charity. Kids like her grow up wary of traps or don't grow up at all.

We'd met when she'd been drawn into the scam that had ended in Morgan's brother's death, and a sort of trust had developed between us. I'd managed to get her hospital care when she'd been involved in a building fire; she'd given me the key that told me who was running the scam. Since then she'd come under Tom Lee's protection. Town Hall would have been appalled. For Luna it meant some backup, more regular work, probably an almost-safe place to sleep. She was moving up in the world. I hoped she hadn't decided I'd be best left behind. But she had set up a meet: this morning. At the corner of what had once been a park, Sutton's civic pride.

I was glad she hadn't asked me to meet her inside it.

And I had half an hour to get there.

Morgan didn't need to know his credits for investigating Andy were going fast on cabs. I could see myself becoming as reluctant as Millie to use buses.

35

The park isn't far from Town Hall. It's a feral sort of place: too many people with nowhere else to go hang out there. You need to know who owns which bit of territory if you're going to walk through safely. Even if you do, the chances of being rolled for the clothes you're wearing are high. And if they get you naked, there are plenty of types there who'll take that as an invitation to something particularly nasty. People live in the park when there's no place left on the streets for them. Most don't last long.

Luna was at the main gate. Still wore blades, I saw. Could make a quick getaway if she needed, and her eyes scanning behind and around before they settled on me with something which might have been warmth told me she still needed to be quick. Life in Tom Lee's care wasn't luxury.

I stopped. Not too close.

"Luna. Looking good. Nice blades."

A slight smile, pride of possession, as she glanced down. She'd lost her last pair after the fire that nearly killed her. "They're good. You 'kay?"

"I'm good. Can you talk?"

"Depends. No trouble?"

"Not sure." She looked ready to bolt. "I tell you. You decide."

Fractional relaxation. "Tell."

"It's personal. Niece of mine, Charity." Luna didn't quite hide the twitch of a smile. "She's thirteen, run from home and they think she could be here. Thought you might know how I put the word out."

"Depends," she said again. Suspected she used it often. She was getting more cautious. "What's the word?"

"That I'd like to know if she's OK. That she can call me if she wants help. I'm not chasing her and I'm not about to send her home." I had no idea at all what I might do with her if she did make contact, but I wouldn't send her back to the Community unless she wanted to go. Whatever my brother might want. The thought of pissing off Ethan was cheering.

Luna hesitated. "Not easy," she admitted.

I wasn't sure if that was the opening in a negotiation. "I've some credit," I offered.

She shook her head violently. "No. Not the problem. Street's a mess at the moment. Something up."

"Like what?" By my standards the streets have always been a mess. "Peeps flushing you more than usual?" Tom Lee normally bribed too well for that to affect his people.

Another head shake. "No. Dunno. Girls are scared. More so than usual. Say someone's after them. The young ones, round your Charity's age, they're *real* scared." The young ones tended to huddle together for protection from pimps and hustlers and the starving cold. "Say there's something out there. Snatching them."

It sounded scary enough. It also sounded like the plot of some bad horror vid one of them had managed to see and tell the others about. Easy enough to scare a crowd of kids. But Luna wasn't laughing.

"Serious?" I asked.

She wriggle-shrugged. Uncomfortable. "Dunno. They're scared," she repeated. "But I will try to say about Charity. Case she's with them."

I almost hoped she wasn't.

"Thanks, Luna. I owe you." She nodded. Liked the

balance sheet that way, I guessed. "You say thanks to Tom Lee for me?"

"'Kay." She seemed about to blade off, hesitated. Uncertain. "You and me…" Suddenly very young. Not much older than the frightened kids huddled against a world of monsters.

"You and me are OK." I said it firmly. Meant it. "You call anytime. I'll listen."

"'Kay." Casual this time. Too casual for the colour branding her cheekbones. Pushed off on a blade. "See ya." Over her shoulder, careless.

Friends aren't easy to make on the street. Trust is something you earn. I left feeling as though someone had given me a present I didn't quite deserve and wasn't sure I knew how to handle.

36

Byron was waiting on the *Pig*.

I shouldn't have been surprised. He had a tendency to materialise when all I wanted was space and time to think. And he never worried unduly about intruding. But the fact he'd turned up in person meant he had something to say he wanted me to listen to. He knew I didn't rate vid exchanges, didn't trust me not to hang up.

Byron is technocrat in every organised cell of his body and augmented mind. He thinks in binary and doesn't relate well to messy stuff like emotions. Give him a fact and he'll analyse more data from it than it knew it possessed. Face him with a human quandary and his screen goes blank. He also doesn't like the water. Not if it has anything to do with messy, illogical things like sailing or boats. And he makes no concessions. Today, as usual, he was dressed as sleekly as any Family courtier and he still hadn't found a pair of shoes suitable for boatyards.

I had never been sure how tight in he was with the Vincis. Morgan had said he'd been doing work for another Family when this mess started, and it wouldn't be like what I knew of him to have committed his independence to just one organisation.

It was the only thing Byron and I had in common.

He'd found my stock of good wine and opened a bottle. I raised an eyebrow. "Drinking early, Byron?"

"Heard you were doing it late last night." His bland gaze watched as I took out another glass. Waited while I poured my own drink. "Feeling better?"

Damn. "Mark or Morgan?" I asked.

"Morgan was talking to me when Mark called in. Passing out drunk seems exceptional for you." He didn't quite say *even for you*. There was something fastidious about Byron. I wondered if he ever lost control. Probably thought it would fry his circuits. "Tox report is in."

I didn't need to ask why Mark had sent it to his employer before reporting to me. Since the message light was live on my vid, I suspected he might even have sent me a copy. But contacting Morgan meant only one thing.

"Someone drugged me." Not a question.

"Evidently. Possibly even tried to kill you." Uninflected, no shock. "You must have annoyed someone." Again.

I almost smiled. "Good."

"Only as long as he or she failed."

"I didn't know you cared, Byron."

He steepled his fingers, propped his chin delicately. "If you're dead it will be difficult to sort out this problem. Morgan won't like it." He let this sink in. Went on, "I assume you haven't made records of your progress so far?" Barely a question.

"No." Hadn't thought to. Perhaps I needed to be a little more organised. In case someone one day was more skilled with drugs, and Millie didn't happen to be around to hold a basin and call a medic. "But *you* have records?" I assumed.

"Oh yes. I'll tell you what I've found about Perry's after you've told me about last night."

Bargain. Byron believed in trade as much as Tom Lee did, only his business was data. With Byron, my instinct was to tell him nothing and leave him to find out what he could. Last time he'd had to ruin a pair of those glossy shoes to learn something I already knew. Reminded myself that this time he was meant to be helping me. Squashed instinct and told him most of what I'd learned about Ardco. Included my assumption there was unofficial traffic along with the legit stuff. Left out my encounter with Sal and her lieutenant. He looked at what Simon had given me, and copied the stuff from my screen that I hadn't bothered to read. Suited me. If there was anything in there, he'd be more likely than me to find it.

He looked up. "What else? This wouldn't get you poisoned."

I thought. No point not telling him. Described the visit to *Felicity* and what I'd found. "Andy didn't kill himself," I finished. "Someone drugged him and strung him up and left a note."

"In his own handwriting?" An archaic communication form as far as Byron was concerned, but possibly useful this time.

"Has anyone checked that it is his writing?"

"I'll see." Point to me. Byron straightened. "Morgan's not going to like this. You know what he wanted."

"Suicide. Nothing related to Midway. All tidy before the party," I recited. Shrugged. He wasn't going to get what he wanted. Family disappointment didn't happen often enough as far as I was concerned, but I saw where Byron was going. "He going to shut me down?"

He probably could. Byron was shaking his head. "He remembers last time. Doesn't want you crusading on your own. Might want some promises."

"Like?"

"Like control over action if you do get some answers."

"Family always want control," I observed. "Can't always get what they want." Byron just waited; he did that well. I sighed. "If I do find out what's happening and I can let him know, I will. If I can keep it quiet, I will." The relationship between Morgan and me was peculiar: well-entrenched prejudice on my side and something that wasn't far off bewilderment – mixed with a little suspicion of someone who'd brought down his brother – on his. But, in my more rational moments, I would admit he had what seemed like a sense of justice. Not something I'd heard of many Family types. Credit for that. He was also ruthless. After all, it was he who'd actually had brother Milo killed. Not me. And that was typical Family.

My half-promises seemed to satisfy Byron. He probably knew he'd get nothing better. "So what encouraged someone to poison you? I suppose you don't know who spiked your drink?"

"Don't know, both questions," I told him. "It happened on Stephen and Amanda's boat, so it may have been one of them. Since most of the other dozen or more people on board were their friends or colleagues who also knew Andy, it could also have been any one of them. In fact," I concluded, "the only one I'm pretty sure is in the clear is Millie."

"I've met Millie." He thought. "You're probably right. But have you thought that one of those people, or someone connected to them, also knows how to get through your security?"

I stared. Not because I didn't know what he meant, but because I'd been trying to ignore that thought ever since I convinced myself that I hadn't poured a glass of wine when I returned to the *Pig* last night. I looked into the quite harmless glass I was holding and set it down with care. *Be not drunk with wine, wherein is excess.* Except that I hadn't been drunk.

"You got through it," I pointed out to him. It wasn't the first time I'd come home to find Byron on board, but he was a security expert. The *Pig's* alarms are good, but I'd have been surprised to find a system he couldn't talk into opening up for him.

"Yes." He had no doubts either. "You sure you locked up?"

Thought about it. There was no way I'd left the *Pig* open. She was the one constant in my life, more than a home – storehouse of good times, escape route, bolthole. I didn't leave her unlocked. "Sure."

He didn't argue. "Narrows it down. Someone with tech skills was here. Your system was designed for the Ark but that doesn't make it easy to crack."

Sometimes he managed to surprise me. Not because he knew about Noah – his brain was the biggest database I was ever going to access – but because his comment was almost a compliment. And it wasn't what he'd said when he'd first talked about my system. But we'd both been lying to each other back then.

"Seems I'd better see about an upgrade," I admitted.

"I've been waiting for you for about an hour." For a man whose equipment dealt in nanoseconds, instant access, an hour was a long time.

"What have you done?" Looked round, suspicious. Nothing obviously changed.

"Just a few modifications. I'll show you."

I could rant about privacy invasion but it wouldn't make any difference. And a Byron-coded system would be reassuring. Contented myself with a glare which he ignored, and let him show me what he'd done.

"Subtle," I allowed, when he'd demonstrated the failsafe he'd installed and the supplementary motion detectors. As far as I could see there was no way anyone except me – and probably him – could get round it. Not that my impression mattered: I'd be baffled by an old-fashioned manual key and lock unless I had a large hammer handy. But if Byron thought it was secure, I wasn't going to worry. I sat back, took a sip of wine. It was good. "So," I wondered, "was there anything interesting about Perry's?"

37

"Nothing definitive." He glanced at my screen. Interesting how one gesture can convey contempt for outdated equipment as well as information about what he'd placed there. Byron was economical. "I traced the company. It folded just under two years ago."

"Another ferry operation?" I assumed.

"Not quite. Transport – mostly in this country. Heavy loads, uneconomic for air-freight."

"Uneconomic for them if they folded," I pointed out.

"Not quite. They shut down with a healthy balance sheet. No reason given." He watched me.

If Amanda hadn't exactly lied to me about the business that didn't 'work out as planned', she'd certainly left me to assume it had gone bust. "That explains how they could afford luxury cruisers," I realised, "but not much else. You don't know any details of the freight?"

He shook his head. Irritated. "No one admits to knowing any details. Similar pattern to Ardco: limited client list, promises of confidentiality."

"We still don't know what they're smuggling." It wasn't a question.

"No."

Shared silent frustration.

"You're the people expert," Byron was happy to hand over this area of expertise. "So why did Andy die?"

"Speculation? He wanted to take the company in a direction the others didn't agree with. Or the other way round."

"Murder's a bit drastic – and clumsy," he objected.

"True, though it might have seemed like a simple solution. Perhaps he objected to what they were carrying – maybe they'd changed product. Wanted to tell the world?"

"Still seems over-dramatic."

"Depends what they have to hide."

Back to the same unanswered question. At least we knew what we had to look for. Byron could go back on the cyber-trail; I needed to talk to more people, cover some more ground. Or look more closely at the ground I'd already covered. I wished I felt more hopeful. It's hard to look for something when you've no idea what shape it is.

"If I can't find out about their cargo any other way, I'm going to have to look around one of those ferries – without Simon as guide. Any chance of getting a copy of their schedule for the rest of this week?" I really didn't want to hang offshore in Davy's battered tub, hoping for a ferry to arrive.

A task almost too basic for Byron. He sighed. "I'll let you know. I'll also talk to Morgan."

"Thanks." That was genuine. I hadn't looked forward to telling Morgan that there was a murderer on his new marina. And if he'd tried to persuade me that it would be politic to leave everything until after the celebrations I just might have done something ill-advised – like losing my temper.

"And it might be worth discovering what Stephen and Amanda and Andy were doing before they set up Perry's."

He nodded. "Looking for a pattern?" People who like cyberspace love patterns.

When Byron had gone I played with my security upgrade for while. Decided I could live with it.

Thought about the little we'd learned. Tried to absorb the fact that someone wanted me dead or disabled.

Whoever had done it seemed willing to take drastic steps as a first resort. Which was both alarming and informative. It seemed somehow amateur, almost panicked. It also said there was something hidden which was worth murder to protect. Which meant they might also be led into more revealing action; which could in turn lead me into learning something a little more useful than our present rather thin crop of speculations.

I tried not to think about the likelihood that any revealing action would have its violent aspect.

38

Looking out from my deckhouse, I saw what I should have seen earlier if I hadn't been preoccupied: party preparations. Almost every craft in the marina had been decked out. Those that had masts and enough rigging to allow it were dressed over all, others had bunting strung from every available line. A few had hung out signal flags without much concern for the distress signals they were inadvertently expressing. Besides, who was so old-fashioned they understood signal flags? Ex-Community escapees with one foot in the last century.

I would have to rig the *Pig* out in fancy dress, if only as camouflage.

Somewhere in a locker in the forward hold I had some bunting. It wouldn't take long and mechanical tasks are good for thinking. And it seemed I had a lot of thinking to do.

The hold was in reasonable order. The flag locker even revealed what I wanted after only a brief search. I hauled the bundle – which looked as though someone had tried to crochet a giant's shawl out of it – on to the deck and started to try to restore it to order.

Find the end, pull it through a loop in the line, straighten the first flag. Who was trying to kill or disable me? And why such an uncertain approach? If it was the same mind as the one who'd arranged Andy's death, it suggested that my death hadn't been the principal aim. If it had, I'd have been on that unpleasant steel slab in the morgue right now. My fingers met another unlikely knot – how does something with no free ends manage to tie them? – and began to tease it out. If I'd died, would Morgan have felt offended enough to investigate or would he have given a sigh of relief? Didn't want to know the answer.

The tangle of bunting was beginning to look ordered. My thoughts weren't. I was still trying to work out what was worth smuggling that needed its own freight business. Something that paid well enough that a couple of clients could keep the company fed and profitable and something that was both bulky yet fragile, needing freight haulage. So not drugs or gems. All the commercial secrets and Family spying went through cyberspace – which meant they were Byron's problems, not mine. And they certainly didn't need ferries.

Rare species? Perhaps, but not between this country and France. If the trade had been with Africa or South America or some of the more obscure warring states of what was trying to become the New Russian Federation, it might have made sense. Smuggling anything in or out of China was too scary to think about. Still, I could check the ferry for bio-storage units, just to settle that one. If I could get on board.

The last knot pulled free. The bird's nest had become a biddable coil shot with all the colours of the flags. Some things are more easily sorted than others.

"Dressing up? Not your usual style, sweetie." Millie took a careful step on board.

"I don't have any style. You know that. Besides, if I don't do this Gus will complain even more than usual." I hadn't seen him lately, which could be worrying except that I hadn't spent much time at home since my enforced return to Midway. And he wasn't someone I went looking for.

"He's too busy tearing his hair out over precedence in

the Family party, wondering whether he's invited to anything interesting, and giving the schedule yet another polish."

"Along with every bit of brass he can fit on his jacket?"

"That's it." She looked at my coil of flags which threatened to turn itself back into the Gordian knot if I didn't do something with it. "I'm probably going to regret saying this, but can I help?"

I didn't give her a chance to change her mind. "Take this." She got one free end of bunting.

With someone to hold on to the line while I tied one end of the bunting to the backstay, then used the halyards to lift the body of flags and stretch it out until it reached a forestay, the dressing-up process went almost smoothly. At the end, the *Pig* looked slightly embarrassed, a middle-aged woman conscious she's wearing more make-up than is quite proper, but she didn't look out of place. The whole marina was tarted up to excess, after all.

Millie stood back, nodded. "Very festive. I hope this means you're in a party mood."

"Not really. But I'll buy you supper." The light was beginning to fade. Some of the boats, I noticed, had managed to string flickering lights fore and aft. I ignored them; I had no intention of competing.

"I hoped you'd say that. Are you feeling OK after last night?" she asked with belated concern.

"I'm fine. Do you want to go into town or is there somewhere decent in the mall?"

We settled on the mall.

39

"So, any word on your niece?" she asked when we were seated to her satisfaction.

I shook my head. "Nothing yet. I've checked with Town Hall, and they'll tell me if her ID goes silent." Meaning dead. "And I've put the word around on the streets with a couple of people I know."

"Not the sort of people I know," she assumed. Rightly. Speared a tiny morsel of grouse from her plate. Took a healthy sip from her glass. "But at least you know she's alive. Have you contacted her parents?"

"No." I had no wish to speak to my brother or my sister-in-law. I would have to speak to my mother, but wanted to have something more definite to tell her than *not yet dead.*

"And what about last night's little problem? Have you heard anything yet?"

She wasn't going to pretend she hadn't understood what had happened. A problem with a friend who was too observant and possessed no tact at all.

"Only that I was drugged. Not necessarily with lethal intent."

"Comforting. Have another drink."

I did. Let her tell me that tomorrow's opening shot in the Grand Celebrations would include a walkabout by Family members, live music at a range of sites, a holo show of historic sailing ships, and a barbecue on the seafront. I thanked her for the warning, decided to boycott everything except perhaps the holo display. And possibly the barbecue.

"One other thing," she said. "I was watching the screen

this morning. Local news."

"You must have been bored." Local news was a regular turn-off.

"I was. But I was waiting for a contractor and there was nothing else to do. Saw something which might interest you." And about which she'd hesitated before telling me? Another morsel, another drink. "Some do-gooders are running a hostel for street kids. Yes, I know, yet another one. But this one did seem to be for real, not image. It's probably a total loss but I suppose it might be another dead end for you to head down."

"And you weren't going to tell me because… Let me guess. You think I'm in enough trouble already? That I shouldn't be worrying about a girl who's probably not even in the city?" And she'd still bothered to tell me. I appreciated it.

"Something like that. And if you do find her, have you any idea at all what you're going to do?"

"I'm trying not to think about it," I admitted.

"People like us are far too selfish for children." She was right: I had no obvious child-shaped space in my life, and no wish to change that life.

I filled my glass. Decided discussing parties and walk-abouts was more comforting than trying to make plans for a girl I might never meet.

40

I woke to the imperative demand of a call on my screen. Someone wasn't listening to the 'not available' noises. Before I'd even scrambled out of bed and muttered my name into the cabin screen I knew who would expect to find me alone and interruptible just after dawn. She was also the only person I knew who would expect me to be awake at such a time.

"Mother. Good morning."

"Humility. God with you. Have you word of your brother's child?" No *how are you*?

Am I my... No. I would not say it. Cain should have known better than to ask. I struggled to pull sleep-tangled thoughts into something coherent. "Not directly. She's definitely still alive and people who live on the streets of Sutton are searching for her." Well, a couple of people are keeping their eyes open. "I'm going back into the city today." Was I? *Wake up, Humility, before you promise more than you can afford.* Thanks, Jack. "Do you know anything that confirms she was definitely trying to come to Sutton?"

The urge to tell me something that would goad me into more activity warred visibly with the ingrained imperative of honesty. I could have told her there was no point struggling: conditioning determined which one would win. "No, daughter. But her friend is sure that is what she intended." I felt her willing me to believe it. Unfortunately, I did.

"I'll keep looking. Call me again in two or three days." I couldn't contact her. Ethan would take it out on her if he

133

knew she'd even spoken to me, never mind confided matters which shouldn't be talked of outside the Community. Especially not with a sister who had been Shunned years ago and therefore did not exist.

"I will." A hesitation. "Daughter, we need to know she is safe. We could not save you but perhaps there is a chance for her."

I didn't know what to feel. Glad to glimpse that hint of real concern, rage that anyone would think I was lost, manic laughter at the idea that salvation from the Community would have been in any way possible. My sympathy for Charity increased. If I found her I would also find her an option that did not include a return to her father's mercy.

"I'll do my best," I promised. Didn't define 'best'. We were bound to disagree.

"Thank you, child. Be well."

The screen blanked.

41

There was no point at all in trying to go back to sleep. Driven by the knowledge of mother's opinion of the way I kept my home, I found myself scrubbing and polishing and cleaning before I even indulged in the first caf of the day. I knew exactly why I was doing it, and was angry with myself. That only made me apply cloth and brush and soap with even more vigour.

Mother would have nodded at the results but said nothing. After all, I was only doing what I should, and if I'd done it more regularly I wouldn't have had to spend four hours on it now. *O cleanse thou me from my secret faults.*

I didn't feel better for the work.

The marina was barely stirring when I left the *Pig*. Sleeping in to party more loudly later?

I'd looked up the hostel Millie had mentioned after I came home last night. It was on the border between parts of the city where the no-go rules don't quite apply and those where no one goes who has no protection. Not a comfortable place, but just the sort of territory street kids might drift into out of self-preservation. Also the natural hunting ground of all sorts of human predators.

The hostel had been established for just over half a year. The details on the screen had told me little beyond a list of worthy names willing to get the credit for being charitable in exchange for the more solid sort of credit. There was also a general plea for credit and time from anyone interested enough to have bothered looking it up.

It didn't take long to reach the street I wanted, although

the cab driver refused to wait and dropped me off on a corner of the more respectable side of the square. Then he raced his engine and left for an urgent appointment with someone who didn't want to travel to places where they'd steal his wheels while he was waiting for traffic to clear.

The hostel had a blank brick wall. The usual graffiti. Barred and shuttered windows fronted the road. A fortress, not a prison – I hoped. It didn't look derelict and the absence of more broken glass and litter than usual suggested it hadn't yet been targeted by anyone deciding it crossed his or her territory. After six months, that was impressive. I walked up to the door. Rang. Stepped back for the vid to get a good look at me. Waited.

"Business?" A scratchy voice, gender unclear.

"Talk to someone about sponsorship." I'd decided an implication of credit to offer was probably the only way in. I didn't look rich but I gambled I didn't look so shabby they'd turn me away offhand.

Silence. Waited long enough to watch a scuffle between three youths who weren't serious enough to do any damage, and a fight between two cats which sounded a lot more dangerous.

Buzzer. Door must be sound-proofed: I'd heard nothing going on behind it.

Pushed the door open. Took both hands. Deliberate, I supposed – makes it difficult to sneak in if you've got to put your shoulder to the door to ease it open. Wondered where the kids' entry was: no way could a half-starved child have dealt with that one. They'd have died of heart-strain on the doorstep.

Found myself in an empty-looking lobby opposite a door. Inside, a woman behind a desk, a screen in front. Normal.

"Good morning. I am Jennifer." She sounded like a drone, but I don't think anyone made them middle-aged, overweight and dowdy. And, despite the ads, I've never yet seen one that could pass as human. Unless she was it. "You asked about sponsorship. You want to sponsor a child?"

"Perhaps. I heard about your hostel on the local news and it seemed like the sort of place the city needs. So I thought I'd come and find out more – you learn so much more in person than just watching a vid, don't you?"

She nodded. May even have believed me. Or just thought me eccentric.

"Certainly. We're always grateful for interest." Might not have got much. "Would you like to know more about us?"

"Yes. What age groups do you look out for – and is it both girls and boys you help?"

"Any child who seems to be under sixteen we consider vulnerable. Some of them don't know how old they are. Many are older than they look but still need our care."

"And some are older by far than their years," I said.

A flicker of what might have been genuine emotion crossed her muddy skin. "Quite. I see you do know something of the problems we face. So many people think all we have to do is give out a few good meals and we'll transform these children into sweet little members of society." I couldn't help the grunt of laughter. She didn't seem to mind. "I'll give you some details of our work." She gestured towards some amateur-looking printed leaflets. I thought of Simon's glossy brochures. "And perhaps then," she added, "you'll tell me why you're really here."

She was good. The drone persona was very effective. I could protest and flounce out. Or I could tell her the truth. Couldn't see I'd do much more harm than I already had, so I said, "I've a niece. She's thirteen years old, brought up in a west-country Community, and she's on the run. I did the same when I was a couple of years older than that, and got lucky, but what are the odds it'll happen twice? She's probably come to Sutton because that's where I ran to, but she hasn't tried to contact me, may not know I'm still here. I know she's alive, that's all." It sounded as pathetic as it was. I handed over the picture. Jennifer stared at it, handed it back

"I see." She had her hands folded on the table in front of her. No move to call up any files or data. "And if you do find her, and she's well, what do you mean to do?"

I wished people wouldn't keep asking me that. I still didn't have a good answer. "Depends what she wants. Not send her home unless she wants to go. Find her somewhere safe. She can stay with me for a while but there's not much room and I'm moving all the time. Important thing is to find her. Then I can ask her."

"I see." Was that her standard non-committal answer? Meaning nothing. She thought. Then pushed her chair back. It screeched against the floor tiles. I winced; she didn't even seem to hear it. "Would you like to look around?"

"Very much."

"I will show you the common rooms and the dining area. I can't allow you into any of the occupied sleeping cubicles."

"Of course not." If she was giving them personal space, she was already doing something powerful for them.

"And I must ask you not to talk to the children, unless they approach you. And do not make them any promises."

She was as stern as the preacher at home. Somehow I was more willing to take her orders. If only because they made sense. I had feared arriving somewhere which dealt in sentimentality and illusions. The children she offered to help would have lost both within a week of taking to the streets.

I nodded. She'd obviously expected nothing else. "And don't let go of your sack. Most of them will steal anything you allow out of your sight." A statement, not a judgement. This woman was someone interesting.

The house didn't seem crowded. Difficult to tell, since more than once I had the sense of someone scuttling away as soon as they heard approaching footsteps. I saw about a dozen girls and five boys. All were thin and suspicious-looking and some had the thin, repetitive cough which suggested something badly wrong. All were also clean and dressed in clothes which mostly fitted. I was impressed.

"You full?" I asked.

A shrug. "There's always room. Always kids out there who don't know this is a place that'll help them. Some days we overflow, lately it's been quiet."

She didn't sound entirely pleased.

"I heard a rumour…" I started.

"Plenty around."

"Something frightening the street kids. The youngest."

She stared hard at me. Mouth pinched tight. "Come back into the office." She pointed back at the chair I'd left half an hour back. "What rumours?" A sharp voice, eyes intense.

"Just what I said. Heard it from a street kid I know. Wasn't sure what it meant – if anything."

"Maybe nothing. But the children are uneasy. More nightmares than usual – even the smallest have usually learned it's wise to sleep quietly. And they don't tell their dreams to anyone. We haven't been here long enough for me to know whether it's just one of the normal cycles.

Your contact says it isn't?"

I shrugged. "Not sure. She's a runner for Tom Lee." A raised eyebrow showed me she wasn't wholly ignorant of what went on in Sutton. "So she counts herself safe. Perhaps it's a gang thing." I thought of Sal and the other girls in the docks.

"I haven't heard of any gang feuds at the moment – no more than usual. But the girls in gangs don't normally end up here. They think they've already found a home." She didn't share that belief.

"Do you know anything about any of the gangs?" I asked.

"A little." Lips pursed in thought. "They mostly keep to their own territories. Some are more violent than others."

"Gang leader called Sal?" I wondered. "In the docks?"

She shook her head. "Could be one of those who keep well away from here – and the docks are the wrong side of town for this place. I've heard rumours of some very tough crowds in that area."

"That would fit." Tough was an understatement, I was guessing.

"Perhaps we could help each other," she suggested. "Am I right in thinking you don't in fact have funds to invest?"

"Hardly any funds at all," I admitted.

"We may be better off than you, then. I could keep my eyes open for your niece. What is her name?"

"Charity. And I'm Humility."

Credit to her, she didn't even smile. "I see. Well, that certainly supports what you have told me about her background. Although, if she's as ill-named as you…"

"Thanks." It wasn't the first time someone had said it.

"I will see what we can do. In return, I would like you to pass the word where you can about this place to other street children. And if you hear more unpleasant rumours…"

"You want me to follow them up?"

"I was going to suggest something less hazardous. Like letting me know."

"Right." Made no promises. I was already reporting to Morgan and my mother; the idea of anyone else expecting regular updates on what I was doing held no appeal at all.

42

Even when I'd left the place, I wasn't sure what I made of her. If she was what she seemed, she was the driving force behind something that Sutton badly needed. Since I don't take people on trust these days, I kept an open mind.

Needed to talk with Luna if she was around. Only one way to make contact.

At the caf-house I managed to snag one of the high-speed wait staff and persuade him to get a request to Tom Lee. Took less than ten minutes before I heard he'd pass on a call. Told me I'd have a reply within an hour.

Which made me very suspicious. Tom Lee was not a philanthropist. If he was encouraging contact between one of his runners and me, there had to be an angle for him. I sipped good caf and ate a salad which, from its cost, should have been dipped in gold. He was also making it oddly easy for a water-gypsy with nothing to trade to get a seat in his place. So he was likely using me. Thought. If he knew what I was working on for Morgan, he might be interested. Had he heard something about whatever Ardco was smuggling? Or did he suspect something was happening there which might cross his territory? A fence who isn't getting his cut of the profits can be a dangerous enemy.

"Message." The same server. As puzzled about my status as I was, but barely showing it. "You can meet the girl in the market Above Bar."

The market. It's a nice cosy word. Where I grew up it meant stalls with fruits and preserves and weaving. A few home-made toys and trinkets round feast times. Plenty of gossip, a tavern for the men – ale, not wine, of course – and women sitting under trees to watch children playing. Sometimes my background does seem idyllic. Until I remember the rest of it. And the market in Sutton bears no resemblance at all to my rustic memories.

It's a sprawling mass of people with things to trade and things to buy. Most of the stuff is damaged or stolen. You won't lose your life but you'll lose every credit chip and loose coin you possess if you're not sharp. I wouldn't buy food there and expect to stay well, but when Jack and I needed mugs and cutlery and a kettle for the *Pig* and had no credit to spare, we found most of what we wanted there. If you didn't want to be noticed, it wasn't a bad choice of meeting place. As long as we could find each other in the crowd.

44

The stalls which offered shade did the best business. Shade meant anything: old cardboard, torn polythene sheets, rough cuts of warped plywood propped on shaky posts. The uneven paving was slippery with spilled oil and squashed vegetables. The less damaged of these would quickly find their own scavengers. I kept my sack in front of me, my hands round its weight. Not much of value in there but value was relative: a few coins meant not having to try to sleep hungry.

Decided to let Luna find me. She knew the market better than I did, might even have left word. I would browse the fringes and wait to see what developed.

I nearly bought some more glasses. Several of mine had been casualties of the gale. Then I thought more seriously about how I would get them home, and noticed that two of them had stems barely glued to their bases. No deal.

You can make some bucks over there, girl.

Jack surfaced whenever a sure way to lose money showed itself. I wandered over to the huddle around the kid with the three cups and the pebble. The plant in the crowd had already proved how easy it was to pinpoint the pebble under the rapidly shifting cups. Now he was silent as the audience began to shove and urge each other to have a go. There was always one willing to show off. Born marks.

No way, Jack. Even you never really expected to win at this.

Didn't stop me trying.

True enough. I'd had to haul him away from more cons

than most people knew existed. I kept my hands on my sack and watched. The kid was good.

"Hey, Humility."

Luna. I hadn't heard her come up behind me. Odd to see her on foot, blades slung on her shoulder. She was a lot shorter this way. Looked younger.

"Hi." Gestured at the game. "You ever try this?"

"Hands not quick enough. It's a good lay if you can do it, and someone lets you have a pitch." No one would set up without knowing whose territory they were in. Irony: illegal games were far more tightly regulated than the legal stuff. She watched a man shake his head after failing yet again to spot the pebble and give up with a grimace. Not before he urged his neighbour to give it a try.

Great thing about running a game: losers always like company.

Jack loved the way mugs fooled themselves. Even when he was one of them.

Luna shook her head, attention back on me. "You wanted to talk?"

"Yeah. Got a picture of Charity for you. Thought you might show it round."

She nodded. "'Kay." She looked at the crowd, comfortable with the crush. "You want to go somewhere quieter?"

Thought. The market was private just because of the numbers of people barging and shouting, but it would be easier to concentrate elsewhere. "Would be good. You know a place?"

"Down here." An alley I might not have chanced on my own. She stopped. "You want to talk to some other kids?"

It was an unexpected offer. More than I'd hoped. "They know about me? Don't want to scare them any more."

"There's two, said they'd talk if I said it was 'kay. No

names."

Of course. "Yes. I'd like to meet them. Here?"

'Here' was the doorless entry to a skeletal building which had once housed shops or offices. Now the bits of it which were more or less weatherproof were home to anyone who could defend their squat. A sort of community, not quite stable but with its own rules and order. A step up from the street. When she pushed past some sacks of rubbish and through a doorway into a small space with a boarded-up window I wondered whether this was Luna's own bolt-hole. Knew better than to ask.

Two faces stared at me. Girls. Skinny, dirty, one white, one black. Both with the same expression. I could feel their urge to run. Out the escape route I couldn't see but which had to be here. Probably behind the two or three ragged garments hanging from nails in the far wall.

"'s OK." Luna had gone in first. Might have given some signal I couldn't see, or perhaps they trusted her, because I felt a fractional easing of tension. Flight instinct on hold, not switched off. "This is Humility. She's good. Treated me right, helped me."

"And I owe Luna," I told them, in case the idea of me as some sort of saint was too much too accept. "She tell you why I'm here?"

They looked at each other. Some unrecognisable process made the smaller one, the one with some sort of skin rash and a missing front tooth, the speaker. "Said you looking for someone." The gap in her teeth made her lisp slightly.

"That's it. My niece. Girl, little older than you. Run away and doesn't know the streets like you. She's probably scared stupid and getting herself into more trouble than she can handle. I'm looking for her. Want to help if she wants help. Hoped you might see her, know someone who had." I reached into the sack, saw them tense again. "Got pictures."

They eased back. I gave them copies of the dismal shot of Charity and her family, pointed out the one I was looking for. They seemed fascinated by this glimpse of a world outside their experience.

"Them real trees and such?"

"Yes. My brother's a farmer." No point attempting to explain communal living – even if I understood it myself. "All the family help out in the fields." They stared at the pictures, trying to discover more than was to be seen. "Charity thought the city would be more exciting." I let them think about the urban excitements they knew all about.

"She don't know about the streets and stuff?" Hard for them to believe.

"She's probably learning," I admitted. "May be in real trouble." I hesitated, then said, "Luna said there's bad stuff out there right now. Worse than usual."

I thought they would run. The little one grabbed the hand of the other girl. Held her still. "Don't know nothing." She squeezed her lips tight shut.

Luna had been watching. Now she went over and sat on the cloth-covered box that was both table and storage. Reached out her hands to the kids. "She's OK. Could be she can help."

No. I wouldn't be dragged into hunting down nightmares for street children. I wouldn't promise them anything, not even when they looked at me with eyes big from hunger and sleepless nights. I couldn't let Luna give them dreams which would never come true. Disillusion was harder to live with than fear. I knew.

"Don't know about help. But I do want to find Charity. Can't do it without you. I'll owe you."

Fascination with the idea that an adult might be in their debt had them staring at me. The one holding the speaker's hand, a taller girl with long dark hair and a black eye, tugged at her friend who bent her head. Whispers. Some head-shaking. A hard stare in my direction. Then nods. Reluctant.

The speaker sat down cross-legged on the floor, tugged the other girl down with her. Luna looked at me. I sat.

"We ain't seen nothing, but we heard things. Might be your Charity got mixed in something messy." Messy would be very bad in their language. "See, there's kids not here who was. We used to meet at the market or down the docks or in that bit of the park where there's still lights." Places where there might be crowds, purses and pockets to be explored. "Don't do that now 'cause it ain't safe. Kids, 'specially us girls, come one day and then no one's seen 'em again."

Somehow the shapelessness of her fear made it more chilling. "You never see any of them again?" Kids would drift off, some would find a gang or a protector, most would drift back again when things went wrong. This sounded different. And nasty. Two solemn heads moved sideways. "Any word on where they go?"

Another shake of the head, silent consultation of exchanged glances. "No word. Not proper word. Just someone says…" She brushed off the hands that pulled at her. "No, I'm gonna say. Someone says they're *taken*."

I understood the bad dreams. It was the bogey man made live. The irrational that couldn't be defeated because it could come from anywhere. Whether their fears were real or not, the nightmare was terrifying for them. I felt a chill at the thought of Charity walking innocently into this world.

Luna was watching me as intently as the children. As if I could make it right. "I do owe you. If I find out anything I will try to help. If you need help you tell Luna to reach me." It was terrible how the weak and empty offer of help which I hadn't meant to make, and which was bound to come too late, made a little life come back into the drawn faces. I knew there was nothing I could do, but I couldn't look at them and tell them that it was hopeless.

The speaker made sure her companion had a picture of Charity tucked into her rags. Carefully gave me back the spares, straightening a crumpled corner and brushing it smooth. "We'll look out. Luna'll say if there's anything."

They eased past me, heading back to the market and the streets.

"Wait." I fumbled in the sack. "You gave me time, you should get paid." I only had a handful of coins but they were more than these kids earned most days. I gave them to the one who'd done all the talking. She was going to be a real leader some day. If she made it. Her two fists tightened on the money. She understood what was due, wasn't going to pretend it didn't matter. That sort of pride comes with not having to worry about the next meal.

"Thanks." The other one clung closer. Turned to stare once before scuttling through the doorway.

45

I let out a heavy breath and stared at Luna. "I don't know if I can help them."

"Sometimes just listening helps." I wondered how young she'd been when she became a street kid. If anyone had listened to her.

"Perhaps." Thought a bit more. "There's this woman I met today. Called Jennifer, looks a bit like a sack of trash with legs and talks like a machine." Luna gave what passed for a smile with her. "She runs a place north of the park. It's a shelter." Saw Luna tense with the instant rejection I expected, lifted a hand. "I was just there to ask about Charity," I answered the unspoken accusation. "But she seems to understand a bit better than some. If the little ones want a place to sleep, clean up, eat something, it might be OK. Not a prison. You could probably find out."

"Where is it?" Not much friendliness in the demand but not a complete refusal. I told her how to find Jennifer's place. Hoped I wasn't making a mistake. "Might check it out." Luna might be reluctant but she hadn't survived this long by dumping ideas just because she didn't like them.

"Thanks." Remembered what I'd been thinking about earlier. "You and Tom Lee working out?"

A real smile this time. "Sure. It's good. Proper work."

Running errands for a fence who controlled a large section of the south coast. A new definition of proper. But it suited her.

"He's being helpful to me at the moment. You know if he's looking for something?"

"Tom Lee's always looking for something. You know

150

that." A frown. "Told me I could see you whenever, if I wanted. Said you was in with some Family type?"

Disbelief threaded the question. I just nodded, didn't feel like explaining.

She grinned, real feeling this time. "He said you was always poking your nose into things and sometimes it could be useful to see what scuttled out of the heap when it was kicked."

I wondered which of the heaps I was currently kicking was the one Tom Lee was watching.

46

The noise of the market crashed on my ears after the relative quiet of Luna's place.

We'd parted before we left the alley, which somehow didn't seem quite so alien now. I spent another half-hour browsing the stalls and failing to find anything useful for the *Pig*. Then I headed home, braced to meet the joys of the first day of Midway Port's formal opening ceremony.

My life is full of contrasts.

47

The Port was busier than I'd ever seen it. Flags fluttered, there was music from a small orchestra under a tented pavilion; in the breeze its classical sounds were thin and scratchy. Morgan needed to organise a little more amplification or something more suited to the outdoors. A wind ensemble or brass band? No doubt it would be sorted by tomorrow. I had a feeling this first day was for the common people – all the worthies from the local village were on show with their chains of office, their attendant partners and deputies. The annoying little buzz cameras of the press flitted around catching shots. They had to be licensed. No one would let unregulated press remotes into a Family event.

I stopped to listen for a while, wandered off to look at some of the stalls that had appeared in the space in front of the marina, now transformed and calling itself a piazza. Found myself making comparisons. The stuff was as useless as most of the goods in the Above Bar market – gadgets which would break if I owned them, fragile model yachts, souvenirs in every shape from phallic lighthouses to scarves – and many times the price. I didn't feel a need to keep a tight hold of my sack. Any purse-snatcher who was enterprising enough to work this crowd wouldn't be interested in the small change which was clearly all I carried.

There were no three-card tricks, but I stood for a while and watched a juggler and a pair of tumblers.

I might have sneered at Morgan's plans, and I had definitely not wanted to be here, but I suddenly felt better.

This sort of entertainment, the smiles and lack of care on faces, the sense of celebration – even if induced by free drinks and the prospect of being able to say you saw Family members and the local mayor, possibly even have your image caught on local vid – was what I needed. Sutton's relentless grimness had begun to touch me a little too deeply.

I eased my way through the crowd, down through the security gates to the marina itself. I could watch from the deck of the *Pig*. Go out again in the evening for the barbecue. Meet up with Millie.

"Humility."

It was Lloyd. Looking smart in a dress uniform with the sort of sharp edges which suggested it was either new or it only emerged from its box for interviews, appointments and Port Openings.

"Hi. Things are looking good."

He cast an experienced eye over at the crowd on the shore. "Yes. Pretty quiet just now." Quiet was relative. "Apart from the music, it's going well."

"Get a brass band," I told him.

"Not Morgan's usual style. But it might work." That encompassing gaze took in the moored boats. A knot of people at the far end of the marina. "He's going to call in. Look interested in your quaint vessel. Talk about things like suicide." His voice wouldn't have carried past my shoulder even if anyone had been listening.

My moment of carefree cheer evaporated.

"Thanks." His mouth kicked up at one corner. Something to do with my tone. "I don't suppose you can tell him you haven't seen me?"

"Not a chance."

I hadn't expected any other answer. Went back to my

home and waited for the invasion.

Morgan and his entourage progressed down the line of pontoons. Exchanging greetings with eager boat-owners, finding something good to say about every cherished yacht and cruiser. Which can't always have been easy. Whatever Morgan's other limitations, he had a real passion for boats and sailing. And little time for upmarket junk.

My turn arrived inevitably. He greeted me and asked if he could come aboard.

"Of course." What would have happened if I'd left Byron's revised security system on alert? Some very wet dignitaries, at the least. I set the wistful thought aside and showed him round on deck, then offered him a glimpse below. "It's a bit of a tight squeeze," I admitted.

"Barges always are. More crew space equals less cargo space. Your holds must be sizeable."

"They are. No cargo just now." I wondered if I could sell a tankful of wine to the mall. Might be worth having another outlet if Tom Lee ever let me down. "We were a little battered by last week's gales. Came back here for repairs." Which he already knew, but I wasn't going to make excuses for a less-than-perfect-looking boat.

"I heard." He turned to his courtiers. "I'll be a couple of minutes here. Gus will show you back ashore."

I'd missed Gus in the clutter of people. He gave me a hard and suspicious stare, then straightened an already ramrod back and led his little flock back up to the gates, taking a wide path past me. I pointed Morgan at the companionway.

My saloon is normally the deck-house. If I entertain men in my cabin it's not usually a formal occasion. Morgan was as uncomfortable as me in the confines of my living quarters, but he perched on the bunk edge when I gestured. I found a locker to park on.

"I've spoken to Byron," he said. "Had a look at *Felicity* myself."

My surprise gave way to understanding. He knew boats. He didn't want to bring in more people than he must, and he could assess what I'd found for himself. I met his look.

"And…?" I queried.

A reluctant nod. "You seem to be right. Unfortunately." The unspoken wish that he'd never approached me, that he could have let Andy's death pass as suicide and have avoided the consequences, was clear. But Morgan had a kind of honesty. Whatever he wanted, it seemed he wasn't here to tell me to forget it or leave the marina. "Are you any nearer learning who's behind it?"

"I don't think it's aimed at you or Midway." I offered the only consolation I had. "It's almost certainly linked to Ardco and whatever's going on there. I think the couple on board *The Happy Family* either know something or suspect. I had a drink there last night."

"I heard." He glanced at his chrono. Neither of us wanted it to look as though he'd spent more time here than on the other boats he'd explored. "I won't try to stop you, but I want you to keep it quiet. I do not want anything to disturb this Opening. If you have to cause chaos, it had better be in the city. Not here."

As he left I wondered whether that had been an order or a rather desperate hope. Or a threat. He probably didn't know himself, and I didn't want to find out.

48

I could either sit at home and resent the way fate had dumped on me, or I could decide there was nothing more that I could usefully do today. And go and enjoy the party.

I'm not sure that a surly determination to have fun is the right mood for celebrating. Fortunately, once I was ashore again, I bumped into a crowd who didn't know how not to enjoy themselves. Quite how Em and Clim and Rusty and the others had managed to get themselves admitted to the Opening was one of life's mysteries, except that if there was a party around they would crash it if it was humanly possible.

They were a crowd of adolescent geriatrics who lived on a group of rusting hulks moored in the mud berths further upstream. I'd helped persuade Morgan that there were better ideas than throwing them off their moorings or towing them out to sea to sink. Last I'd heard, there were plans to turn their bit of the river into some sort of museum or park, complete with the boats of the last century and their inhabitants from the same period. Local colour.

I still felt faintly guilty about not making it clear to Morgan that they were a bunch of unscrupulous pilferers who considered anybody's boatyard their private hunting ground.

"Humility!" That was Em. "Come and have a drink. It's free!" If it had been free meths, she'd probably have given it a try. Fortunately, Morgan's dignity didn't allow him to sink that low. The wine was good.

An almost fairground atmosphere was developing. The

tumblers and jugglers were being replaced by sword-swallowers and rope-dancers. I expected to see fire-eaters once the late afternoon light dimmed towards evening. The holo displays looked almost dull beside the medieval atmosphere of the live acts. It wasn't life as I knew it, but it was beginning to seem an attractive alternative.

I wasn't sure how many people here knew, or cared, anything about boats, but they all seemed to be having a good time.

"I like this place," declared Em with the solemnity of someone well on her way to incapacity. "Morgan's a good type. For Family." She was having trouble with sibilants but was otherwise coherent. Just.

"So your end of the river's still on its way to becoming Heritage Hulks?"

She drew herself up, cropped white hair bristling. "We're doing very nicely, thank you. Even got water laid on."

"That's good." Water was an expensive necessity and her crowd had had to steal it from nearby supplies or collect and carry it over some distance until now. Morgan seemed to be keeping his promises.

I wandered round with Em and Rusty for a while, noted that Clim had slipped off with a deceptively large bag in the direction of the building sheds. Not worth a comment.

The central area of the piazza had been set aside for the barbecue. Al fresco dining was a quaint reversion to the primitive for most people here. The chefs had done their best not to make the flesh they were cooking look too like the animal it came from. The smells were enough to overcome any inhibitions from delicate-palated carnivores. There were plenty of veggies for others. I grabbed a napkin and prepared to get greasy.

Millie had been directing all this as though it were her movie. Perhaps it was. She liked dealing with crowds, manipulating the raw stuff of emotion as long as it could be directed towards having fun at the frivolous end of the scale. I was one of the few people who knew she'd trained as a neuroprofiler before deciding that organised fun was as good for the psyche as designing targeted ads or counselling the rich and miserable. Not that she'd chosen to go very far from the rich end of the scale. She called it a design niche. I thought of it more as playing to her strengths and admired her for it.

"It's going well," I told her.

She looked pleased, wanting the praise that every show-person craved. "Tonight's just the warm-up," she warned me. "Things will get more lively tomorrow and the day after – and the last day should be talked about for the rest of the season."

"You'll make the Vincis envied by every other Family."

She grinned. "Exactly what I had in mind." A theatrical sigh. "What I really want is to find someone who sees things like this the way I do."

"Difficult. Besides," I reminded her, "you've driven every assistant you ever took on to suicidal despair."

"No stamina, dearie." She brightened. "Perhaps I'll train up someone a bit younger this time."

"There are laws against that sort of thing."

I felt the sharp end of her elbow for that. Then she sobered. "Funnily enough, I think I might even mean it. If I can find the right person."

"Someone as stubborn as you, who loves fuss and entertaining, is willing to try things just because they're new, wants everything of the best, done in her own way or not at all. Now. And is ready to listen to you," I summed up. "I'll keep my eyes open." For the impossible.

"I can dream. When I'm not busy." She'd spotted someone on the far side of the piazza doing something that didn't quite suit her demands. I'd no idea what it was, could barely see anything over there in the darkness, which was lit mainly by flaming torches. The safety lighting was the only thing discreet about the evening.

49

I'd enjoyed myself. More than I expected. After the seediness of street life and the frustrations of making no sense at all of Ardco's dealings, an evening of frivolity appeared to been exactly what I needed. I plunged into sleep with a smile on my face.

That's always when the dreams come.

I was shut in. It was dark but I wasn't alone. There were crying children and a smell I feared but didn't recognise saturating the air, almost to gagging. No one knew I was here. No one cared. There were monsters out there and they would come and get us in their own time. We couldn't get out.

"You can if you find the pebble! It's under the cups. Look, here it is. Now shuffle the cups. *Away it goes. Where it's gone to nobody knows.*" The thin sexless voice mocked and challenged.

I could hear the little brass cups shifting round, scraping against a metal floor I couldn't see. The taunting chant grew louder and louder and I had to get the answer right first time or we were all dead.

Louder and louder. I was one of the cups, twisting and weaving with the others, not knowing whether I hid the pebble or not. Then it wasn't cups, it was cards, and I could see them even in the dark, but the card I was looking for eluded me. Every time I tapped one it slithered from under my fingers, leaving a slimy taint. I shook my fingers to rid them of the clinging stuff. It wouldn't let me go, crept up my arms, binding me in slime. Smothering me.

I woke with a shout. Sweating.

It was still dark. I could hear water lapping against the *Pig*'s hull. Out in the marina, halyards that weren't properly tied off tapped against metal masts. A mooring warp creaked. The *Pig*'s own familiar, almost undetectable motion cradled me. My pulse shuddered towards normal. Sweat chilled on my skin.

Knowing the ingredients that cause a nightmare don't make it any better. It didn't take a shrink to remind me of the children I'd talked to in Above Bar, of the pressing need to find Charity, of Andy's death. And of plenty of wine last night. *Look thou not upon the wine when it is red.*

Not even bad dreams were going to convert me to white. I got up, knowing I wasn't likely to sleep again. Rinsed the foul taste from my mouth and showered.

It wasn't yet dawn. I lit an oil lamp, preferring its softer glow against the darkness to the boat's electrics. Up in the deck-house I brewed caf, curled my hands round the largest mug I owned and tucked my feet under me as I wedged myself in a corner of the settee berth.

Why had Byron ever thought I could solve the problem of Andy? And why did my mother assume I would drop everything and look for a girl I'd never met who might not even be in Sutton? And what drove me to make the attempt to deal with both these things?

I ought to have more sense and accept that this was something beyond my power. Last time, I'd been driven on by anger at the indifference of others and a sense of injustice. This time I should have known better.

And you're not still angry?

Butt out, Jack.

I could give up. In theory. But one night of bad dreams was enough: I wasn't sure I could live with them haunting my life. I couldn't give up until I could say with certainty that I'd tried everything I could think of, and pestered everyone I knew who might – willingly or not – help me.

Whatsoever thy hand findeth to do, do it with thy might.

50

I finished breakfast and tried to work out what I needed to do today. First, I supposed, remembering Byron, I ought to make some notes just in case I did wind up dead. Not a pretty thought but I had to admit its justice, considering what had almost happened the other evening.

In the end it proved a useful task, if only because it brought some order to the tangled lines I'd been working with. At first I'd intended just to write down what I had learned about Andy and Ardco, but somehow it seemed sensible to do the same thing for the parallel investigation into Charity's whereabouts.

Neither set of notes provided any dramatic insights, but my head felt a little tidier. That might have been the caf working, of course. I was just filing them, and deciding between another visit to Jennifer and a talk with Amanda, when a message signalled itself on my screen.

Not live. A recording downloaded somewhere a long way from its point of origin – on the other side of the city, at least. And the last person I expected to hear from.

"Humility? Sal. From the dockyard. I want a meet. Go to the old chain ferry dock at midmorning and wait there. Don't bring troops."

A prudent person would contact every troop she knew. She would also wonder what was on offer and not move until she had a much better idea of what the leader of a vicious girl gang could possibly want with someone who'd twice invaded her territory.

I couldn't think of anyone to consult. Anyone I thought of would have told me at once: "Don't go." "You're mad."

"Don't trust her: take backup."

I supposed they were right.

I added a brief note to the file I'd just closed on my screen, put an iron rowlock in my sack, and engaged the *Pig*'s security system.

I was back to taking buses. This one creaked and groaned and swayed itself round the foreshore and across the bridge to the docks. I had more than enough time to wonder about the choice of rendezvous. Coincidence? Or had Sal recognised Davy in his tub and asked a few questions?

The open nature of the old ferry landing was an advantage to me as well as to whoever Sal chose to send with her message: any backup or threat would be very visible.

I arrived early. Walked over to the cluster of ruined cottages. Waited. After what seemed like a deliberate pause for thought, Ma emerged. Didn't come close.

"What?" she demanded.

"I'm meeting someone here. Any chance of Davy hanging round offshore?" As observer, back door, forlorn hope. I didn't mind how visible he was.

She sniffed. "P'raps." Waited while I handed over the last few coins from my pockets. I'd have to find some more – people like her didn't deal in credit.

Two grubby fingers to her mouth and that enviable whistle blasted out across the water. "Thanks," I said, and went back to stand in the middle of the landing place feeling only fractionally less alone. And no less exposed.

I tried not to look an idiot as I stood there, doing nothing. Tried not to seem like someone who'd been set up as a target. Tried not to feel like one.

'Mid-morning' is a vague term. By my reckoning it was

well past that time when a figure emerged from the shadows at the roadside and moved into the light. Tall, thin, wearing black. No backup visible. Sal herself.

That did surprise me. If she was here in person, she had something important to talk about.

She walked down the landing area towards me. Swaggered. Nodded at me. "Humility."

"Got your call."

"No troops?" She'd swept the place in one comprehensive glance. I didn't doubt she'd have spotted any lurking watchers.

I jerked a thumb over my shoulder. "Only him."

A feral grin. "Davy?" She waved. I looked back enough to catch his return wave. Wasn't quite sure what that meant about his allegiance, but I'd been right to trust him once. This time I hoped I wouldn't need him.

Sal had called the meet. I left it to her to start the conversation.

"You still looking for that kid? Charity?"

I nodded. Tried to suppress the flare of interest. I might need a bargaining card later. "Sure."

"Heard something. Might interest you."

"I'm listening."

"Rumour says a girl like her's around the docks some-times. Maybe I could make contact, arrange something."

It was too easy, if the girl really was Charity. "And what's it going to cost?" I'd pay whatever it took, but Sal didn't have to know that. She wasn't stupid: she might guess. But there was no need to make it easy.

Sal wasn't comfortable. It was the first time I'd seen her not quite in command of the situation. She wanted something from me, and it wasn't something she wanted to ask for. Gangs don't ask. They take. She wasn't comfortable.

Suddenly I was tired of bargaining rules.

"I want to find Charity. I'll owe you, even if this is a dead end. Just say what you want."

A surprised bark of laughter. "You for real?" Shook her head. "If your Charity's as simple as you, I'm not surprised you're worried about her." I just waited. "And I'm worried about my girls."

For one second I thought she was saying she had children. Then I realised what she meant. "Your gang? What's happened?"

"Couple been gone two days. No message." She didn't pretend not to understand my silence. "No. If they'd wanted to break away from us, I'd have known." A sudden nasty grin. "Might not have liked it, but I'd have known. This is different."

A chill seeped into me. "And what can I do about it?"

"Stick your nose in. You seem to like that sort of stuff."

How many things would I be investigating before I gave up and admitted defeat? "Any suggestions where I would even start? I don't know anything about gangs." Except that they were best avoided.

"Want you to start right at the docks. Ardco. There's a chance the girls went on one of the ferries. For a bet." The furious sneer told me she didn't gamble, and that she'd made it clear to whoever had reported this story to her just what she thought of idiots who did. I felt the first twinge of fellow-feeling.

"And how do I get on board? I've had the tour. Seen the security," I reminded her, even as I realised that she was offering me the solution to the next step I'd wanted to take in investigating Andy's death.

"You haven't had Sal's tour. We can get you on board.

Give you about two hours while the ferry's unloading."

"When? I don't know the ferry timetable." Byron hadn't come through with it yet.

"Tonight. Ferry docks from France just before dark. Meet you here, show you the way in." She stared at me, willing me to make a decision. "Will you do it?"

It was insane. Tonight gave me almost no time to arrange what little support I could get. No time to think. Perhaps that wasn't such a bad idea. "And what about Charity?"

"Can't get to her today. Should make contact tomorrow. You'll have to trust me."

Oddly enough, I did.

"'Kay. I'll do it. Meet me here this evening. I have to get back."

She nodded, stepped aside to let me go. I waved at Davy and walked off up the slope towards where I hoped a bus would soon be passing.

51

The files Byron wanted me to keep, so that he could find out what I thought and planned if I wasn't in a position to tell him myself, needed updating. If I was going to trust a gang leader to get me on board a ferry which might be smuggling something someone was prepared to kill to protect, the chances of them being needed had increased. I debated calling Byron but reckoned he'd think me mad – which I might be – and would try to stop me. I'd borrow from Sal's communication technique and leave a message. I did want him to know where I was, but not in time to do anything about it.

What I was having difficulty not thinking about was whether the missing street kids, or Sal's gang members, might have some connection with Andy's death. There was probably nothing there: if the two gang girls had been caught exploring the ship, and had stumbled on the key to the smuggling operation, Ardco would have had its own reason for their disappearance which had nothing at all to do with street kids' nightmares.

It made no difference to what I had to do.

I was glad I'd told my mother to wait before she called again: now there was a chance I'd have something to tell her. For the first time I had a real hope I might find my niece, might have to face that question about what to do next. My dominant emotion surprised me: excitement. I was actually looking forward to seeing the girl who'd made the same journey I'd made myself less than two years before she was born. I took the photograph from my sack. Tried to give life to that still face, imagine what was going on behind the dark eyes. Imagined I could sense the seething rebellion which would end in the most terrifying and exhilarating decision of her life. I hoped the weeks she'd spent in the city hadn't damaged her, had helped her decide what sort of life she really wanted. Feared she'd been alone and cold and scared. With any luck that would soon all be over.

It took about an hour to pack my sack with a torch that worked, a notebook, a small vidcorder and, after some thought, a knife. I took the rowlock out, weighed it thoughtfully, tapped it against one palm, put it back in again. There are times when a blunt instrument can be useful. And a rowlock is such an innocuous object. The rest of the hour was spent worrying about what I'd forgotten. Deciding it was too late to worry. But where's the off button for worrying?

Files updated. Sack packed. It was like being ready for sea. But less fun.

I had hours to kill yet. Reminded myself not to think in terms of killing. Went out to see what was happening ashore.

52

Ashore was as busy as yesterday but a little more dignified. I knew they'd planned a series of dinghy races out in the Solent, so Morgan was almost certainly out there watching. Possibly competing – which would be making life hard for his courtiers, most of who didn't share his passion for sailing. There would be some bedraggled aristos by evening.

And I wouldn't be here to see them. Trying not to think of that led me over to the mall to see what displays the outlets were putting on. They would be hoping for major profits from these festivities. The free drink and public shows were impressive, but they also put people in the mood to be freer with their credit than they might otherwise have been. I planned to keep my chips well hidden and to try to remember I might still have to pay for whatever repairs the *Pig* needed when I eventually had the chance to have her hauled. Despite my contract with Morgan, I wasn't counting his credit until it was in my account. Especially since he wasn't exactly happy with what I'd uncovered so far.

It was the first time I'd been in the mall since it was declared finished. The drones had largely gone, though there were a few making sure that litter barely touched the floor, accidental spills or scratches disappeared unobtrusively and immediately. Human attendants offered welcomes and promised personal service, ushered valued clients to chairs and kept them there with refreshments while parading their range of goods: body ornaments, clothes with the newest technology built into trimmings and belts and beaded scarves, rare items with some vague connection with sailing, and personal services from hair styling to underskin holos and full-body treatments. It was as much a show as last night's fair. I wandered round, my casual clothes and obvious lack of anything like styling deterring most attendants from approaching me with real enthusiasm. I just didn't look rich.

I was looking at an old deck watch and wondering whether I could afford a couple of the early twentieth-century Admiralty charts, carefully rolled and kept in sun-proof scroll boxes. They wouldn't get such loving care on board the *Pig* but they would see some use. Today's sat-track stations and ship lanes weren't marked, and one or two of the low-lying coastal features were mostly underwater these days, but they were still remarkably accurate. And beautiful. I don't have much in the way of decorative art on board; these could be framed up and fit right in.

Before I let enthusiasm override sense, I caught a glimpse of someone waving from a shop across the way. Mark. The medic who'd helped me the other night and tested my stomach's rejects for poison. I guess that made us friends of a sort. I shook my head at the woman who thought she'd almost sealed a bargain, made a mental note to come back when the festivities were over and prices were down from astronomical to merely extortionate, and walked over to see what Mark was watching.

"I can never work out how people can put themselves through all this." He nodded in the direction of a window opaqued by swirling images which concealed what was going on inside but still managed to suggest a transformation from age to youth, plainness to glamour.

A body-sculpting studio.

"And you a medic?" I mocked.

"That's exactly why. It's covered in training, of course – anyone who wants to make real money in this field wants to be a sculptor – but I've never really understood it." He shook his head, secure in his own young skin and undoubted good looks. Though he might work for a Family, he wasn't near enough to being one of their courtiers to make the discovery that a Family likeness was suddenly desirable. I liked him better for it. He turned his back on the teasing imagery. "How are you? Recovered?"

"Sure. I got rid of everything and, whatever was used, it doesn't seem to have left any lingering effects. Not even much of a hangover." And I could have brought that on myself. "Sorry you had to be called in – and thanks for what you did." I thought about the analysis as well as the on-the-spot treatment.

"Made a change from blisters, headaches and precautions against seasickness – especially from people on boats which are unlikely ever to go to sea." He grimaced. "Don't often get poisoning or attempted murder."

"I'm not sure it was that dramatic." I tried to damp the enthusiasm I thought I saw. "More that someone wanted to make me feel awful – which was successful – and confine me to my bunk for a while. Which failed, mostly thanks to you."

"My pleasure." He sounded as though he meant it. I had a feeling his interest could be a little more than professional, with any encouragement. Couldn't make my mind up how I felt about that. Flattered, of course, but I tend to be more cautious in personal relationships than in blundering in to investigate things like murder and missing relatives.

And, thinking about that, I saw two people possibly involved in the first of my problems. Clearly the lure of the mall was drawing everyone who didn't feel up to going to sea – even in the launches laid on by Morgan – to watch dinghy races.

I didn't much want to get into a conversation with Amanda and Stephen while Mark was still around, so I agreed to his suggestion to meet up for tea or caf or something in a couple of hours and watched him walk away before I walked over to bump casually into my hosts of a couple of nights ago.

"Amanda, Stephen," I greeted them, trying to decide whether the look on Stephen's face was discomfort at meeting someone he'd fed drugged wine or simply that I wasn't the right type to be seen with here.

"Humility. How nice to see you." Amanda's smile was more open so I immediately suspected it hid more. "I'd have thought you'd have been out with the races."

"I don't do dinghies," I explained. "Too cold and wet. And they tend to capsize."

"So you prefer shopping?" Not exactly, but I allowed myself what she could take as a smile of agreement. She glanced around. "I know it's not exactly the right place, but Stephen and I –" Stephen looked a little hunted – "were wondering if you'd found out any more about poor Andy?"

I wasn't about to tell them Poor Andy had been murdered. Just in case they didn't already know it.

My smile faded into regret. "I'm sorry. I've been a little off-colour lately." They both looked appropriately distressed. "I haven't done as much as I'd have liked."

"My dear." Amanda was all sympathy. "You shouldn't be rushing around if you're not well. Come over to one of the lounges, we can have a nice talk and you can rest." I remembered she'd said something about medical training. Hadn't been sure she was serious.

I allowed myself to be shepherded to the seating area where Amanda fussed over what sort of water she wanted to drink and I accepted a pressed lemon juice. They told me of the boatyard tour they'd been on, the talk on great voyages of the century, and the plans they had for taking their cruiser out once the lock reopened in two days' time for the grand sail in company.

"I'm afraid my boat won't be seaworthy for that," I told them in response to their questions. "I have to have her hauled out so I can look at the rudder hangings before we go anywhere."

Without saying a word, Amanda managed to let me know she wouldn't know a rudder hanging if it fell off her boat and hit her.

"But then you must join us!" Stephen was delighted with his idea. "We were going to be going out on our own and we'd love the company – especially someone who really knows about sailing, like you. We can watch the fireworks from the boat when we come back in."

In the face of Amanda's support for the idea I couldn't think of a way of turning them down flat. I could always be rude nearer the time if nothing else came up to stop me.

I thanked them again for the tour of Ardco, told them how interesting Simon's publicity material had been and wished them every success for their company while agreeing that it was terrible about Poor Andy. And, no, I didn't think it was right for me to join them for the funeral when at last the authorities – who were so slow about these things, as if the situation wasn't distressing enough – released his body.

53

I only had time for a half-hour break with Mark before I had to face my return trip to Sutton. Enough time for both of us to decide we should bump into each other again some time quite soon. Since his job here wasn't just for the festivities – and since he had replaced the earlier medic who had seen my humiliation in the morgue – there seemed to be plenty of possibilities and no real rush.

I took a cab to the waterfront. It didn't seem like a good occasion to risk being late. It was Sal's lieutenant who was waiting for me. She didn't look glad to have been given the job.

"You're to come with me."

"Hello, Annie," I said, not moving to follow her. "Nice to see you, too."

She stopped. Turned. Stared back at me and sighed. "We have to get to the ferry before it's finished unloading. We're going in through the dock gates since the sea approach is too visible in daylight." It was dusk, but a small boat might well still be visible to alert guards or sensors. "I can show you how to get on board, but after that you'll be on your own."

"Just how I like it."

She ignored the tone and made off. I had to hurry to keep track of her as she made her way partly along the roadside, partly through derelict yards, always sticking to whatever cover was available. I wasn't sure whether this was habit or if she was trying to impress me. I didn't think there were vids surveilling the road or, if there were, anyone would be checking them. Unless they saw a pair of females behaving in a very surreptitious manner. It didn't make me feel any more hopeful about tonight's entertainment.

And I still wasn't sure if I wanted to find answers on the ferry. I was growing more and more afraid that I wasn't going to like them if I did find them.

Just beyond the main entrance to Ardco was a small blind alley.

"We wait here." Annie's voice was barely a whisper. She was watching, listening, eyes on the gate. I barely existed for her except as a complication to a familiar but tricky procedure.

As soon as she saw the gates begin to widen, Annie moved.

It wasn't as easy as sneaking in behind a truck that was on its way in. Slipping in behind one that was on its way out meant finding cover as soon as we were through. I became Annie's shadow, ducking where she ducked, weaving as she did, in case her slightest deviation from a straight course meant evading some vid or alarm. By the end of the ten metres which took us from the main gate to the other side of the small inner hut where the tekkie, No-neck, had waited, I felt as though I was breathing with her lungs.

The ferry was moored up. Stern gates gaping wide and unloading on to the line of waiting trucks. Not a big cargo, I thought. The ferry wasn't even half full. At least its main cargo deck was almost bare. Either Ardco was operating at a loss or it was carrying something that wasn't stored on the main deck.

I'd seen the balance sheets. Now I wanted to see where else cargo was being held.

Annie led me round the perimeter of the warehouse,

keeping the ferry in sight all the time. There were drones working the cargo: I didn't see any sign of human intervention.

"Is unloading wholly automated?" I wanted to know.

She nodded. "Don't often see any people here – just a tekkie in the box by the gate in daylight. Couple of office staff. And the guy who thinks he runs things, of course." That was a definite sneer for Simon. "But the alarms are live and sensitive. Saw some street type looking for a place to crash here a few weeks back. Must have thought the ferry would be more comfortable than the sheds." A grin showed bared teeth, one missing. "That's how we know security's set at kill."

I winced. Took her word for it. Didn't want to hear any more details. Didn't need convincing. And I was going to try to get on board? I'd a feeling I knew why Sal had decided to nominate me rather than one of her gang for the job. My guess was that her assurance of a safe way in was mostly theory. My privilege to make the first live trial.

We waited at the edge of the warehouse. Now I saw that, beside the trucks off-loading and leaving the yard, there were smaller drone vehicles taking crates into the warehouse. They didn't all pass under the security gantry. Some of them were working through a small entryport in the ferry's port side. I had no idea what they carried but, as long as they weren't rigged to be weight-sensitive to detect unscheduled loads, I could use one as my boarding pass.

"Was this how the two from your gang went in?"

Annie nodded. Mouth tight. "Idiots. They know what Sal thinks of betting. And neither of them were good at getting around quietly. They liked centre stage."

Sounded as though Sal wouldn't have been too sorry to lose them from her gang – except for the insult if someone else had made that decision for her. When you haven't got much else beside your pride, insults can be deadly.

"What sort of age are they? Any clue how I'd know them if I saw them?" I asked.

"They're around my age, I s'pose," said Annie with the inflection of one who wasn't sure how old she was. "Acted like kids, though, sometimes." She might have been sixteen, no more. "You see any kids on board, you bring them off. If they're ours, we'll sort it. If not, we'll kick 'em off our territory. 'Kay?"

"'Kay." It seemed clear enough and I nodded.

A crawler was coming out of the warehouse. I braced myself. Annie pulled something off her belt and passed it to me. A com. Hi-power/lo-range. "Sal said to give you this. Don't use it unless you have to. We'll buzz you if it's time to run. Get off anyway after an hour. You won't be able to get away once they've locked up after off-loading. This one's not scheduled out till tomorrow night's tide. They'll load then."

I looped the com to my own belt. Useful item.

The little low crawler was moving slowly enough for me to swing aboard on Annie's gesture. "Stay low," she ordered. Then, almost unwillingly, "Luck."

Hoped I wouldn't need it. Tucked my head down level with my hunched knees and clung tightly to a handle on the side of the crawler furthest from the security gantry. Didn't want to be jolted off.

54

The ride was short and straightforward, lumpy but not desperately uncomfortable. I didn't really need the death-grip on the handle. If it hadn't been for my brain telling me it was going to be fried every two seconds, it might have been nothing but a rather foolish joy-ride. I was wet with the sweat of fear by the time we lumbered through the entryport.

Not the same ferry Simon had showed us round. Had to expect differences.

It was reasonably well-lit inside. Floor-level lighting, mostly. One or two floods over the great cavern of the main cargo area, nothing on the stairwells. Drones seldom do stairs. I had to assume there were lifts to the upper decks but they would certainly be monitored. Time to stop hitchhiking and hit the stairs.

The crawler didn't seem to notice my departure. I slithered round the steel bulkheads towards the enclosed stairwell. Got round the first turn before I reached in my sack for the flashlight. Its beam was narrow and I held my palm over it to cut the glare. Allowed just enough light to show me the angle of the stairs and the way they spiralled round. Doors off at each deck level, I guessed.

Decided to start at the top and work down.

I didn't know what I was looking for or whether I'd find it. All I could do was look at as much as I could in the time allowed and hope I spotted something that would give me some idea of what was going on, something just enough off-key to let me know it was significant.

The rail was clammy, sweating slightly in the damp salt

air. Or perhaps that was my hands. I stepped carefully, anxious to make no noise on the metal treads whose ridges pressed through the thin rubber soles of my shoes. I clutched my sack to my body so it wouldn't swing and clatter against the bulkhead.

Counted the decks as I passed. Just two above the cargo deck. Reckoned the bridge would be on the lower one. Waited with caution as I came to the top of the stairs. Saw nothing, heard nothing except the almost subliminal hum of electronics, the vibration – more heard than felt – of generators on low power. Somehow dusk had given way to night in the time it took me to climb up here.

Stepped out on to a small gallery platform looking aft. Nothing here except a view of Ardco's docking area. Trucks still moving around. No sign of Sal's girls. Went through the doorway behind me into a corridor with doors off to either side. Carpeted floor. Cabin space. For crew or passengers? A look inside a couple of the rooms – washing facilities, wide berths not yet made up, upholstered seating – gave me the answer. Passengers: drivers and their mates from the few non-automated trucks I'd seen on the main deck among the containers, the foot-travellers who could afford a cabin. Besides, there weren't likely to be more than three or four crew.

A quick check told me that all the cabins up here were alike. All stripped and bare of anything of interest.

Softly down one flight of stairs at the bows.

Yes. Here was the bridge. Usual layout: banks of touch-screens and a couple of keyboards. A wheel, for tradition's sake. Links to the engine room and what looked like mostly automated controls. Various lockers and a chart table which was probably never used. Communications. No room for anything out of place and the least likely site for it. Hurried on, conscious of time passing.

The crew's quarters were just aft of the bridge. Single-berth cabins where the proverbial cat would have had a hard time swinging. No carpet here. Few facilities and no luxuries. Nothing more than basic regs laid down, I guessed. Berths for seven, which was more than I expected – but perhaps this ferry had once done longer runs. Signs that not all the cabins were in current use.

The rest of this deck was lounge seating, a bar, dining facilities. Open walkways to each side of the big public areas for those who couldn't manage without fresh air. Screens inside which probably had all the popular shows and games on permanently. Everything easy to clean, not yet torn or too shabby, a few signs of wear. No better or worse than most Channel ferries I'd been on board.

Depressing.

It was beginning to look as though I'd find nothing. All that adrenalin wasted. At least I could cross this ferry off my list of places to search, even if I was no wiser about what Ardco was dealing in. And it didn't seriously cross my mind they might be legit: it just wasn't profitable.

Only one place left to look.

Below decks.

It hadn't been my claustrophobia that stopped me trying there first. At least, I didn't want to think so. It had seemed more likely that valuable cargo would be kept somewhere a little healthier, a little more accessible, than in the space left after you'd accounted for the engine room and the galley. The bilges.

55

The companionway leading below decks was steep and greasy: a ladder with hand rails. I stepped even more cautiously and began to ease down backwards. I stopped after the first dozen rungs and allowed my flashlight to spread a wider beam. No portholes here to let a glimmer of light escape ashore and raise the alarm.

Nothing showed up in the light except the pipework and internal framing of the ferry. Down a little further to a tiny landing which allowed the ladder to take a one-eighty turn and go down again in its near-vertical run. I was glad to get to the bottom. Conscious of the dangers of slipping in a mix of oil and water if the engine-room was sloppy, I shone the torch at my feet as I made my way past the machinery. No need to linger here. Whatever had been concealed was unlikely to be anywhere there was a chance of it getting tangled with the drives.

I was rationalising. If I was looking for drugs or uncut gems or ancient manuscripts, they could be hidden under my hand and I'd have had no way of knowing. I just had to hope I'd see something more obvious. Or at least find a trace of the girls from Sal's gang. Who might be somewhere in France right now, working out how to get back and wondering if it was worth risking Sal's anger to do so.

The engines were aft. The galley, reassuringly clean and grease-free – the drones probably steam-hosed it after every trip – was just forward of the engine room. There was unallotted space forward again. Unless my mental image of the ferry's dimensions had become completely turned around in the dank and clammy darkness with the weight of the upper decks pressing down on me.

Crew's dining area. Not much used by the look of it. A watertight bulkhead door with a heavy handle that needed all my weight and both hands to turn. There was something here. Emergency lighting edged the deck by my feet. Dim, but enough for someone human to move around in. I killed the flashlight and kept moving forward. Shut doors, one on either side. I pushed against the one to my right: it opened on to darkness. Shone the torch all round. Empty. Metal floors and walls unsoftened by furnishing of any kind, unless you counted the series of wide iron shelves riveted to the hull wall. Six of them. There were ring bolts along the other walls, about a metre up from the deck. I couldn't work out what the room was for. Storage, obviously, but someone had gone to some trouble to make sure there was no trace left of whatever had been stored here. The steam cleaners had been busy again. A faint glisten of moisture hung round the drain hole in the room's corner. Some unidentifiable smell, half-sweet/half-rotten, hung teasingly faint in the stale air.

The place made me uneasy: conscious I was below the ferry's water-line with no exit except along the corridor I was in. A man at each end could block it. Hell, a child with a gun at each end would be enough to make me surrender.

I wasn't sure what was making me think of guns. Perhaps it was the claustrophobia after all.

I moved towards the door on the opposite side of the corridor. Felt something brush against my thigh. Froze. Thought about dropping dead from terror, and realised that the brushing was the com unit Annie had lent me, doing its discreet best to attract my attention.

"Shit." I leaned against the bulkhead and lifted it to my mouth. "Yeah?"

"Sal. Find anything?"

"Don't know. Not your girls, anyway. Almost done now."

"You'd better be. At least, you'd better get out now whether you're done or not. They've finished unloading. Closing up in minutes. Don't get locked in."

The com went dead. Thanks, Sal.

Just the cabin across the way to look in. Chances were it was the duplicate of the one I'd just left, but no point in leaving it unexplored. I might not get another chance.

Pushed on the door. Harder this time. They'd cleaned this cabin, too. Just not quite so thoroughly – manual, not steam, I guessed. The smell was heavier here.

And I recognised it.

The brush against my thigh this time was a buzz. Sal probably had the com fixed so it could cause real pain if you didn't do what she wanted. I grabbed at the small heap of dust and debris driven into one corner by an inefficient sweeper drone and stuffed it in a pocket.

"Coming!" I snarled into the unit and moved fast.

Down the corridor. Up the ladders and froze at the entry to the cargo deck. It was deserted. No sign of truck or crawler and the stern doors were swinging shut. I could still dive out through them, either on to the dockside or, more likely, straight into the Solent with all that meant in terms of needing a stomach pump.

Was just deciding I didn't have a choice when a last crawler emerged from behind a bulkhead and moved towards the entryport. I made a dash and climbed on board.

56

I was well clear of the ferry and back into gang territory before Sal solidified out of the night and said, "Well?"

"We need to talk." And I needed another couple of minutes to decide what to tell her.

"Over here."

'Here' was one of the abandoned containers. Only it wasn't abandoned any more. Someone had cut an opening in one end and welded a narrow door in place. Gang HQ. Inside were a couple of chairs which looked as though they'd been retrieved from the nearest dump, a table made of ply laid on trestles and some shelving. Light was good. Guessed Ardco paid their power bills and didn't know it.

I slumped in one of the shabby chairs, shifting to avoid a broken spring. After the lower deck of the ferry, this container seemed almost homelike. Although I was glad the door remained fractionally ajar.

"Well?" Sal felt I'd had enough recovery time.

"Bottom line: there's nothing there." I paused. "Now."

The disappointment gave way to a frown before it could form. "What do you mean?"

"I started on the top deck," I began and explained how I'd found nothing out of the ordinary up there. "Then I decided to look below decks."

"And?"

"And nothing. Except two rooms that looked a bit too clean, and which didn't have any function I could tie in to anything else going on. Could just be storage, but it didn't feel like it. And ships don't usually indulge in useless space."

"And what do you *guess* they were used for?" Sarcasm and curiosity in equal measure.

"I don't know," I admitted. "But I think your girls may have been in there." I fished in my pocket, pulled out the scrap of waste I'd retrieved. "What's their hair colour?"

She stared at the small handful of fluff and dust tangled in a hank of a dozen or more long reddish-brown hairs.

I dropped it into her hand so she could see more clearly. She looked hard. Clenched her fist and glared at me. "That's hair roots. This was pulled out." Opened her hand for another look. "Beany had this colour hair."

Past tense. I thought she was likely right. Nodded.

"I'm sorry." Two unknown gang girls, probably floating somewhere in the Channel.

"So am I." There was grief there, but rage was also growing. An insult to one gang member was an insult to all. "What you planning?"

I wasn't sure, yet. And I didn't want to confide all my plans to someone who was likely to send her whole gang out looking for retribution and blood if she was given anything approaching a target. "I need a thinking space. Looks as though someone at Ardco's got something he or she wants to hide, but I need to know more."

"We could just torch the place." She liked the idea. I didn't mind it.

"And lose your lair?" She looked thoughtful. "Besides, you've no way of knowing if whoever's responsible would go up in flames, too. Be a shame to miss him. And I suppose there's a chance your girls might still turn up – just a bit battered."

A hard look. "You believe in fairy stories, too?"

Not really. "I want another look at the ferry. After the cargo's loaded, before she sails."

"Not easy. You could end up sailing with her."

"I'll take the chance." And possibly get some backup. "I'll come over again tomorrow evening. Same time. Before then, though, I want to see this girl who could be Charity." Who might still have a chance of a happy ending.

"You want her to come to Midway?" A bargain was a bargain.

I thought. I'd rather not meet her on gang territory, but she might not want to come to mine. "If she'll do it, yes. If not, we could meet somewhere neutral." I considered. Not Tom Lee's, too conspicuous. Thought about Luna's hang-out. "What about Above Bar? It's open ground. She wouldn't feel I'd want to force her to come with me."

"Possible. I'll check. Call you tomorrow, early." I hoped my mother didn't have the same idea.

"'Kay. You going to do anything about that?" I pointed to the hair still gripped in her hand.

She stared down at it. Dropped it on the table and straightened the limp strands with surprisingly tender fingers. "I'll wait till you've been in again. After that, we'll torch the place if you haven't come up with a better idea. To hell with the lair." Her voice was soft, almost emotionless. It scared me.

I left.

I hadn't told her about the smell in the cabins. The smell I remembered from my nightmare. The smell of blood.

57

I felt as though I'd spent whole nights in the docks, but a quick check told me there were still hours to go before midnight. If I went back home I'd either get caught up in whatever partying was going on or have to sit on board the *Pig* and listen to others enjoy themselves. I didn't find either prospect appealing.

In the end Tom Lee's was the obvious choice.

It had what I wanted: bright lights, lots of glossy surface, people pleased with themselves, full of talk and noise. The sounds of a life that didn't recognise the stench of blood or the threat of violence.

Of course both those things were there. But Tom Lee didn't let them out into the restaurant.

I walked up from the docks. It took half an hour and should have been a stupid and dangerous decision. Somehow the hour I'd spent on the ferry made the streets safe. If anyone intended me ill that evening, they saw enough to make them step aside, decide to wait for a better time or place. No one even crossed my path.

It was late enough for all the tables to be crowded, but the queue was almost gone. I found a seat at the bar as I'd somehow known I would, and cupped a fragile goblet of deep red wine in both hands. Its enigmatic depths gave nothing back.

Wine's like that.

"Want company?" Tall guy. Quite pretty in a sculpted sort of way. Around my age, perhaps a year or two older given the sculpting. Nice smile, not much behind the eyes. I shook my head.

"No thanks."

A shrug. "Your loss."

Perhaps. I went back to the glass I was nursing. When a hand tapped my shoulder I sighed, ready to be a little more forceful with the tall guy this time.

It was Byron.

"Don't tell me this is coincidence." Somehow I couldn't even summon up surprise.

"Hardly. May I?" He indicated the stool next to me. I decided he was probably the only company I could put up with tonight. He wouldn't want to play games. I nodded. "I asked Tom Lee to contact me if you came in tonight. I live nearby," he added.

That was a surprise. If I'd thought about it I'd have assumed he'd have a roost somewhere out of town in one of the upmarket fortified compounds. Then I thought again: I knew quite well he could handle his own security and, even if cities were unfashionable, dangerous places these days, he was urban right through. A blade of grass would only puzzle him. Perhaps Sutton suited him in an off-beat sort of way. Was that where he'd been when I'd first called him to discuss Morgan's offer?

"And Tom Lee gives out info on me for nothing?" I was insulted.

"Not quite. He needed a favour – and I don't think he'd have done it at all if he hadn't watched us the other day when Morgan was here. Seems he thought the signals were friendly."

Interesting. Tom Lee read body language better than most.

"Hope it was an expensive favour." A girl needs to feel valued.

"Oh yes. It was."

"Good." My wine tasted better. "What do you want?"

He signalled for wine for himself. Sipped. "Wondering how you got on tonight. Thanks for the belated message, by the way."

"Pleasure. I did upgrade my notes on this business." And I'd copied them to him – a courtesy, since I knew very well he could easily have extracted them from my system himself. "It was just a recce. On and off the ferry with no one noticing, no trouble." If you didn't count my own emotional switchback.

"And did you learn anything useful?" Always precise, Byron. He didn't doubt I'd have learned *something*.

"I think I got more questions," I admitted. Gave him a potted history of what had happened, didn't cut out the gore this time. "I'm going back tomorrow."

"I see." He probably did. "Is this still about Andy?"

I tried to be honest. "I think so. I think his death is linked to whatever's happening at Ardco. If I find out what that is, and who's behind it, I think I can pin down whoever killed him."

"You already have a good idea about that." He had read the files.

"And no proof or motive. It's not enough." Not for me. Not for Andy, either. He deserved for someone to understand what had happened. I was beginning to think he hadn't been quite the nice fun guy everyone talked about, but that didn't mean he deserved to have been murdered. Perhaps Byron understood. Certainly he understood me well enough not to argue.

"You need support tomorrow?" I told him what I wanted. He thought about it. "I'll talk to Morgan."

"Is that why you were looking for me? To get a report for Morgan?"

"Obviously. But it could have waited. Or I could have called you. No. There's another project I would like your views on. This seemed like a good place to talk."

Or drink. He'd bought me a refill. Still, talk and drink are only incompatible a long time after the second glass. "Go on."

I wasn't used to seeing Byron pause to collect his thoughts. I assumed they always moved at nanospeed and he just pressed the equivalent of a mental button to bring them into coherent order and slow them down to realtime.

"You're naturally curious." He could just have said nosey. "You deal well with people: listen to them, notice how they think, deal with their emotional complications." He gave the impression of listing tasks which any normal person would find distasteful and difficult. Normality can have a lot of guises.

I thought about it. "True. In a way. But I'm not into communal living." Had too much of that as a child. "I couldn't survive without somewhere to get away from people."

"Understood." Much more easily than the rest.

"So?" He couldn't rouse that curiosity he'd mentioned and not supply an answer.

"You know I do investigative work? Mostly for the Vinci Family, but not solely."

"Facts and figures. Data. Numbers." I listed them much as he'd listed my traits. He'd been masquerading as an auditor when I'd first been introduced to him.

"That's it. Seems to me there's a symbiosis there." I just stared, wondering what mutual benefit he could possibly see. "Investigation." Byron did patient superiority too well for someone of my more emotional traits. I went on staring, beginning to see where he was going but not sure whether I believed it. Or wanted to. "I have a good business." It kept him in very expensive hand-made shoes and tailored suits. "I think it might be even better if we combined our skills."

"But I'm never here," I protested.

A raised eyebrow. "No? You've got a permanent free berth in an exclusive port. You have to come back to England to sell your cargo, and your contact with Tom Lee means you'll probably choose to do that here more often than not." I had always hated his habit of reciting a series of logical points as though explaining basic math to a seven-year-old. "So why not earn extra money as a consultant to cases I might not otherwise choose to deal with?"

I could think of a million reasons. Wasn't quite up to listing them in any sort of logical sequence. Could feel a splutter coming on. "Apart from the fact that you've clearly just gone crazy? We think differently. I like sailing and you don't. I can't touch the most basic tech without it disintegrating, and there's no way I'd even contemplate having any augments. I don't like Family, I don't like technos, I *hate* being told what to do. And, added to all that, what on earth makes you think that now – when I've come from a ship that reeks of blood and gives me claustrophobia and is run by a set of murdering crooks – is a good time to ask me something like this?"

I wanted more wine.

"Because, knowing all that, you're still going to go back tomorrow and find out what's going on." I gaped at him. Heard what he was saying and realised we were both insane. "And you stand a much better chance of surviving, *and* getting the answers you want, with some tech backup from me."

The worst thing was that, even with my mouth open to tell him just how ludicrous his idea was, I knew he was right. I really hated that. But I was also hearing the answer to a question I'd been asking myself ever since I was dragged into this whole mess.

"Just when did you start thinking about asking me to work with you?" I demanded.

He didn't blink. Didn't look as though I'd caught him out. Just nodded fractionally as though I'd reached a very obvious solution. "I thought about it soon after that last business ended. When Morgan tried to bring me in on Andy's death. It looked like suicide, then. I knew you'd be able to look at motives, work out why he'd done it."

"Except he hadn't."

"You've still got at least as far as I could have done, probably further. I'd have seen through the suicide, but there's not much data here. Too much money around for anything honest, but no cybertrail to follow. You're getting closer than I could."

I shook my head. "I can't deal with this right now. You can't just spring things on me and expect an answer."

"Did I say I wanted an answer right now? I just wanted to give you something to think about. You can let me know your decision before you sail off again." He put his empty glass carefully in the centre of an immaculate white coaster.

Something to think about? Something *else* to think about? "I'll let you know," I managed. My wine coaster had a nice red circle on it. Blurred. Off-centre. I knew how it felt.

"Good. Come on, I'll get you a cab."

I'd only had a couple of glasses; I didn't need transport,

or an escort. What I wanted was to stay here until I needed both. But if I was going to be any use tomorrow it was an offer I'd better accept.

58

Funnily enough, I didn't dream. I don't know if it was the wine, or Byron's 'something to think about', or simply the fact I'd had enough of fear and revulsion during the hours in the dockyard. I was just grateful.

I wasn't allowed a chance to lie in. Sal had said early and meant it.

"Humility?"

"Yeah?" I wasn't very awake.

"Above Bar. Two hours. She says she wants me nearby." I thought she was going to blank the screen before I could even say thanks. She'd turned away, now she looked back. "I think it's your kid."

The thought that I might be trudging back into the city for a disappointment had already crossed my mind. The reassurance, whether based on anything real or not, helped. "Thanks. I'll be there."

Blank screen.

At least I had a reason to leave home before mother called. I was nervous. Thinking about Charity. Found myself fussing over what I should wear. Tried to anticipate what I would say, what she would say. Wondered if we'd have anything to say to each other. Would she be frightened? Defiant? Angry she'd been found? Hungry? I stuffed some bread into my sack, then took it out again. I could buy her a meal if that was all she wanted from me.

Had she found someone? Someone who liked her, and worried about her, and didn't want to make her into any-thing she didn't want to be? I couldn't imagine two people being that lucky.

Thanks, Jack. I didn't always remember to say it.

In all the fuss of the past few days, Gus had been too busy to harass me. Or perhaps I'd just not been around, except when Morgan was also on the scene. Now I saw him at the head of the gangway down to the marina.

On days when you just want to get on with important things, people and events keep interrupting. I nodded, said "Morning, Gus," and went to move on. Perhaps it was my politeness that unsettled him.

"You up to something? You make sure that barge of yours doesn't let the Port down this week."

The Flying Pig was not one of the glossiest, newest or most luxurious boats in the marina. She had probably seen more sea miles than all the others combined, and she was my home. She was also damaged. She wasn't in any condition to do harm to anyone. He really shouldn't have started it.

"The *Pig*'s not let anyone down yet. We're saving it all for the fireworks display. Should be fun." My grin was not friendly.

He didn't exactly believe me but he didn't think I was lying, either. "You do anything…" His imagination didn't run to details. "Those fireworks have been specially licensed. The precautions we've had to take…" He shook his head at the memory. There had probably been a mountain of forms. He was clearly torn between delight in Midway's being able to produce such a rare show as a real firework display – no holos, everything guaranteed flammable and explosive – and terror at a growing list of Things That Might Go Wrong. I had some sympathy, but not enough to tolerate insults to my home.

I was looking forward to the display. But a few incendiaries of my own weren't going to burn the port down. "How could

I do anything? The *Pig*'s drive isn't quite stable, of course, but she's not going to blow up. I might bring a few friends around, though. In fact, I'm off to the city to see a couple now. 'Bye."

I left him gobbling. Suddenly felt weary, rather than cheered, by the exchange. Gus loathed me on what he probably called principle, because of what he thought he knew about my background. To him, the Communities consisted of irresponsible drop-outs capable of disrupting anything respectable folk might organise. They opposed the Families and civilisation and had no proper sense of order. The fact that I'd rebelled against them made me worse, not better – a drop-out's drop-out. And he probably remembered a couple of wild parties on the *Pig* when Jack was still around.

And I suppose I hadn't done much lately to improve my image. But if association with Morgan wasn't going to do it, nothing would.

It usually amused me. It bothered me today because I was just about to meet a girl who'd exiled herself from one community and hadn't yet found a place in another, and was probably too young to deal with people like Gus who would reject her for something she'd never stood for.

I was angry with Gus because I was uncomfortably aware how angry I'd been with Charity for disrupting my life here, which I wanted – desperately wanted – to keep separate from the life I'd fled.

Knowing it didn't make me feel much better. The morning's caf turned sour on my tongue.

The next interruption was less unwelcome, but I still felt time passing. Mark was walking towards me.

"Don't you have people to heal? Wounds to bandage? Drugs to peddle?" I demanded.

"Not even a sprained finger. I missed you last night. The party's beginning to hot up. Tonight should be a bit special – and then there's tomorrow's fireworks."

"Tell me about it. Sorry about last night but I had business in Sutton. Same again tonight, I'm afraid. Have a drink for me." Or several.

"I'll do that. You'll have to tell me about your city friends sometime." I didn't think so. "You got a couple of minutes for a caf break?"

Considered. I wanted to rush off, arrive early, but I had at least an hour in hand. I'd planned a cab. Knew myself well enough to know I risked doing something misguided if someone on a bus pushed me in the wrong direction this morning. So I could spare some time. And talking with Mark wasn't a hardship.

"'Kay."

I walked with him to the mall. There was one of the smaller caf outlets which seemed to have become the place where people who worked here, not the paying clients, drifted in. It always happens: no one quite knows why, but one place ends up preferred. Often the choice seems to have nothing remotely to do with the quality of the food or the service. This place at least had the virtue of trading on the phenomenon, and opening early.

"You've been busy lately." Mark was too polite to ask straight out. Saved me lying straight out.

"Business in town. A bit complicated."

He looked sideways. "To do with the state you were in the other morning?"

I grimaced. "In a way." Thought a bit. "Did you ever check out the suicide guy for the same stuff I took in?"

He nodded. "Eventually. Nothing showed on the first tox screen. Even the second, when I was really looking,

I wouldn't like to bet heavily on it. But there was a trace of something like it."

I had a feeling it would be safe to bet on it. Mark took his work seriously enough to have chased down the last few molecules of something and given them a name. It wasn't a surprise; I'd have been disappointed with any other answer. Andy must have been knocked out somehow, because there'd been no sign of a struggle. I remembered my tour of his boat.

"I don't know if it's still there, but there was an unfinished bottle of wine on his cruiser." The tidiness of the saloon hadn't just been his killer's work: every drawer and locker had been obsessively neat. Andy had tidily put the opened wine away before its contents had had time to work on him. "Could be you'd find another trace there."

He brightened, a hound on a scent. "Could be. I'll look at it. More interesting than sprains and hangovers."

"And body sculpting."

"Definitely. Not that there aren't some impressive specimens of the art wandering round the marina. Beautiful work, some of it." He drank caf. "If you like that sort of thing." Grinned. "Won't stop a couple of them coming in for new livers before long, the way they're putting away the free stuff."

I was curious. "You don't mind doing that sort of work – even though the harm's often self-inflicted?"

"It's different. Sculpting – most of it – tends just to be vanity, or fashion, or fitting in with the Family. Organ replacement saves lives. Whatever you think of the lives involved. If you can afford it, tissue engineering means you can even build your own organs. And since they knocked out the rejection problem, the only problem with the donor route is supply."

Too many people living long, healthy lives. China controlling the Asian market. No one wanting anything from Africa or India because of Aids – and modern superstition making too many people believe that the only safe donor organ was from someone the same ethnic stock as themselves, believing young and healthy donors would make them young and healthy too. "And the synthetics just don't do it for most people."

"Not these sort of people," Mark agreed. "Strictly organic."

We drank caf, talked of lighter things like fireworks and meeting for a meal when all the fuss of the opening had gone away. We were both comfortable in our opinions of the over-indulged and pampered rich. Everyone's allowed a couple of prejudices.

Mark looked at his chrono. "I'd better move. Sure to be a blister needing attention somewhere."

I saw the time. "Shit!" My plan to arrive early was suffering a setback. "I've got to rush."

Grabbed my sack, waved. Was gone.

59

It wasn't full market today, but there was still plenty of buying, selling, trading, going on. Even at less than full volume the place had an energy the Port wouldn't recognise. Today I hardly registered it. Just scanned, searched, went on. If I knew Sal at all, she'd be waiting in the shadows. Checking that everything was clear and clean before appearing from nowhere. If she had the full gang with her, of course, they'd have swaggered their black-clad way straight through the market, making way for no one. Since this was a personal encounter, favour for favour, she'd be alone. Or Annie would be well-hidden, at least.

Pride had me wanting to get a fix on them before they materialised. If Sal had been alone, it wouldn't have happened, but her companion hadn't had a chance to develop that mix of patience and alertness which keeps you ahead on the streets. I doubted if I'd ever really develop it either. Started too late.

They were at the opposite side of the area from the alley leading to Luna's hole. I glimpsed a back wearing the unmistakeable tawny-brown of Community homespun. My fingers had been worked raw on the stuff too often not to recognise it and, amid all the syntho-stuff and garish mismatched tatters of the rest of the crowd, it could hardly have sent out a louder signal.

The lingering doubt, the conviction that this was a set-up, a chase after fool's gold, faded.

I let Sal make the move. Paused by a clothes stall as though something among the much-used stuff might be useful. Shook my head and drifted a bit further towards the busy shadow into which they blended. Ice-cream concession. Oh yes, Charity would like that. She was thirteen years old and the restrictions of Community life would still be vivid, still feel like something to be half-guiltily defied.

It seemed a good place to wait.

"Hi." Sal's voice, behind me.

I turned. "Sal." But it was the girl with her I was looking at, knowing at once that this was my niece. Unsure what that meant.

Her picture had been more accurate than most: despite her time away from the Community, with food in shorter supply than she was used to, she was still plumper than the average street kid. Glared at me with defiant eyes which might also be a little scared. Neither the photo nor her present mood told me what she'd look like if she smiled.

Below the homespun she wore trews. They looked OK on her, but she shifted awkwardly as though still conscious what her mother – worse, her father – would have said to find her dressed as a boy. She'd hacked her hair short. I smiled. It was what I'd done my second day as a runaway. I remembered how odd and light it felt. How good.

"Charity." I kept the smile, didn't move to touch her. Nothing that would make her think I wanted to take over.

Still no smile. "I'm Cherry now." Half sullen, half defiant. Expecting shock? It was a good idea, and a much prettier name. Hanging on to my own name had caused me far more problems than changing it to something more acceptable would ever have done.

"Good name. I'm glad to see you. Sal told you I was looking for you?"

She glanced over to the older girl with something not far off worship in her eyes. Sal nodded. Permission to speak.

"She said you were my aunt? Humility?" Something, less a touch of awe than the inevitable disappointment of seeing your exemplar made flesh, tinged her voice. "So you are well. My father…"

"Ethan thinks I'm damned and I guess he's beaten you for even listening to someone mention my name."

She flushed. Looked down. "Yes." A soft voice. *It is a shame for women to speak.* In church or anywhere else, if Ethan had his way.

"Don't worry. He tried to beat me often enough when we were children. But I could run faster, and could throw a rotten apple more accurately." My father had administered the beating for that incident. It was a couple of weeks later that I'd heard him discussing my marriage with my mother and had known I would have to leave home. Charity, *Cherry*, was staring, open-mouthed.

"It's all right. He's your father, but that doesn't mean he's not a narrow-minded bully." I considered: Ethan wasn't someone I thought of often. "It's probably not his fault, really. Just the way he was brought up."

She didn't know whether to run from me or embrace me. It was one thing to hear the careless blasphemy all around from heathen who knew no better, but from someone brought up among the godly… Well, she'd just have to learn to deal with it.

Sal was staring. "You two really are from off-planet." Near enough. "But I guess you still eat?"

"Sure. The ice cream poisonous?" She would know. Cherry was suddenly looking very young and too hot.

"Be better off over there." Sal hitched one thin shoulder in the approximate direction of one of the stalls trading out the front of a derelict building. Her voice didn't quite carry to the ice-cream seller behind us, but we still got a killing look when we moved off. We'd used her shade and bought nothing. No fair trade.

The tables and chairs were mismatched, but their presence made this a restaurant, not a stall. Prices to match, probably.

Cherry went for the ice cream. So, after a moment's hesitation, did Sal. I chose a cold lemon drink and felt older than my years.

It was a couple of minutes before Cherry looked up. Her dark eyes were frowning. "How did you know I was here?" She'd abandoned the long-winded courtesies of the Community, not yet adjusted to the way the World spoke. Not deliberately rude, I thought.

"My mother called me."

"But no one in the Community knows…" she protested.

"Where I am? Mother has known since about six months after I left." When Jack forced an arguing and stubborn runaway to tell her parents she wasn't dead. I still was, as far as father was concerned. "We don't talk often."

"She speaks with thee?" The old forms still lingered. She heard herself and blushed. "I mean, you're not really Shunned, then?"

Sal looked confused. I was resigned. "I certainly am. Mother risks all sorts of things by talking with me. But when she believes she's right about something…"

Cherry winced. "Grandmother Judith can be strong in a righteous cause," she admitted.

Weird to hear my mother spoken of as someone's grandmother. Made her seem old. "That's one way of saying it. So you came here because the rumours said this was where I'd come?"

Embarrassed, she pushed the wooden spoon around in her puddling ice. Nodded. "I had to get away. Had to come

205

somewhere, and Sutton was one of the cities I'd heard of. I thought if you could make it, then so could I." She met my eyes. "And I did. I came here, and I made it without any help."

I looked at Sal, silent beside her. Cherry didn't know how much help she'd had. How lucky she'd been. But I'd been lucky, too. It was the only way to survive.

"What made you run?" I wondered. "I waited till I was fifteen and they started talking about life partners."

"I couldn't stand it. They, *Father* mostly, wouldn't let me do anything and it was always work and 'look after your little sister'. I couldn't do anything *I* wanted. Ever." Now she did sound her real age. Or younger. "And I talked to my friends and told them my aunt had run off and they said why didn't I do that if it was so great. And I said I would and…" Somehow it didn't sound so grand even to her as she told it. I thought about boasting to a group of sulky teenagers and being dared to make good my words. I might even have found myself doing the same thing as she'd done, however mad.

I could see why she didn't intend to go back. Meeting her friends again might be even more humiliating than whatever Ethan had in mind.

"And since you've been in Sutton, how have you managed?" I asked.

Cherry looked as though she was remembering something she'd prefer to forget. "It was horrible at first. Not like I thought it would be at all. One of the traders to the Community gave me a lift to the city but then he just left me here, said there were plenty of ways for a girl like me to make a living. I didn't understand what he meant." She looked up from her ice cream, expression hard and scared together. "Then."

"I know." I didn't ask what she'd done, whether she'd chosen or been forced to make the kind of decision no child should. She'd tell me if she wanted. My guess was that she'd somehow managed to avoid that, so far. Selling yourself leaves scars that are hard to hide.

"There are some good kids on the streets," she told me, as though she had to defend them from some unspoken accusation. "They helped me, stopped me getting into fights." I winced at the thought of what would have happened to her in any street fight. "Showed me how to scavenge, a bit. Even shared, though there wasn't much."

She'd learned more than most city people ever learned about the good side of those who led their lives on the edge of the abyss. Some fall off, others are hauled back.

"And now?" It was too soon to expect a decision from her, but I wanted to know if she had somewhere to sleep at nights. Somewhere to eat.

Another of those glances at Sal. "She," and there was no doubt who that was, "says I can bunk with her gang for a few days."

"Sal?" I queried. Gangs didn't open their doors to any waif, particularly not one who had nothing obvious to contribute. They were emphatically not anyone's idea of social security. I thought of Meera: I needed to tell her I'd found Charity. Wondered if I'd need to tell her my niece was in the care of a dockyard girl gang.

Sal's smile had a hint of wryness. "She's *not* gang." Something in the look she gave Cherry stopped the girl's indignant protest. "She can stay until you've sorted the other business." Whatever was going on with Ardco. "After that, we'll see. Unless she'd rather stay with you?"

I might have imagined a hint of appeal in the question. Clearly my niece was used to getting her own way and, for her own reasons, Sal hadn't yet chosen to show her just how ruthless a gang leader could be.

"Do you want to stay with me, Cherry?" I asked. She was watching us both. Something in the set of her mouth said she wasn't going to let adults make her choices for her. But sulking wasn't going to get her far. "Why don't you come back to the Port with me now? You can look around, see what my home's like and, if you want, come back to the docks tonight. I've got to come anyway." And I wasn't looking forward to it. I trusted Sal to make sure Cherry was well away from what I was going to be doing.

"You'll bring me back? You promise?"

As if words could guarantee anything. "I promise."

She considered. Nodded. "All right. Do you really live on a boat?" She was suddenly an eager child again. I was finding the shifts between defiant independence and clinging childishness hard to handle. Had I been like this at thirteen?

"Yes. She's a barge, officially, called *The Flying Pig*, usually just known as the *Pig*. I used to sail with the man who owned her, and when he died I inherited her." With a little help from Byron.

I could see her wondering how to ask about the relationship between the barge's original owner and myself. Decided not to make it easy for her, since I really didn't want to try to explain Jack to anyone.

Sal stood. Brisk and keen to return to the shadows and her gang. "That's settled, then. See you this evening. You think you can get in?"

I remembered last night's moves. "Think so. It'll be easier following in-bound trucks."

She nodded. "See you then."

She was gone. I paid the bill.

208

60

Cherry was seeing Midway at its best. She looked dazzled by the flags and banners and holos; the music from floating speakers drifting among the shrubs; scent-spilling arrays of flowering plants. I looked around. Today's theme was clearly associated with the tranquil side of sailing. One whole wall of the mall had become a holo-screen projecting images of sunlit waters, yachts surrounded by frolicking dolphins, beautiful young men and women diving into clear waters. Better not try that in the Solent.

I wasn't surprised my companion was looking stunned. The contrast with where she'd spent the last few weeks was powerful, and the show was certainly impressive. Even I had to admit it looked good.

"It's not always this glossy," I warned her, although Morgan wasn't ever going to let his pet project look drab. "It's just that we're celebrating the port's official opening this week. No expense spared."

"Are you really rich now?" Cherry's wide-eyed stare and direct question, which showed she still hadn't worked out the more rigid privacy conventions, made me laugh.

"I'm lucky if I've got enough credit to feed myself and fuel the *Pig* most of the time," I admitted. "I do some casual work and trade in what I can carry on board. Wine, mostly." A sideways look at that. For the first time I wondered if my preferred choice of cargo had as much to do with the Community's disapproval of drink as with my own tastes. "A couple of months ago I got involved in something which worked out quite well. I got mooring and water rights here as a reward."

She could have no idea of just what that was worth. With any luck she wouldn't even want to know the details of what I'd done to earn it.

"Can we have a look in the mall?" she asked. "Just a look. I haven't got many credits, either," she admitted. I didn't expect she had any. "There aren't any proper shops in Sutton, or none that I could go in." She sounded wistful. In the areas of the city where real shops did business with the better-off end of the market, traders tended to keep their premises code-locked. Entry by loyalty card-code or appointment only.

"Why not?" She wouldn't find much to do on board the *Pig* and it sounded as though she was more interested in shops than I've ever been. And what do I know about entertaining thirteen-year-old runaways?

She stared at everything as though she could consume it all. I'd felt intimidated by the conspicuous display when I was new here – and I suspected I hadn't really got used to it yet. Charity, no, *Cherry* was absorbing it as though this was what she'd dreamed life in the city would offer her. I didn't want to tell her that having to stand outside and gaze in could be more painful than never knowing. But there was no chance I could see of my being able to offer what was on show here.

Didn't think I'd better suggest Tom Lee might recruit her as a thief. Besides, I doubt she had the talent. It was one that was best cultured in the very young.

"Humility!" A voice that could score glass. Of course Millie would be here. She'd barely step off-site while her show went on. And it was hers, whatever Morgan thought. He just paid the bills.

"You're going to meet a friend of mine," I had time to warn Cherry. "She doesn't really bite." Much.

Millie took in my companion at a glance. "You," she accused me, "never wore homespun that well."

I stared at Cherry. There was something that might have been the first, uncertain twitch of a smile touching one side of her mouth. And yes, the homespun jacket did have a more individual look that those I'd worn. I couldn't quite work out what she'd done, but Cherry had definitely altered the garment's usual shapelessness.

Unusually tactful, Millie ignored the rest of Cherry's clothes. She grinned in a vulturish sort of way. "So you found her, then? Your aunt's been looking all over this godawful city for you. I don't suppose you're grateful, are you?"

Cherry didn't know whether to answer the question or be horrified by the profanity. She was staring at Millie as though she was meeting an alien and discovering they talked – almost – the same language.

Of course, Millie could look quite alien to a lot of people: she'd never believed in following trends. "I don't believe in copies," she told me once. Today she was on duty so she was naturally wearing her take on the day's theme. Turquoise robes, hair gel and nails. Robes which billowed even when she wasn't moving: waves, presumably. Body ornaments of nacreous shell. The pale face-paint and green-blue shifting contacts completed the other-worldly outfit. In a peculiar way, it suited her. The smoke- and alcohol-ruined voice didn't quite fit, but there wasn't much she could do about that without surgery. Besides, she was too good a businesswoman not to know it was part of her trademark.

Seeing that Cherry was still lost for words, Millie let a wide arm-sweep encompass the mall. "So give me an outsider's view. What do you think?"

61

Cherry looked embarrassed. Met Millie's eyes and quickly looked down. Clasped her hands in front of her. Don't fiddle, child, the devil will take your fingers. When Millie just waited, she started off with a "very nice".

Millie snorted derision. Cherry swallowed hard. Glanced up, round cheeks scarlet, and then turned and took a really good look around.

"I like most of it," she said in a breathy voice.

"And what about the rest?" Amusement, and a hint of sharpness, were in Millie's eyes. I wasn't sure whether she was humouring Cherry or if she'd seen something I hadn't.

She got a long look from the girl, weighing up the same thing. Wondering if this odd adult – who would be appalled to know she'd probably been classified by Cherry as an Elder Mother – really wanted an answer. Something convinced her.

"I thought there were some –" she searched for the right word – "sort of *muddled* bits."

"What do you mean, 'muddled'?" Millie preparing to tear a critic to bleeding shreds was a daunting sight for anyone. I wondered how much flesh I'd lose in the rescue attempt.

Cherry was obviously not the type to recognise danger. *How* had she survived six weeks in Sutton? She was frowning. Thinking. "It was when we came in, just past the place where they sell all that old boat stuff." My turn to wince. I liked the 'old boat stuff'. Millie nodded. "I just thought I couldn't tell what was going to happen next.

I mean, not in a *good* way, like over there – " She pointed to a cluster of outlets which seemed to have a completely random assortment of stock – "but in a sort of," she shrugged, "well, messy way." Millie was staring. Hard. Cherry looked down, clutched her fingers together. Bright red again. "I'm sorry." A whisper. "I don't mean to be rude."

I waited for the outburst.

"Why not? I always do." It was my turn to look slack-jawed. Millie sounded inordinately pleased. "Let's go and have a look round and you can tell me about any other bits you think are messy." A dismissive look at me. "Humility can go back to play on her boat. I'm sure she's got plenty to do there."

I did, but some instinctive protest struggled to be born. And gave up. I wasn't sure whether Millie thought she was helping me or whether she was teasing Cherry, cat playing with mouse. Or whether something else was going on which I didn't have time to think about. I gave up and went home, stopping at Gus's control tower to pick up a package I'd asked for – he wasn't there to comment. Sent a message to Meera.

Read the message from Byron which told me he'd laid on the backup I'd requested. Probably overkill. Wished I'd thought of a more fortunate word.

I called Jennifer. Told her I'd found my runaway and what I'd heard from the street kids. Said a girl called Luna might be around.

The stern face smiled. Didn't make her look much better. "Blader? She's already been here. Made your inspection look soft. Don't know if she's approved me or not, but I've got a few extra beds made up just in case I passed."

"She's OK." I smiled at the idea of Luna being mother

hen to the little ones. "Thinks she's all grown up. Whoever she passes word to, you won't get her staying under your roof."

"Yes. She made that quite clear, too." Jennifer looked as though she might have come off worse from an argument I wouldn't even have attempted.

"I'll stay in touch." Signed off. Not sure why I wanted to keep that contact. But I traded just above street level, and Byron's proposition still nagged like mild toothache at the back of my mind. She could be useful.

I'd just about finished loading my sack with what I thought I might need this evening. Including the neat com unit which had been in the packet I picked up. I'd asked Byron to lend it to me: more powerful, bigger range than Sal's. And small enough to strap to a wrist. He'd preset a call number I didn't recognise. Looked at the tag display: SOS. That was clear enough. Panic button. Not entirely reassuring.

A call from the pontoon.

Millie and Cherry. Both looking slightly ruffled but no signs of real violence on either of them. I wondered for a second just how wise I'd been to leave Cherry with someone who was a stranger to her – and very well known to me – then knew I was worrying about nothing. Millie didn't poach, and Cherry really was too young for her.

"I've brought your missing chick back." A look I didn't identify passed between them. "I suppose you're both back to that frightful city tonight?" As though she and I hadn't passed some memorable evenings in the 'frightful city'.

"Yes. I've got to go," I told her. I felt as though I was dampening what should be a major celebration: in some corner of my heart I'd feared I'd have to admit Charity would never be coming home. In a way, I was right. Unless

I guessed wrong, the girl who used to be Charity was gone for ever. I looked at her. "You want to stay on the *Pig*? I can tell Sal you didn't want to come." It would be easier without her. Someone less to worry about. And I didn't want her involved in what I was very afraid I might be going to find out.

"No! I have to come!" She was alarmed and wary.

"OK. Your choice." I held my hands up. I couldn't afford to let Cherry think I was going to take over from her father in the order-giving area. The docks might be the last place I'd choose to take a child of her age, especially if trouble was likely. But if I tried to force her to stay away, she'd run. She'd done it once. It would be easier next time round. And she might run back to Sal at the worst possible moment. I'd have to trust the gang leader to keep her safe.

"I promised Sal. She said she'd look out for me." Her voice was torn. She'd had something like fun this afternoon, but I knew she'd glimpsed something in gang life that drew her. Probably a sort of loyalty she hadn't found at home. And she'd seen the girls had respect. She couldn't understand the sort of fear and loathing it was built on; she was too new to the idea that females had any value or control over their lives.

Let's hear it for girl power.

I wondered just what she'd say to Mother when they eventually made contact. Decided I wasn't yet ready to hear it. This evening already looked like being more trouble than I could handle.

How had I come to this point? It had started with a simple request from Morgan and a more difficult one from my mother. It was looking as though Morgan's attempt to keep the curious away from problems at his new marina would prove far more intricate and deadly than my mother's wish to find a single child in the chaos of the city streets.

I'd thought about backing out. Didn't know whether it was curiosity or stubbornness which kept me in. Did know there was a slow-burning rage inside me that would not let me sleep without being afraid to dream until I had solved the problem of Ardco's smuggling and the stench of old blood in a ferry's hold. I felt tainted by the knowledge of its existence and I needed to get clean.

And I was taking a thirteen-year-old girl along with me.

Transport to the docks had been arranged. I'd asked Byron to set that up, and to have the cab cruising somewhere and well-paid enough to come when I called. I didn't want to have to wait around in the dark, and I had no idea what state I'd be in when I came out. Or if I'd be bringing Cherry back with me.

62

Cherry was silent for most of the journey into the city. I'd asked her how she'd got on with Millie and had a wrinkled nose and "She's OK: she's odd," in reply. I didn't think it bad as summaries went.

"What's happening tonight?" she asked as we crossed the river.

"You're staying with Sal and the others," I told her. "I have to go on board the ferry that's loading there and have a look around." I can do summary, too.

"Are you allowed to do that?"

"I'm hoping I won't be noticed," I admitted.

Wasn't sure if it was admiration or shock I saw in her face. "You're going to break the law?"

"A little trespass and possibly some breaking and entering." I left out the possibility of more major crimes occurring on either side. "But you won't be involved." Not after the initial trespass. I saw her mouth open, heard the unspoken protest, the offer of a sidekick. "No. I won't be able to do what I have to if I'm worrying about you. I've only just found you after some very uncomfortable searching – you think I'm going to take any risks with you now?"

It deflated her a little. "I'm sorry." Then, "Did you really want to find me?"

There was something else in the question. I looked at her, saw the tension, the doubt. Gave in to impulse and reached out to grip her hand. "*Yes.* I did want to find you. And, no, I have no intention at all of sending you back to your father unless you get down on your knees and beg me to." She was staring. "And even then you'll have to beg damn hard."

Her hand turned under mine to return the clasp. "Thank you. I don't think I can face him again. He'll beat me and *pray* over me."

He would. And keep reminding her for the rest of the time she spent under his roof how ungrateful she was. Then he'd make sure she married someone who felt the same way.

"It's not going to happen," I told her. "We'll talk about what you want to do, and what's possible, after tonight."

"I know what I want to do," she declared, suddenly bright and cheerful again. "I'm going to stay with Sal and the other girls. I'm going to find out what it's *really* like to be one of a gang."

I hoped not. Managed not to sound shocked or disapproving because it was what I'd expected to hear. "OK. But we'll need to sort the details later." And I needed to check what Sal intended. "Right now we need to get on with the trespass bit of the evening's entertainment. Once we're out of the car you'll have to follow me, do what I do. And *don't talk*," I added as her mouth opened.

63

Getting in to Ardco wasn't difficult. I followed the route I'd first seen one of the girls use. It seemed like months ago, but it had been only a few days. I followed the truck, one hand holding tight to Cherry. I didn't trust her reflexes. If we had to dodge and weave I would tow her behind me and hope she could keep her mouth shut and wait till we were clear before she made any protest.

There was no need for any towing. The truck headed straight for the ferry which looked as though it was already part-loaded. I peeled off to one side and headed for gang territory.

Annie stepped out of the shadows.

"Cherry?"

"Yes." Sounded a little subdued. Annie wasn't looking welcoming; I doubted if she knew how.

"You're to come with me. We'll find somewhere to stash you while Humility gets herself in trouble on board." A glance at me. Not friendly, not entirely hostile. "You know what you're doing?"

"No."

She nodded. "What I thought. Luck." She turned back to the shadows and I gave Cherry a shove. "Go on. I'll see you in a couple of hours."

It wasn't quite the welcome she'd expected. I guessed she'd hoped to be fussed over, be centre stage. I felt sorry for her, but not sorry enough to wish Annie had behaved any differently. I began to think Sal knew what she was doing. Hoped so.

It was a relief to be on my own. I checked the com unit

on my wrist. Live. Checked my pockets. Knife, short length of line, gloves, vidcorder. No sack: it could snag just when I wanted to get clear, or knock into something with more noise than I dared make.

Bulky though it was, I'd also kept the rowlock. Jammed it in my belt.

I couldn't keep checking details. Daylight was beginning to fade but the arc lights had the ferry exposed. No little crawlers going through an unguarded entryport this evening. I would have to use one of the trucks.

No point in waiting. I didn't know how far off the ferry was from being fully loaded. I knew its scheduled departure time was 2200 but didn't want to depend on it. I *really* didn't want to find myself trapped on board when she sailed.

The next truck followed the same pattern as the others: through the gates, slow to swing round to pass under the gantry, then up the gangway. I swung on board as it slowed. Trusted to luck that, like the crawler, it had no sensors to take alarm at the added weight, no heat-detectors. No reason it should, as long as its cargo was legit. And I was betting only a small, and very special, part of this cargo was illegal.

I don't think I breathed between the heave which got me on to the gap of space behind the container at the very back of the flatbed and the moment the truck slowed to a halt in its allotted space on deck.

Tonight everything seemed automated: my guess had been that night crossings wouldn't carry many people, but the glimpse into the lounge upstairs had told me that there were sometimes passengers on these runs.

I was frighteningly aware that everything I was doing tonight was based on a series of guesses and, if even one was wrong, I might find myself in more trouble than I could deal with.

I slithered from the flatbed to the deck. At least I knew where I was going: no need to bother with the upper decks tonight. Unfortunately, I had to get through the engine room and the galley without being seen. And not only did regs say there had to be human crew on board, but I was guessing there had to be men around to deal with the cargo they held below.

The engines were fired up. The steady rumble reached up to me from the steps down to the lower deck. There were lights on. Voices.

I held my breath, flattened against the bulkhead. Waited.

How long could I wait? Not until the ferry sailed. Not even until the loading bay doors were sealed. I strained. Couldn't hear the voices. Did it mean that whoever was there was on his own now, or had everyone gone?

No way of knowing. I put a cautious foot on the first step, hoping that silence and my dark clothes and dazzle from the bright lights beneath me illuminating the engines would keep me hidden. Hoped that whoever was there didn't look up.   Step by cautious step. Feel for the metal rung. Let my weight come on to it. Don't make a noise. Remember to breathe. Down to the first landing. No sign that anyone had noticed me – no reason for anyone to be lying in wait with a large wrench poised to beat my brains out as soon as I got to the bottom.

My hands were sweating. Slippery on the damp metal. Thought about Byron's panic button and wasn't reassured.

My feet touched flat metal. The deck. Above me, the companionway which had seemed endless rose only about fifteen metres. I unclenched my hands from the railing. No one tried to beat my brains out. No one was in the engine room. Voices coming from the galley.

I peered round the entrance. No one in sight. Glimpsed the flicker of a screen and realised they'd left some talk show running. Swore under my breath. Didn't they care how much they scared people? Don't answer.

Through the galley. Nothing happening. No cooking smells. No one in the crew dining room. Where were they all? Not waiting for me beyond the heavy bulkhead door. I hoped.

Opening that door was one of the hardest things I've ever done. Not the physical difficulty; I already knew it would take muscle. It was the sense of exposure: with both hands working on the door I couldn't check whether anyone was sneaking up behind me, and I knew anyone waiting on the other side could just watch the circle of the handle turning and wait for me to step across the sill.

64

There was no one there. The lighting was full on: bright and stark, no shadows. I walked softly. The door to the starboard cabin was shut. Not locked. The other door had a bolt drawn across it.

I listened. Nothing from the starboard cabin. Tried the other side. Thought I heard something but the heavy steel muffled sound. Couldn't think of any alternative, so I slid the bolt aside, turned the handle, and pushed the door open.

No lights inside. I heard the sounds of indrawn breath, a sob – stifled – and a hiss as though someone was trying to smother pain. The light flooding in from the corridor lit up the five girls inside.

The youngest must have been around seven and was half-asleep, dozing with her thumb in her mouth, leaning against the oldest. Who might have reached eighteen. Not much more. She hugged the little one to her, while one of the others clung to her free hand. Two more scared faces peered out from behind the fragile shelter she offered.

"Please," she said, her voice weary as though she'd shouted too long for help and was reduced to pleading. "At least let the little ones go. Don't hurt them."

I pushed the door almost shut behind me, took the precaution of jamming my rowlock in the door-frame – it wouldn't stop anyone coming, it would prevent them slamming the door on us. The cabin darkened and I thought I heard a tired whimper.

"Ssh. I've got a torch. I'm here to help. We mustn't make a noise."

The older girl's eyes flickered with a hint of hope, quickly flattened. "Is this a trick? Because we made a noise? We can scream a lot louder and someone will come."

She didn't believe it. The other kids wanted to. "You don't need to scream. Not any more," I told her. "My name's Humility and I came here to find you, to get you out of here and stop the people who are doing this. I've some friends with me who'll help you, but we need to be quick and quiet. You're on a ferry. It's going to sail soon and you need to be back on shore before that happens." I waited, watched the war of hope and dread on her face.

If she didn't quite trust me, she knew she'd be better off out of this stuffy hole. She'd already worked out there was no escape from here. She'd turn on me with teeth and nails if she decided I was part of this nightmare she and the others were in. "There were two men. They were angry when we wouldn't eat what they gave us." A sideways glance down. "Ellie was thirsty and drank some water. She's dozy now."

Drugged. As long as Ellie was the only one, it might help. She was less likely to cry out.

"OK. If I lead, will you follow me?"

A quick exchange of glances. However they'd been lured here, they weren't careless now. Nods. The older girl looked up. "We'll follow. I'll carry Ellie at the back, the others in the middle."

"Could the others help Ellie? That way you're free if something happens…" If the men reappear, you can go down fighting.

She heard what I didn't say, nodded, turned to the others. "Here, take her. She ain't heavy and you can swap her between you."

With hands gentler than her voice, she eased the child

from under her arm and allowed the girls behind her to take the slight weight.

"Good. Let's go. There's a door, then a sort of eating place and a kitchen, then the engine room. Straight up some ladders and we're on deck. If you hear anyone coming, freeze. Hide if you can. And make as little noise as you can. I don't think we've got much time."

They hesitated at the door. Stepping out into danger, even if it was also the way to safety, wasn't easy for them. Action's hard when you've been driven into submission. But they did come, stepping as quietly as they could into the bright lights of the passageway.

I retrieved my blunt instrument and re-bolted the door behind me.

I hadn't shut the watertight door and the dining area was still empty. I could hear the sound of the vid playing in the galley. Nothing else. At the sound the younger girls scattered, finding what concealment there was behind a table or spindly chairs. The older girl didn't move. Just watched me, and let her eyes flicker round, assessing danger. I glanced into the galley. Still clear. We were in luck.

"Into the engine room and up the ladder," I whispered. "Hide in the shadows at the top but *don't* make a dash for the shore – the alarms are set to kill. I know how to get round. Understood?"

Four nods. Ellie didn't move. "They understand." The tall girl's voice floated across to me.

"Right." I led the way, waited in the engine room and sent them on up ahead. "You'll have to take the kid now," I told the older girl. "Go on up. Wait for me. If there's trouble, get them ashore. I'll call ahead. Go along the mud and you'll get picked up. *Don't* duck under the gantry: that's where the alarms are. Friends are looking out – girl gang. Don't worry, you can trust them."

"I'll do it." Didn't even blink at the idea of being helped out by a gang. Just hefted Ellie and used one hand on the ladder railing to haul herself up. I waited below.

I hadn't meant to do it, but I *had* to go back and check the other cabin. It would only take two minutes and I'd ride my luck a little longer. This group stood a good chance of getting clear. I needed to know there were no others.

I took one of the minutes to send a message to Sal. Text only: talking wasn't a good idea. Then I hurried back along the route that was becoming too familiar: galley, dining area, passage. Door.

65

One hand on it. Eased the handle down. Leaned my weight on it so that it swung slowly open.

This was the stench that had haunted my dream. Thick and nauseating and dark red. One of the shelves bolted to the hull was no longer empty. Coarse sacking covered the shape but didn't really hide it.

I should have got out then. Instead, I took the three steps across the little cabin and reached out to pull the sacking aside.

They hadn't even left her face untouched. The eyes were gone. Her hair was matted with blood, dried hard. Just a few fine wisps to tell me she'd been fair. I began to lift the sacking further but the way it clung told me I wouldn't be able to bear what I found: everything gone. An invasion worse than any rape. She was only still here because someone had decided that the crossing would offer the easiest opportunity for disposal.

I made myself look into her face, note the small teeth exposed by the drawn-back lips. They didn't look like adult teeth. Her cheeks had once been soft, rounded. They'd started to sink now.

I didn't recognise her. I'd dreaded I might see one of the girls I'd met with Luna. This child was a stranger. A stranger who had been kidnapped, terrified. Eviscerated.

I hadn't known I was crying until my eyes blurred. I wiped them on my sleeve. Sniffed. Drew the sacking back over the ruined face as tenderly as I could. I couldn't take her now but I would see that she had the dignity of a funeral.

"I promise," I told the shrouded form.

"Promise what?"

I almost fell, trying to turn fast enough.

The voice belonged to a man wearing rough work clothes, his back to the bright light of the passageway. He sounded colder than the dead child behind me. Not even angry. He held a snub-nosed gun in his right hand.

"Move away from the trash. Hands out. Empty."

I moved, shuffling sideways so that he had to take another step into the cabin to keep me in full view. He looked over at the sacking. I couldn't work out what he'd thought I might do: it wasn't as though the kid had anything left worth stealing. Then he looked in the other direction, out through the door and across the passageway. Saw the bolted door. Looked back at me. Kept the gun and his eyes trained on me but backed away until he could lean against the locked door. Listened.

Then he reached out to pull the bolt back. It stuck. He had to glance down, put his weight into it.

Gave me a five-second break. Time to press one button on the wrist unit and palm the rowlock.

"Bitch!" He'd opened the door on the empty cabin. Spun round, rage showing now. "What have you done?"

"Me?" I shrugged. Edged a step closer to the doorway. I might be able to make a run for it.

The gun was alarmingly steady. "Where are they?"

"Safe." I hoped.

"You're not." A sudden grin with no humour in it at all. "We'll need to replace that cargo."

I knew that. I also knew there was only one way out of this too-small cabin. Despite the gun.

Had to gamble on a reluctance to damage 'the cargo'. That he'd hesitate, just a second, before he fired.

I couldn't get past him. I'd have to go through him. I'm quick and fit, and I was motivated.

I went for him mid-body. Tried to push him off-balance and used the iron rowlock gripped in one fist to hammer at him. He swore. The gun in his hand made him clumsy. I was too close: he couldn't bring it to bear. He was effectively fighting one-handed. For a moment I thought I was getting through. That I could pass him and get away into the corridor. I had no illusion I could do any more than run faster than him. Knew I couldn't take him down.

I couldn't even get past him. After his first step back from my assault he began to fight seriously. He didn't try to get the gun back into action. He just used his greater strength to grapple me and push me back into the cabin. I used teeth and nails but he only swore and tightened his grip on my wrist. I heard my useless weapon clatter to the deck.

Then he brought the gun up. Used the butt.

I didn't pass out. Not quite. I saw the deck coming up to meet me and couldn't do anything about it. Felt another wrench on my wrist. Felt the boot meet my ribs. That was when the world went away.

It came back.

It came back pitch black and utterly silent.

He'd locked me in the cabin.

66

It was black. There wasn't any light, however hard I strained to see. When I held my wrist to my face there was no gleam of illuminated figures. My chrono had gone.

I grabbed at my other wrist, knowing what I'd find: the com unit had gone too. No chance of calling for Sal. Perhaps a good thing: her gang might consider themselves invincible. I doubt they'd ever faced men armed with guns and willing to use them. Men wanting to take on the girls, keen to replace the cargo they'd lost. They'd prefer to take live captives, but my silent companion in this black hole testified that they had ways of processing the dead.

"Think, girl." My own voice: even Jack didn't have anything helpful to tell me. I didn't like the way my words sounded here: lifeless. No echo. No resonance. No response. Think. It was the only weapon I had to ward off the terror that was clawing at the edges of my mind. Telling me the walls would close in and crush me. The room would fill with water and drown me. That no one, not even the man who had closed it, would ever open that door on to light. That I was entombed.

An horror of great darkness.

The only thing that didn't fill me with terror was the memory of the body on the shelf.

I made an effort to rediscover the door. Crawled round patting walls until I discovered the pathetic shelf against the hull. Knew I was going the wrong way. Crawled back. Found myself at the inside bulkhead. Let my hands travel across the metal surface, feeling the rivets and seams I hadn't noticed when there was light. Hinges. Hands scrabbled against the door until they met the handle and an unreasonable hope surged through me so that I tugged and pulled and twisted it, somehow convinced that it couldn't possibly be bolted.

I could feel the stickiness of blood on my fingers and my nails were torn before I gave up, collapsed against it and gave in to the fear.

I don't know how long I lay curled against the unyielding door. It couldn't have been as long as it seemed. Nothing could. And I hadn't heard the tell-tale change in the engine note which would have told me the ferry had sailed. Surely I would have heard that? Or felt the change in the vibrations of the ship's hull?

Think. I knew what Ardco was smuggling. I'd guessed, but not wanted to believe, before I came aboard tonight. The delayed, last-minute loading had told me the cargo was perishable. The time-scale of Ardco's prosperity coinciding with street kids' nightmares meant that a link between them had always been a possibility. And I knew whatever Ardco was smuggling had to be worth a lot to whoever was running it. That some threat to it could have ended in Andy's murder had also told me it was likely to be bad.

At first I'd thought it was prostitution, but that hadn't quite made sense. Prostitution might mean exploiting children – all ages, both sexes – but there was no profit in exporting them. It was the conversation with Mark which had given shape to my formless fears. All the old nightmares, going back two hundred years, made real. Body-snatchers. Flesh-traders. *Harvesters.*

These people might have started out as pimps and procurers; perhaps that was why they concentrated on young girls. Now, however, they were dealing in body

231

parts. Transport them fresh to France where no one was looking for them. If they died en route they could take the organs, chill them, and dump the bodies overboard. Better for them to keep living donors who could be used as need arose. Like a grotesque, living organ bank. My gorge rose.

They would keep me alive, I reasoned. They wouldn't think I could escape – hell, *I* didn't think I could escape – from this hole. I had a few hours to decide what to do before they opened the door to take me away.

I thought of those hours and wondered if I'd be sane enough to do anything but fall into my captors' arms, sobbing with gratitude for the return of light.

67

When I heard the noise I shuffled back into a corner, where I'd be behind the door when it opened. He'd taken the com unit but hadn't bothered with the rowlock which was clenched in my fist. I wanted to take out his eyes with it. Let him lie in the dark like the two of us he'd left in here.

I tensed. Squinted, knowing I'd be dazzled by whatever light came in. Braced myself. *Go for the eyes.* I held a sprinter's crouch, ready to leap up at my target, knowing he'd be even less able to see than I was. I couldn't afford to think of anything except getting past whoever was out there, taking him down and getting away.

The door eased open. I'd expected it to be flung wide. The single line of light was a spear of hope and terror.

"Humility?"

For a moment, nothing made sense. I hadn't allowed myself to think about rescue. Feared a trap even though my captor hadn't known my name. Kept quiet.

"Humility? If you're in there, say something. If not, I'm going home. I don't like boats."

"*Byron?*" Not my idea of a heroic rescuer. As far as I knew, he didn't do physical.

"Of course. You pressed the right button, didn't you?"

His panic button. The one thing I'd been able to do before the com unit had gone. Later I wished I could have been cool, found something clever to say. Something that would stop either of us remembering me curling up even tighter and weeping. Snivelling.

"How did you find me?" I managed eventually. My voice was still unsteady, disbelieving. He unbent far enough to reach down and help me to my feet. I was still half-crouching. I straightened clumsily. Eased my cramped grip on my useless weapon.

"Homer signal. No point in a panic button without one." His voice was steady enough. But he was holding me tightly, hands gripping my shoulders. "You OK?" Was he asking if they'd hurt me, or afraid I'd keep on crying?

I sniffed. Hard. "I'm OK." As long as no one shut me inside again. "And Byron…"

"Yes?"

"Thanks."

He could have sent someone. He'd come himself. I wasn't sure he knew just how much that meant.

He wasn't going to let me tell him. He gave me something between a shake and an awkward hug, let me go and stepped back. "Are you coming out now or do you want to stay in your nice dark hole?"

"I'm coming out." I stepped from behind the door, towards the light. Looked back. "There's a girl in here. I promised her I would help."

He stepped quickly in. "Who? They said you were on your own."

There was no time to ask about 'they'. I nodded towards the shelf. "Over there. I told her I'd see she was buried decently."

He took in the shape of the bundle. Nodded. "Yes. You can keep your promise. I'll see someone brings her back to Midway. We can arrange something from there."

It was enough. I followed him out of the cabin, but I didn't close the door behind me. Left it wedged open with the rowlock, so she wouldn't be in the dark.

The ferry hadn't sailed anywhere. On deck five men were being held by people I'd never seen before. I assumed they were in Vinci service. They looked reassuringly tough. The crewmen had bound hands and looked subdued. There were some split lips and a few black eyes. It hardly seemed enough.

Byron wasn't far from my side. "These men aren't saying much. Can you identify the one who locked you in?"

He was the first one I'd seen. I pointed. "Him. I don't know if all the others know what was going on down there, but he certainly does."

"Good enough. I'm sure the others will be as helpful as they can be when we get them ashore." His voice was bland. "And, speaking of going ashore…" He indicated the open stern doors.

As simple as that. I hesitated only one moment. "The alarms? They're set to kill."

"They were. Now, if you're sure you don't want to go to sea, would you mind if we got some land beneath our feet? Boats don't agree with me."

The ferry wasn't moving. There was no swell and the tide wasn't running hard. There was no way anyone could be seasick on a moored boat. If his black skin looked grey-tinged it had to be something to do with the harsh lights blazing down at us. Or what he'd seen below. But he had come through for me.

"OK." Then I remembered. "But there's someone I have to stop and see."

"Do you mean that terrifying young woman in black?"

I nodded. "Sal. Yes. You met her?"

"She did her best to lead the assault on the ferry. After we'd persuaded her whose side we were on. Said something about 'torching the place.'" It wasn't quite a question.

"That fits. How did you stop her?"

"With difficulty. Had to convince her that we needed

'the place' intact in case there was evidence. Pointed out that not all the villains – probably not the ringleaders – were going to be on the ferry and we just might need to have a look around." A pause. "She said you'd said something similar." He sounded slightly surprised by the evidence of common sense.

"True. My niece is with her." I'd told him about Cherry when I'd realised there was likely to be a link between missing street children and Ardco.

"Interesting. For both of them. Does she plan to stay there?"

"I don't know." Reaction from the horror of the past few hours was setting in and I was beginning to feel exhausted. I wanted to go home. Alone. But I needed to talk to Cherry first. "That's what I need to find out."

"I've got a cab. I'll wait for you outside the dock gates."

68

There were cars in the space in front of the warehouses. More light than when I'd sneaked in. One of the cars had a stocky female figure leaning against it. She waved.

"Jennifer!"

She straightened. "Good to see you. Got the message you'd found some of the missing kids. Thought they might want a place to stay."

I looked beyond her, into the car. Five girls inside. One asleep with her thumb in her mouth. The window came down.

The older girl, whose name I might never know, said, "We owe you. So does every kid on the streets of Sutton. We'll put the word around."

A few little kids would sleep better. "Will you stay with Jennifer? She's straight. Won't hold you if you don't want to stay."

She grinned. "She's something, isn't she? She said she knew you. And yes, we'll stay for a while. Then think about things. Ellie here needs somewhere steady. Me?" She shrugged. "I can make my own way. And this time I'll be more careful."

"Can I call you tomorrow? Talk?" I asked. "If I'm going to pin down whoever's behind this I need as many details as you can give."

"I'll tell you all I can. You just make sure you get them." Savage anger in her voice. No blame for that.

"'Kay. Speak to you tomorrow. You can sleep sound tonight."

"Sounds good." She leaned back in the car; the window

shut.

"I'll call tomorrow," I told Jennifer, who nodded.

"Fine. It'll seem a bit further off by then. Not good, but not quite so immediate." She paused. "Just get the rest of the scum."

It seemed to be a unanimous thought.

69

I walked over to the edge of Sal's territory. She was standing there, most of the gang behind her in the shadows. Cherry was beside her.

"Hi." I was really tired. Hoped I wasn't going to have to deal with much more emotion tonight, because I would either lose my temper or just sit down and cry. I wasn't sure which would be worse. I could do with a boost shot. Why does no one offer you drugs when you actually want them?

"Hi." Sal's expression was more serious than I'd seen it. "No trace of Beany and Jace?" Expecting the answer no.

I gave it. "No. Send me what info you can, I'll try to find out if their IDs still register. Let you know." Shook my head. "Don't hope too hard."

"They're gone." Hope wasn't stuff she dealt in. "You stopped them?" Meaning the traffickers. The harvesters.

"Stopped this load. Should stop the organisers tomorrow." Byron had said Morgan was going to cover this. Word wouldn't get out for twenty-four hours. I wasn't sure it could be done. If it couldn't, we'd lose them.

Sal nodded. "OK. You held up good. Crazy, like I said. But sometimes that's what it takes."

I agreed. Looked to Cherry, whose face was stark white in the lights from behind me. "You know what you're doing next?"

She'd been told, or learned by listening, what had gone down tonight. Perhaps she'd met the kids who'd gone to Jennifer's. Any idea that life on the streets was an adventure had surely gone south. It was a hunting ground, and kids like her were prey.

She stared back at me. "I said I was with Sal and the gang. Gave my word." Her voice was steady. Only her eyes showed a hint of panic. But she still believed that a promise meant something. Couldn't fault her for that.

"Sal?" I asked.

She read me well. Looked sideways at Cherry. "You ain't gang. Told you. What skills you got? You can't fight. Don't know the streets. Scared shitless all night." She hadn't been the only one. "You'd be trouble for the gang and we already got trouble enough to deal with. Go back home. You got folks looking out for you. Don't need us. We don't need you." She turned her back. Some signal I didn't see to Annie and the others and they started to move away. I'd never know if they would have taken Cherry in but Sal had given me the only thing she had to give.

It was brutal. It worked.

Cherry half-turned to follow. "*Sal!*" Pleading. Turned back to me. "I can't go home!"

"You can't go back to the Community," I corrected. "So you need to find out where home is. Come back to Midway with me. Tomorrow we'll talk, think of something. You've got choices and you're safe." I thought about that. "Puts you a couple of points ahead of a lot of people here."

She looked back over her shoulder. No one. The containers and crates of the gang's home still stood in their careless tumble. I knew now that they were a community with rules as strict and merciless as the one I'd run from. Though they were less self-deceiving. Cherry could have done worse, but I doubted she'd have been any more content under Sal's law than she had been under Ethan's in the long term.

"Cherry?"

She turned back to me. Tears streamed down her cheeks. She thought she'd failed. Had to ask for help. It was as though all her brave attempts at independence, about choosing her own way in life, had fallen apart and now she had to be rescued by the grown-ups.

"You're even younger than I was when I ran," I told her, searching for the right words. "You've been on the streets for more than six weeks and you're still safe – not bad for someone from our background. You can be proud of yourself. But it's hard to do the next stage on your own."

"But I don't want to *have* to stay with you. I mean," she sniffed, "it's not that I don't like you, but…"

"But you ran away from family and don't want even a relative like me to make decisions for you."

She sniffed again. "Yes." Just a whisper, but a definite one.

"That's OK by me. I like my independence too. But when I ran off I needed help and found it in the friend who owned the *Pig*." I smiled to myself at the old memory. "Some day I'll tell you about Jack," I promised, "but what you need to remember is that it's OK to take help. I'll give you space to think about things, might even give you some ideas. But it's going to be your choice. Which can be scary. You might even choose wrong. And that's when you can ask friends for help, or even just a space to breathe in while you think."

"Just a few days with you? And you won't tell me what to do?"

"I might tell you what to do on the *Pig* – she's my home, after all. What you do with your life is going to be your problem. But you don't have to solve it all at once."

She thought about it. She didn't have much choice, but

241

I needed her to believe she'd made this one. And I wanted to get home before I passed out in front of her and went to sleep on this bit of industrial waste ground.

Another sniff. A shrug. As if she didn't really care. "OK. If that's what you want."

I reminded myself she was only thirteen. "Come on then. Byron's got a cab at the gate."

70

I gave Cherry my cabin and bunked in the deck-house. I wanted to sleep for ten hours straight and I told her she could do what she liked as long as it didn't involve waking me before noon.

I'd reckoned without Mother.

The call came about an hour after dawn. I pulled blankets over my head and turned my back on the screen and shouted at it to tell the caller I wasn't home. But my mother has never given up easily and I hadn't been home when she'd called yesterday. And I knew what she wanted to hear.

"Mother," I said at last.

"Humility." She took in my surroundings. Saw that I'd been camping in what looked to her like a space not meant for sleeping. The look of reproof was too familiar: I felt the automatic defensive reaction rising even as I told myself that I didn't care what she or anyone else in the Community thought about how I'd chosen to live my life. I sat up, pushed the blankets aside and made myself not straighten them.

"Charity is safe and well," I told her. "I found her yesterday and she's unharmed."

The fractional relaxation of tense muscles betrayed her. She *had* been truly anxious. "And you will send her back to us."

Not a question, although she must have known what my response would be.

"No. I'm not sending her anywhere. When she's finished sleeping I will talk to her about what she wants to do. And

I already know she has no wish to return to Ethan's home."

"But she is a *child*! Even you must see she cannot be allowed to do just what she thinks she wants. She needs guidance."

"Yes." I couldn't help sounding bitter. "She needs guidance. But not from my brother's belt. She does not need to be compelled into marriage with a man of his choosing. She does not need to be told she has no choice and must bow to the words of her elders." Mother's expression was growing more rigid with every word I spoke. "She needs to be valued as more than a drudge. She has survived in this place for more than six weeks and that takes a kind of courage you can't imagine. It also takes quickness and intelligence and a willingness to adapt. Are you telling me these are things that would be welcomed if she were to come back to you?"

The eyes that looked back at me from my screen were both hard and puzzled. She really didn't understand. "Have you tainted her so quickly, daughter? And will you not let her come and speak to me, tell me for herself that she has chosen ingratitude? Have you no care for her brothers and sisters, or for others who might be tempted by her example?"

"I pity her brothers and sisters. If any want to follow her example, I hope they take fewer chances, but I would give them my support."

Someone behind me drew a quick breath.

"Grandmother Judith." Cherry faced the screen, determination in every line of her body. If her hands were clasped to stop them trembling, no need for anyone else to know. "Good day. I am sorry to have distressed you but you can see for yourself I am well."

Mother's face softened. "Child. You must come home.

Your father and mother need you. The city is not for you. It is a place of sin and damnation."

"I know that." She had discovered it last night if she had not already learned it. "It's also a place of opportunity. A place where people do not force you into the shape they want for you. There are kind people here. People who care even when they have much to lose themselves, and little to spare."

"Charity. Granddaughter. You do not know what you are saying. I will send money and make arrangements for your return."

Her hands whitened on each other. "No. I won't go." The strong young woman would slip back into the defiant child in a moment.

"You heard, Mother. I told you I'd find her and I've done that. I'm glad you cared enough to ask for my help, but now you have to let her go."

She ignored me, still focused on the girl. "Charity. Disobedience is a sin. You must honour your father and your mother and return to them."

My mother could hardly have said more to strengthen my niece's resolve. I was proud of her when she said, "I am Cherry now, not Charity. I know I've a lot to learn out here, but it's my choice. Please tell my parents I am safe. That's all they need to know." She reached out and blanked the screen.

"Well done."

"Was it?" Her eyes were wet now. She was about to lose what she'd managed to hold back.

"Yes. You had to tell her directly, she wouldn't accept anything less." I thought about how she'd responded to my situation. "She probably still won't accept it, but she can tell Ethan she did her best. And your brothers and sisters will know you are well – if only because he'll make a sermon out of it."

"They'll Shun me, won't they?"

"Yes. But it's not bad being Shunned. The really good thing is, you don't have to stay for the ceremony." Which took hours and involved a lot of guilt being thrown around. "I've lived with it for long enough."

She looked around the deckhouse. I could see her thinking of the small, spare cabin she'd slept in. "And you're happier here than you were in the Community?"

"I don't remember being happy there, not once my grandmother passed." I made a vague gesture. "This is what I want. It's not what you want, but you've time to think about that."

She sat down hard on my rumpled blankets. "I have, haven't I?" She looked terrified.

Choice can hit you like that, especially when you've never really had it before. All she'd had was stubbornness, a streak of mutiny and enough lack of self-control to back herself into a corner she couldn't get out of without losing her pride. Tough situation for a kid of her age. I knew exactly how she felt.

"You can start by doing chores. Doesn't matter where you end up, chores still need to be done."

A flicker of what might have been mutiny touched her mouth. I waited. She looked around the messy deckhouse. "You're right. They do."

She had inherited something from my mother's genes after all.

I let her get on with it while I brewed caf and tried to make plans. I do impulse better than strategy, but today definitely needed a plan.

71

I'd arranged to meet Byron and Morgan at 1030 in the Family housing unit. Another place which held no good memories, but we needed the security. Lloyd was there, too, when I arrived.

I'd left Cherry behind. She'd let me know what she thought of my idea of cleaning and was doing something about it. Old habits. It had taken me long enough to shake them; I might as well benefit from hers while they lasted. I'd told her she could go to the mall or just wander round if she wanted. Also told her not to go anywhere near *The Happy Family*. Her mouth had tightened at what I hadn't said but she'd nodded.

I looked at Lloyd; he was the Port Officer so I'd use his systems. "My niece is on my boat. Can you track her? Or at least let me know if she goes aboard any other boats – or anyone calls on her?" If there was a problem I could always ask Byron to do it.

He nodded. "I'll have her tracked." A command passed through the slick unit built into Morgan's desk and it was done.

This wasn't the suite I'd been in with Morgan's brother Milo, with its slightly decadent luxury. I hadn't seen any other of Morgan's rooms but this one was functional. Furnishing was new and sleek, but it had a purpose. The only decorative details were the nineteenth-century marine oil paintings on the walls. I coveted those.

Morgan, looking more serious than usual, had taken position behind the desk. In charge. Lloyd, once he'd input the request about Cherry, had backed off, was sitting to one side. There to run errands, give info, not necessarily have other input. That might have to change – this might be Morgan's project, it was Lloyd who knew just how the marina ran.

Byron was at a smaller desk with absolutely nothing showing on its surface. Which meant he had more circuits plugged in than I could imagine. He'd already updated Morgan on last night. We were meeting to work out how to close the last of it down.

Team playing isn't my strength. I knew what I had planned. They were going to have to work around that. Although, as I'd discovered last night, it would be stupid not to take backup.

"You think Stephen and Amanda are responsible for this…" Morgan hesitated, mouth twisting in distaste. "This obscenity?" He'd found the right word.

"Right." Byron had been through my files and had his own records, including the deep search he'd done last night. "Amanda trained as a medic. Body sculptor. Good one. Means she knew easily enough to drug you. And to –" Byron's turn to search for an appropriate term – "process her victims."

'Process' was one of those neutral words I loathed. *Butcher* would have been my choice but he'd have argued that it was more skilled than that. At least he'd recognised they were victims.

"Does one of them have tech skills?" I asked. I still wanted to know who'd broken into the *Pig*.

"No data. Neither of them has training, but it's possible to acquire the sort of skills needed for by-passing alarms without formal training." Hire a thief to teach you?

"What about Andy?" I wondered. I didn't want his murder to get lost in the greater horror. "Did you get any comeback on the handwriting?"

Headshake from Byron. "No. So little handwritten stuff around these days. No records on file. A couple of notes on the boat but no real comparisons. Could be real, could be fake." Likely fake.

Morgan straightened in his plain chair. Calling the meeting to order. "We need to establish their guilt without question. At the moment the people we picked up last night aren't saying enough to identify them positively. Simon's claiming total ignorance of anything illegal."

"That's got to be a lie," I protested.

"Of course." A touch of impatience in Morgan's voice. "He has to have known there was smuggling going on, but that doesn't mean he knew exactly what was happening."

Perhaps he hadn't. I thought of him. Yes. He was young and eager and proud of his new company which was doing so well against Family competition. He might have been happy not to know just what extra freight the directors were shipping as long as it helped bring in the bright and shiny profits. I hoped he felt his willing ignorance had some part in the horror of what had been done to the city's children over the past few months. Hoped next time he'd look a little harder at what was happening on his own turf.

"OK, but you've got him under wraps?"

"He's being co-operative." I liked the way Morgan said it. Gave me a nice picture of a very scared Simon who was thinking hard about his future. "I suggest I go over this morning and invite Stephen and Amanda in for a talk."

I didn't like it, was about to protest, but Byron was ahead of me. "They won't talk. As soon as you let them know what you want they'll deny everything, buy in a good lawyer and lay the blame on everyone except themselves. They've been here in the port, entertaining. People can vouch for them. How could they possibly have done these terrible things you're blaming them for?"

"It must have been Poor Andy and he couldn't stand the guilt. That's why he killed himself," I added.

"But he didn't," Morgan pointed out.

"They don't know we know that," I reminded him. He looked about as yielding as a rock. "You can probably get them in the end – after they've made enough fuss and got enough publicity for your Port to be associated with child abduction and organ-trading for as long as it lasts."

Which wouldn't be long, with that sort of press. That message did get through.

"So what were you planning?" Resignation in his voice now. Good.

"I've already accepted an invitation to join them for the parade of yachts this afternoon, staying on board for the fireworks. I want to be able to record what they say – evidence admissible – because I'm fairly sure I can persuade them to show off to me. After all, they probably plan to kill me anyway, so why not let me know just how clever they've been?"

There was a sort of appalled silence. Spoken aloud it did sound mad, but I didn't really have a death wish.

"You'll be listening in," I said to Byron, who nodded. The tech stuff would be his; he wouldn't delegate. "I'd want someone on the next boat in the parade – something fast enough to pick me up if I have to go overboard."

"And something with enough armour to board if you press the panic button." Again.

"Thanks, Byron." I meant it. In a way.

"You're convinced you can make them admit it?" Morgan didn't rate my persuasive powers. Didn't want publicity. I could see the balancing going on in his head.

"Yes. And if I can't, you can always go back to Plan A."

"You have a point," he conceded. "Lloyd, we need to look at the parade order. Byron, is the recorder going to be any trouble? It might need to be waterproof."

He didn't quite shudder. "Sea water, too. Technology really doesn't like it. I'm sure I have something that will serve the purpose." He looked at me. "I'll leave a package with Gus this afternoon. Instructions on your screen. You're scheduled to sail at…?"

"Fourteen hundred." Those were the sort of details Lloyd didn't need to look up.

"You'll have it an hour before then."

"Do we all know what we're doing?" Morgan still had his doubts, but he wasn't going to waste time rehashing the scheme. It was cobbled together out of hope and string, but I couldn't see another way of nailing Stephen and Amanda for all the children's lives, and Andy's death. And I really wanted that.

I pushed back from my chair. "I know. And I need to make sure my niece doesn't foul things up by exploring the wrong boat. Excuse me?"

I left before they could raise any more objections.

72

Cherry wasn't on board, but the *Pig* was gleaming clean. There was fresh-made soup in the galley and bed linen drying on the rack in the forward hold. She'd had the sense not to hang things out in what both her mother and mine would have described as God's fresh air. Not bad for someone who didn't know or care anything about boats, or about the conventions of what not to do during an official party like the one still going on all round.

I didn't panic when I didn't find her. Apart from the note she'd left, I had Lloyd's update. Since they both said the same thing, more or less, I was inclined to believe them. *Gone shopping.*

Before I braved the mall, of which I'd seen too much lately, I contacted Meera. Left a message with the details Sal had given me about Jace and Beany, her two missing girls, asking her to try to track them and run an ID check. Knew what the result would be, but did it anyway. Then I called Jennifer.

"Hi. You look better than you did last night," she told me.

"Feel it. Would have been even better if people had let me sleep, but that's how it goes. How are your new guests?"

She grinned. Looked even fiercer than usual. "Ellie's a cutie. Doesn't remember a thing but knows she's safe now. I think she'll stay on a while. May even be willing to accept fostering if I can find a good family. She still likes being cuddled."

Kids who've been brutalised don't like physical handling. Don't trust people. Ellie might even have a home somewhere and parents who missed her. Or she needed a new set. If anyone could find them, I was beginning to feel it might be Jennifer.

"Sounds good. And the others?"

Her hand moved in a so-so gesture. "The three younger ones might stay, might go. One of them talked about learning a trade – might mean it, might be saying what she thinks I want to hear. I'll try to get them to stay until the nightmares ease back a bit. Give them some choices."

"And the other?" The older one with sense who'd known what was happening and tried to shield the younger ones. Who'd taken the risk of trusting me.

"Says she's going. Back to the streets."

I suppose I'd expected it. She was old enough and knew enough about street life to make the decision. Something in Jennifer's expression made me think she wasn't so comfortable with it. "You going to do something about it?"

"Might. I need some help here. Someone who can speak to these kids. A bit of cleaning, a bit of counselling, that sort of thing. Might even help with a bit of schooling."

"If she's had any herself." I was beginning to smile.

"We could put that right. I'll put it to her, let her go. See if I can reel her back in."

She just might. "Good luck. Tell her I called. That things should get sorted today – I'll update later. May need some details from her to close the case." Jennifer nodded. I was beginning to get ideas of my own about her. She wasn't quite what she seemed. "You need patrons and things? Short of cash?"

"You lending?"

"No."

Her smile made her look like a frog. "Thought not. It's good if I can get people with more credit than's sensible to pass some of it on. Spend a lot of time telling that to my

Family."

I heard the capital letter. So. She was Family. Didn't ask which one, I've better manners than that – Byron would find out for me if I needed to know. But she certainly didn't need credit. Which made me think I might be able to do a little good for someone else.

"What about an assistant – heart too soft for her current job, lots of data skills, used to confidential stuff?"

She frowned. "You're not talking about yourself and that niece of yours isn't going to have much in the way of data skills yet. Who've you got in mind?" I explained Meera. "Could be interesting. I'll send her a message. Mention your name. See what happens. You let me know about the scum?"

I promised. Blanked the screen. I'd done all the good deeds I wanted for the day. This afternoon was going to be self-indulgence. But I supposed it was time I checked that Cherry hadn't found trouble.

73

I suppose it depended how you defined trouble. She'd managed to hook up with Millie, who had to be too busy to take time out for a shabby child with few social skills.

Except that Cherry didn't look all that shabby. I couldn't work out what she'd done – I recognised some of what she was wearing as mine, but it didn't look like that on me. And her cropped hair was spiky but not hacked. I'd seen a few hairs in the recycler: she must have had another go at it this morning. Whatever she'd done, I could see it was an improvement. And the way she was laughing at something Millie said told me she was getting her confidence back, fast.

For one minute, I was angry. Didn't she understand what she'd been through? What might have happened? What I'd gone through last night?

I wanted to shake her, and I was ashamed. I envied her. When I'd first arrived in Sutton I'd been scared of everything for a lot longer than the six weeks Cherry had been out of the Community. If I wasn't careful, she'd be getting cocky and I had no idea at all of how to deal with an over-confident child who was just discovering what it was like to be a teenager out in the world. My turn to be frightened.

I pinned on a smile, picked up my courage and walked over to where they were sitting.

"Hi."

They both looked up. Cherry beamed. No other word for it. "Humility! How did your meeting go? Did I tidy up right? I borrowed your clothes; you don't mind, do you?"

"She probably didn't notice," Millie pointed out. "And if you found something wearable on that barge you've got real talent, girl. Have a seat." I assumed that bit was meant for me and, feeling a bit dizzy, sat. "Well? You going to tell us about this meeting?"

I considered. "Some. It went OK. How much has Cherry told you?"

"Enough to confirm that there are some creatures around who should never have been allowed to see the light of day. Which I already knew."

"Sums it up," I agreed. "Should finish this afternoon. Cherry, I need you to be clear of the marina, or stay below on the *Pig*, all afternoon. Can you do it?"

"Why? I want to help you. I want to make sure those people never try to hurt any of the street kids again. I *knew* some of the ones who went missing."

"And the only damn thing you can do to help Humility is to stay safe," Millie said. "Don't whine, kid. You're alive and looking good. Not many people who've been the road you've just run can say the same. And you owe your aunt for that. She wants you to stay clear, you stay. Understood?"

I could have hugged Millie. Cherry stared, mouth open. The pout that had been about to develop was aborted. She looked from Millie to me. Shut her mouth. Nodded. "OK." It was subdued.

"Good kid. You can hang with me if you don't get under my feet and don't try to tell me my job." Cherry opened her mouth again to protest. "Oh yes, you do. But not this afternoon. We might get to watch the fireworks later."

The prospect cheered her up.

"Now that's settled," I said with relief, "can I get something to eat while you tell me what's going on with you two?"

"Done."

Lunch was good, but I was convinced there was some pact between my old friend and my new niece to keep me out of whatever it was they were plotting. Didn't much mind. My own plots were taking up enough of my attention, and I had a packet to collect.

74

I picked up the packet. It weighed light for something that was going to hang two murderers out to dry. Gus passed it over with a sneer, which I ignored. Because he didn't try to deny it existed or pretend I didn't have authority to collect it, just said, "This isn't a delivery office," I guessed Byron had handed it in himself.

He'd be glad to get back to his remotes. Cyberworld. Dealing with me was all too rough and real, not to mention the risks of contact with salt water. Was he regretting the deal he'd offered in Tom Lee's two nights ago? Probably.

Instructions were clear enough. Designed for a dumb rat or a techno-idiot. Basically: wear it. Body heat kept it charged. Vox activated it. If I wanted vid I could wear it as a pin and keep it open. Direct feed to Byron so no limited storage capacity.

The pin was in the shape of a pig.

I wore it.

All around me the marina was bustling. Drives came on line, bunting was taken down by the few who thought they could hoist sail and still stay in parade line, others were freshening up by adding yet more flags. Lines were singled up. Marina staff appeared as if by some conjuring trick: wise move, making sure at least casting off would go smoothly and in the right order. I almost regretted that the *Pig* would be one of the few boats staying in her berth while everyone else went out on parade.

No time for sentiment. Picked up my sack, patted my new pin, and went off to have fun on *The Happy Family.*

Stephen was on deck, coiling a line and looking nautical in a peaked cap and white shoes. Amanda was on the bridge. Looking ornamental. I assumed every detail of the parade, the proximity alerts, the tidal info, the place in the line, had all been programmed in. Dockside staff could have tended lines. They could have been sitting back in deck chairs with a cool glass of something in their hands. Fussing around looked better. More seamanlike.

Stephen saw me. Raised a hand and stepped back from the warp he was handling. "Humility. Welcome aboard. Amanda and I can do with some expert help." He laughed to show he didn't mean it. We both knew the boat could do all the work.

I hadn't been absolutely certain their invitation to me had really meant I'd be their only guest. Extra company could have wrecked everything. I was relieved to realise that there was no one else around.

"Thanks. Looks like we've got a good day for it." Talk about the weather if you can't think of anything else polite to say.

In fact it *was* a good day for it. A light breeze to cut the heat, but nothing that would do more than ruffle the water's surface. Bright sunlight. I know all about UV burns – with my red hair and light skin, I'd better – but I had good screens on every exposed surface. In other circumstances, it would have been a delight.

The cruiser eased away from her berth with impeccable manners. Fenders not needed. Proximity sensors working overtime, making constant minute adjustments so we were never within a metre of any of the thirty other boats joining the decorous scramble for the lock gate. I guessed almost every other boat had the same equipment. Made it almost dull, but saved a lot of lawsuits for damages.

It took about an hour, following the maroon which announced the start of things. We left the marina in due order, the yacht ahead of us hoisting a multi-coloured butterfly sail which wouldn't do much for its speed but looked gorgeous. Sails were going up all along the line which was heading downstream slowly against a tide at half-flood.

Astern, a black-hulled hi-performance cruiser idled in our wake. Its presence was comforting, once I'd digested the shock of seeing Morgan at the helm. He'd a cap on and wasn't obviously recognisable, but I knew him at once. I wondered how many of his security staff were down below in what must be limited accommodation. The only others I could see on deck were a man and a woman, dressed as casually as he was, handling lines with an easy efficiency not quite typical of most of the flotilla.

The plan was to move out in a line into the Solent. Circle so that the local and national vids could get some good shots and individual vessels could pose for their own special images and holos – to be displayed on board or in board rooms – and return to the river around dusk, just before high water. We'd moor up in time for the fireworks, which would look much better illuminating the river and Port rather than the mud banks which would be exposed at low water.

Gave Morgan credit for planning this event for evening tides.

My own planning was slightly looser. I helped Stephen tidy up the minimal mess left from our departure, agreed with Amanda that the celebrations this week – most of which I'd missed – had been fabulous, and admired the boat's skill in handling herself. Which meant it was time for a long cold drink. Nothing as vulgar as champagne for them, which was a pity, but the white burgundy was good. My own lack of enthusiasm for white wine meant I'd have no problem keeping a clear enough head over the next few hours.

We pointed out familiar landmarks to each other as we cruised down river. Commented on the other boats in the parade, exclaimed over a flight of oyster catchers flying overhead. Watched the Isle of Wight emerge in the distance. Agreed it had been a good idea to declare it a nature reserve; a pity it had to be a prison island too. Still, it kept the criminals away from people like us.

I wondered what Byron was thinking as he absorbed all that from his secure office in the Port.

"Did I see you had a visitor?" Stephen asked in a lull.

I blinked. He must have seen Cherry this morning. Frantic calculations to work out whether he could make any link between her and Ardco. No. So I smiled. "Yes, my niece. She's visiting for a few days."

"You should have brought her along," Amanda protested. "We'd have asked her if we'd known you were going to have company. She looked a nice little thing." I hoped I had a chance to pass that one on to Cherry.

"I'm afraid she's not really interested in sailing. She's going to spend the afternoon in the mall, shopping. I hope she won't have cleared out my credit before we get back." Smiled to show I didn't mean it. "She only decided to visit because she heard there were going to be real fireworks."

"Yes, that's quite a coup for the Vincis. You know Morgan, don't you?" A probing question from Amanda. Could be innocent. Trying to place me in the social order. Or trying to gauge how much fuss would be made if I were to disappear?

"Sort of," I admitted. "I told you I'd been involved with

261

something linked to him a few weeks back, and he asked me to look into your friend's death." So I was really just an employee. Waste-disposal level.

Appropriately sad expressions on both their faces. They'd been reminded of Poor Andy. "We don't like to keep asking, but we do need to think about funeral arrangements." Stephen looked uncomfortable: this wasn't the right time and place to talk of such things. "Have you any idea when they'll release him?"

I could be reassuring. "I'm sure it'll be in the next day or two. I put my report in to Morgan this morning and I know he'll sign off on it as soon as he's free from all these festivities."

A little tension that hadn't been apparent eased.

"That's good news. After all, the only thing we can do for him now is to make sure he has a decent funeral."

I thought of the girl in the darkened cabin. I thought of Sal's two missing girls, I thought of the unnumbered children who had had no funerals, whose organs had been harvested to fund this cruiser and the wine I was drinking. It tasted like vinegar. The bright day was suddenly garish.

"You're good friends." Bloody murderers.

We progressed at stately speed down the river and into the open water of the Solent. Vid units buzzed us occasionally. We smiled, waved. Everyone having a good time. Not sailing as I knew it, more a performance. The performers were loving it. I wondered when I'd get the chance to bring up the subject of smuggling.

75

The free sailing was fun to watch. The light breeze allowed the yachts to show off their new sails as they tacked elegantly across the water. There were a couple of misguided moments from an inexperienced crew when everything suddenly tangled. I've been there myself, but seldom been filmed doing it. They recovered themselves, laughing to show they were good sports, to display their colours and lines. There were even a couple of yachts I'd really like to have been out on. Had a feeling Morgan would have felt the same: today was business, but I knew he preferred sail to power.

I spent some time not looking at the black cruiser astern of *The Happy Family*. Amanda and Stephen seemed to have dismissed it as rather small and irrelevant and I didn't want anything to change their minds. When they waved at acquaintances from the marina, I waved too. When they asked me about the *Pig* I told them about the storm damage, admitted that, even if she'd been seaworthy, I'd have found her hard to handle by myself in such close order as this procession.

"So you're really doing me a favour by letting me join you," I admitted. They liked that. "Are you going home tomorrow?" I wondered.

Amanda smiled. "We think so. It's been fun to take time out, but living on the boat for more than a few days is a bit cramped for us. We've a little business to take care of in Sutton first."

"At Ardco," I assumed, showing I remembered their kindness and the tour they'd arranged.

"That's it." Stephen frowned slightly. "I think there's some glitch in their com unit. We've had message contact, but haven't been able to make live contact with Simon this morning." That was good news. He shrugged. "Nothing serious, just wanted an update on a ferry sailing."

"But the com message confirmed it," Amanda put in, "so we'll just go by in the morning if the system's still out and check that everything's going well."

"You're very hands-on." Hoped I sounded approving. Didn't want to think of her hands and that cargo.

She laughed. "I'm afraid so. It's our new baby and we want it to do well."

"Looked good when you took me round." I was reassuring. "Perhaps Simon knew you were going to be tied up today and decided to take a free day for himself – hoped you wouldn't notice?"

They looked at each other, thoughtful. "Could be," said Stephen. "He's usually as keen as we are, that's why we like him, but sometimes personal stuff does come up."

"We'll have to talk to him about it, if that's what happened." Stern Amanda, wouldn't tolerate slack behaviour from her employee. Not as tolerant as Soft Stephen.

"I wasn't quite clear what your cargoes were," I wondered. "All sounded very confidential." But you can tell me, can't you?

Apparently not. Amanda shook her head. "They really are. It's our main advantage over the big boys."

"Discretion. You know." Stephen smiled and topped up my nearly full glass.

It occurred to me that drinking on board this boat might not be good for my health. Tipped the glass to my mouth, let them think I was sipping gently. Put it down untouched.

"Of course. I hope your friend's death doesn't lead to any complications for you in that direction."

Amanda's glass went down with a little click. "What do you mean?"

I waved a hand, vaguely. "Oh, you know. Publicity. Speculation. Suicide's not so common that the vids don't like to run it. And, of course, because it happened here during such a high-profile week for the Port, they're going to want to get in a dig at the Family."

"I'm sure Morgan will squash that." She didn't sound quite as certain as she wanted.

"Of course. And as long as they get the suicide verdict, it shouldn't be a problem."

"What do you mean?" That was Stephen, not looking at all relaxed now. "What else could it be?"

Amanda's eyes were hard and narrowed. I wasn't her friend any more. "She's talking about murder. I thought you said you'd put your report in to Morgan?"

"I have. Why would I have suggested murder?" I wondered.

Stephen stared. "You don't exactly hang yourself by accident, do you?"

There was a silence which stretched a little.

"I didn't tell you he'd hanged himself," I pointed out.

"The gossip's all round the place," Amanda laughed. "You know what ports are like – no secrets for long. Everyone knows Andy hanged himself."

"No." I shook my head. "They don't. If Family asks its employees – security and medics – to cloak something, it stays hidden. And Morgan didn't want a whisper about Andy to get out during the Opening. The guards on *Felicity* are 24/7, and I know they're alert."

Something in their matching expressions told me they

knew it too. They'd tried to get in to see the boat. Wanted to remove that unfinished bottle of wine? The one they'd forgotten while they were stringing him up because he'd tidied it away. Perhaps. Lied about having his codes so they could lure me in originally to play the innocent bystander, witness to their grief and shock? Mistake.

I wasn't among friends any more. Around us the yachts and cruisers still circled, displaying like birds before their mates, flaunting their beauty and their cost. Here, the attention of Amanda and Stephen was exclusively on me. I hoped Morgan wasn't allowing himself to be distracted by a pretty yacht.

"And just what have you said in your report?" Her voice was soft. Threatening.

"I'm sure Morgan will let you know." I needed to prod, to get the admission I wanted before they moved on to violence. There were only two of them and, though I was certain they could kill – and had already done so with Andy – I thought they preferred their victims passive, drugged.

They'd drugged Andy. They probably only saw the children when they'd been drugged. Never saw or heard the tears and screams and pleading. They had employees for that. Most of who didn't want to know what the end was for the girls they lifted from the streets.

"We need to get back. Now." Stephen was urgent. I'd thought he would be the first to panic.

"No, we don't. We don't want any attention at all. We stay with the parade. And meanwhile Humility can tell us just what she put in that report to Morgan and whether he's had time to read it yet." Amanda was the captain now, not the ornamental crew. I guessed that was how they worked in business, too.

"I'll tell you if you'll tell me why you killed Andy. Perhaps we can come to some arrangement." Hoped I sounded calm, as though blackmail had been what I intended all along.

Amanda relaxed fractionally. Stephen was still on the edge of panic. His knuckles were tight on the glass locked in his hand.

"Perhaps we can. Let's pretend your little fantasy has some truth in it. Why do you think we would harm someone who's been our partner for years?"

"Because your current business was making him sick? Because he'd decided he was going to put a stop to it? Perhaps even turn you in?"

They stared. Taking in that I knew, or guessed, a lot more than they'd feared. And out here, boats all round, people waving and calling to them, and the bright sunlight playing on the water, there was no escape. They didn't even know how to take the boat they'd paid for in blood out into the open sea.

"You're mad." Amanda's attempt to dismiss what I'd said failed. The horror on Stephen's face and the tremor of her hands betrayed her.

"No. But I think you must be. How else could you have done it? No amount of credit's worth what you've done." I could hardly bear to look at them. "I wish I believed in the hell my father used to preach about, because then I'd know you'd get what you deserve." The conviction in my voice surprised even me.

"What are you talking about? Andy killed himself. You told me so yourself."

"That's what it looked like," I nodded. "Except for the drugs in his system and the rope he couldn't have fixed himself and the note no one can prove he wrote."

"He must have drugged himself so he didn't feel the pain," she protested. "There's no proof he didn't hang himself."

"I think you'll find you're not quite as clever as you thought. Andy was murdered. And the chances are it was done by the hand which gave me the same drug as he was given. Leaving that glass of wine out on the *Pig* to make people think I'd been drinking was a mistake."

That stopped them both for a moment.

Around us laughter and shouts rang across the water. Morgan was a black shape twenty metres astern.

"And it's not just Andy you have to answer for," I reminded them. "Selling your own body parts is a desperate business, but legal. Taking children off the streets and selling them off for spare parts is not only criminal, it's obscene. And you *will* have to pay for that."

Stephen's head was in his hands. Amanda was still trying to bluff. "You don't know what you're talking about."

"Ardco's little smuggling operation."

"Smuggling? If any smuggling's being done through our business it's Simon who's responsible. He's the man on site." Her eyes narrowed. "Of course! That's why he's out of contact today – he's heard you've been poking around and you've scared him off. You've been so clumsy, you'll probably never catch him, whatever he's been doing. And if that's what's happened I'll make sure you pay for it, for ruining our business." She sounded almost as though she'd convinced herself. Perhaps a capacity for self-deception went with what they'd done. Then she spoiled it, adding, "And I don't believe it's anything as disgusting as you're suggesting."

"Simon's not on site because he's in custody," I

explained. "Your last cargo was intercepted – and the girls will testify."

In the sunlight, she looked pale. "No one will believe them."

"It is hard to believe," I admitted. "Do you want to tell me how it happened? What changed between the time you shut Perry's down and the time you started Ardco?"

In their faces I saw the growing understanding of how much I knew. Amanda was still defiant. Stephen had sagged. The body-sculpting that made him look only a few years older than me suddenly showed. Behind the youthful skin on his face, eyes that were desperately tired and sick stared out.

"Perry's was almost a hobby at first. Something for me to do. Amanda had her work."

"I was the best body-sculptor in my area." And she'd practised on her partner. She was right: she was good.

"So you started trading goods – and girls."

He wanted to find a way to make it sound OK. Sound like just a type of merchandise. Knew I wasn't going to be convinced. "They were street girls. What did they expect?"

"They were children." It wasn't a question. There was no real need for the Ardco business to have focused on girls, especially young girls – any healthy tissue would have done. There had to have been some special reason they'd got into that particular market. "And you liked children."

He moistened dry lips. The gesture had nothing to do with the heat of the day, nor did the sweat on his forehead.

"They knew what was happening. I looked after them. They went to people who would look after them, give them more of a life than they had on the street."

"You were a procurer who sold them on to pimps. And you made money at it."

"A lot of money." Amanda wasn't panicking, which made me wary. "Enough for me to give up surgery and look a little more closely at Stephen's toys and the market he was playing in."

"And you knew there was an organ shortage. Here and across the water."

"That's it. If you're rich enough, you can have the tissue engineers grow you something of your own. If you're in a hurry or not quite so rich, you need someone to donate. All most people want to know about their new heart or liver or pancreas is that it comes from someone like them. Some," she added as though she were discussing a preference for freshly picked fruit, "will pay even more if they can see the donor and watch the health checks being done." On the living victim.

"What about synthetics? Couldn't you have gone into that market, helped make them more acceptable?"

"Why? No one wants synthetics, they want real organs. Human organs. I just supplied them."

"No, you didn't. You stole them. You *harvested* them. You traded in lives."

"It's a business. And no one cared. I took the girls to France because people are just as desperate there and, as long as there were no reports of their own girls disappearing, they didn't care what the source was. Simple, really."

"And profitable." I'd seen the accounts.

"Oh yes. And Stephen still had the chance to indulge himself from time to time. It worked well." Stephen was trying not to hear, not to believe in what was happening.

"Until Andy couldn't take it."

A mix of rage and scorn touched her. "Yes. He didn't mind the prostitution. Then he saw some of the kids on a ferry. Said he hadn't known they were that young. Told us we had to stop. Go back to the other business. As if we could just sell off the ferries and go back into domestic transport without making a loss. He said he'd have to tell someone if we didn't have an exit strategy this week." She took a thirsty drink – water, as usual. "So I decided that he'd have to be the one to exit."

Logical. "And now you're going to have to go out of business after all. Morgan will have people ready to pick you up when we dock."

"*No!* It's not going to happen. I won't let it. You're the problem – if it weren't for you no one would care what was happening to those kids."

"You'd be surprised." Meera and Luna and Jennifer and Sal, even my mother in her way. They'd all cared enough to take risks, to put themselves out. They hadn't known what was happening, but they'd cared that children were being terrified, were disappearing. *Suffer the little children.*

"If you're not here, they won't be able to prove anything. Who'll believe what a street kid says? They're all liars."

"Morgan won't need proof. He's Family."

"So he's probably done the same thing. All Families make their money in crime, you know that. He'll under-stand, might even want to buy in." Desperation coloured her voice, made her words tumble over each other.

"I doubt it." She wasn't saying anything I hadn't thought. Crime and vast wealth tend to go together, whatever the original intent. I just didn't think Morgan would have anything do with something so vile. He'd kill, but I didn't think he was an abuser.

Amanda wasn't listening. "Get her, Stephen!"

He was slow. Too wrapped in his own thoughts to grab me while he had any chance. I dodged, kicked out and

271

heard a grunt. Pulled away when I felt Amanda's arms round me to hold me still for whatever she wanted Stephen to do. When I managed to turn in her grip I felt the slash of her nails down my cheek.

That really made me angry. I hit her as hard as I could, heard her fall back and didn't hang around to see what happened. I was over the guard rail on the flying bridge and down on to the lower deck. Scrabbling sounds on the ladder told me one of them was following. Amanda. Something in her hand that looked too like a syringe.

I prepared for a dive overboard.

76

The acrobatics weren't needed, and I didn't have to get wet.

Morgan must have moved as soon as the talk shifted from explanation to threats. Two men and a woman were boarding even as I crouched at the gunwale. Morgan had the cruiser alongside and was holding it in position as though it was the easiest thing in the world to keep close station on a boat which was rocking under the antics of its crew and following a choreographed programme of circles and figures in relatively open water.

In other circumstances he'd have been enjoying himself.

Stephen hardly put up a fight. Amanda kept kicking and struggling and lashing out with her claws but Morgan's staff weren't worried about manhandling a woman. Once she'd laid open the back of someone's hands, they put her in tight restraints which they fastened to one of the chairs bolted to the deck. They collected the syringe and put it carefully away in a locker by the helm.

"Want us to take the boat back in?" the woman asked, looking as though she'd enjoyed a little light exercise.

Thought about it. Shook my head. "No. I'll bring her in – it's almost all automated, anyway. Pre-set course and timing to fit in with Lloyd's program. She can probably do it all on her own. You get back on your boat. Pick up these two after the fireworks when no one's interested in what's happening. They'll keep for a couple of hours."

She nodded. Understood that publicity which couldn't be controlled was almost as bad as butchery. I heard a splash. Looked over to starboard where a press vid unit had abruptly lost power and landed in the water. Salt water was bad for technology. And the wrong sort of publicity was bad for the Family. I assumed the drone had been the one which had been buzzing over *The Happy Family* while Amanda and I were squabbling.

Byron had his uses.

The rest of the parade was odd. I stood on the bridge pretending to navigate while the boat quietly got on with her program. On the lower deck Amanda glared from her chair and tested her restraints. Beside me, Stephen had barely protested at his own imprisonment. He didn't say anything, unless you counted a muttered, "It wasn't our fault," which I ignored on the grounds that I was too tired for pointless arguments and didn't want to talk to him anyway.

Eventually a flare went up signalling time to re-form and return upriver. Everyone had enjoyed a meaningless day out. Except that it hadn't been meaningless: they'd had some fresh air, been noticed, enjoyed each other's company. It wasn't such a bad way to pass the time. Unless you had company whose perfect exteriors barely masked the rot inside.

Dusk was creeping in, lengthening shadows, turning the glare of sunlight into something rose-tinged and gentle. On the banks the greens of field, trees and parkland deepened into something not far from black and the glittering grey-blue of the water dulled. Morgan's project, Midway Port, gleamed in the approaching dark. Looked almost beautiful. Points of light beginning to glow against the turquoise-tinted sky; the shapes of sheds and mall and offices becoming silhouettes. Even the yellow glare from the distant city looked mellow.

I wished I were watching it from my own deck.

As we neared the last sweep down towards the marina I realised Amanda's bound figure on the lower deck just might attract the sort of attention Morgan preferred to avoid. In my position she'd have found some drug to knock me out or make me look happy and smiling until the celebrations were over.

I don't carry drugs. A shot of caf wasn't going to do the job. I needed her out of sight down below in the saloon, or up here on the flying bridge where I could watch her.

Below seemed easiest. Safest. Until I thought about the neighbours calling across to ask if she was OK.

One of the things I'd been glad to leave behind when I ran away was neighbours, I remembered. So I had to persuade her up here. Left the boat to steer itself and went down to her.

"You're coming up to the bridge and you're going to keep very quiet," I told her.

"Why should I?"

There are some people you want to smack. "Because otherwise I'll put you in the saloon. Gagged. And tied up very tightly. I really don't have time or energy for you to make a fuss."

"And if I say I'm not going to move?"

I looked from her to the water. "I think I'm strong enough to dump you overboard. Morgan's just behind. He might haul you out."

She looked astern. Until then she hadn't understood who was in the black cruiser, except that it had produced heavies when needed. Now the man at the helm lifted his cap. Stared at her without expression. She shivered. Seemed to shrink back into the chair.

"I'll go up top with you," she muttered.

I trusted her like a snake. Undid the restraints, freed her

from the chair, re-tied the restraints in front of her and shoved her to make her unbalanced way up the ladder as best she could.

On the bridge I pushed her down into the spare chair next to Stephen.. Nowhere to fix the restraints but I hobbled her ankles to the post which bolted chair to deck. If she wanted to fall out of the chair on to her sculpted face, that was her choice.

She looked over at Stephen. He was out of it. Eyes blank, unfocused. Looked vaguely at her. "Amanda? What's happening?"

"Shut up," she hissed. "Don't say another word until we get ashore, then we'll call the lawyers. Piracy. Isn't that what they still call it when someone takes over your boat? I'll bet Morgan knows all about piracy."

With his name he ought to. Wouldn't bank on it. Wondered if I'd ever get round to asking him. I let her rant and threaten until it was tiring.

"We're into the marina in about five minutes. You can watch the pretty fireworks with me, and be quiet. Or you can watch them with whatever this is in your veins. And I hope it's really unpleasant."

I held up the syringe she'd threatened me with. Sudden stillness. Her expression said it was deeply unpleasant. I didn't think Amanda was the sort of woman who'd opt out: she'd keep fighting with nails and lawyers and whatever weapons she could find until someone put a stop to her. I didn't trust her nod of agreement any more than she trusted me. Kept the syringe in my hand. Thought I'd better watch her as much as the fireworks.

77

Marina staff took the lines. Moored *The Happy Family*. I stayed where I was. Watched the other boats come in, make fast. Heard the chatter and the laughter and the excitement: they'd had their splendid sail, they'd looked good on screen, it had all gone smoothly and now they could pour the champagne, set out the drugs of choice, lie back in their loungers and watch the climax of the Opening: the grand firework display.

It was like looking through glass. I saw and heard it all as though it were a back projection for the reality of the two-metre-square area of this boat's flying bridge. In the foreground: me, standing foursquare watching the two other players, both in chairs. Stephen, given up and sorry for himself, lost to reality. Amanda, restless eyes checking everything around, muscles shifting fractionally as she tugged at the restraints. Smiles for the people who called up to her as false as the surgery which had shaped the perfect mouth. Planning the next move: coax, bribe, seduce Morgan. Persuade him it was a mistake. Or all Stephen's fault. Trade publicity against a few worthless lives. Use her profits for a good lawyer. Bargain it down to a minor offence. *Make it go away.* The options flickered across her face as though it were a screen. She wasn't thinking surrender, defeat.

She didn't even glance at Stephen. The loser.

There was music in the background. Something noisy and old and joyous and designed for outdoor playing. Speakers drifted discreetly overhead. Strings and trumpets and drums. I hoped Cherry had a good view. If she was still with Millie, of course the view would be good – and she'd have the debatable benefit of Millie's commentary. Wondered if the girls at Jennifer's, or down with Sal, were watching on-screen. If they'd seen me in the scans of the boats coming back in and wondered what was happening.

An explosion of noise and light across the river from what had once been a spoil heap. *Oohs!* and *Aahs!* from the boats and the crowds on the shore as golden streams fountained upwards and cascaded down, each flickering spark dying in a burst of white light. It had begun.

Spinning circles of fire, soaring rockets whose flames ended in explosions which seemed to make the sky shake. Magnesium white so blinding it left an afterglow of red on the retina. The smell of cordite filling the air and a slow drift of smoke turning the river into a thing of mystery.

I had seen flares before, never fireworks, not live. I was as transfixed as everyone else, held by a primitive awe and delight at the beauty and the wonder and surprise. After each burst of light, the darkness around deepened.

There was a pause and then it began to build: a platform of pure white light, overlaid with gold, then green, each stage rising higher. Everyone knew it would end in the biggest explosion of all. The climax. When I looked away to watch my hosts, my eyes were dazzled by the afterglow. Perhaps that was why I missed it.

Missed Amanda's lurch from the chair and the dive towards a locker I hadn't looked in. The grab and turn even as she fell, still tethered, to the deck.

I didn't miss the way she came up, twisting awkwardly. Or the gun gripped in both her hands as she steadied her aim against her own momentum.

I hurled myself sideways. Knew the muzzle was tracking my movement as I hit the deck which lurched under me as the wake of a passing dinghy slopped against the hull. Felt my shoulder go numb and wondered how badly I'd been hit.

The shot itself was lost in the detonation of fifty rockets.

78

Keep moving, girl!

I was trying. I didn't know how much blood was leaking out of me but at least I wasn't tethered to a chair. I scrambled sideways, hoping my left arm wouldn't collapse under me. Threw myself at her with no expertise, just a desperate lunge to stop her firing again. The hand gripping the gun was twisted under us. Digging into my ribs. She swore and tensed. She'd pull the trigger if she could. Take us both down if she had to.

I did the only thing left to me: I stabbed her with the syringe. Wasn't very careful with it and hoped it hurt. She collapsed, boneless.

I shoved the dead weight off me. Found I could use the arm after all. Shoulder still hurt. I reached up with my right hand. Touched the shoulder carefully. No sudden bolt of agony. Looked at my fingers. No splash of red. Straightened the arm. Slowly. It worked. Nothing broken. Just a throbbing numbness from the impact with the deck. Tomorrow there'd be a bruise. At least there'd be a tomorrow.

Then I looked at the other chair. The one that had been behind me when Amanda shot at me. Stephen hadn't moved. If it weren't for the dark bloom in the centre of his chest, you'd never know anything had happened.

The small, squat gun had fallen to the deck. I didn't touch it. Didn't know enough about guns to know how safe it was. Looked at Amanda. She wasn't dead. Didn't know how I felt about that. Dead might have been simpler but it would also be too easy. She might never understand what she'd done, but I wanted her to know how it looked to others. Wanted them to hold up a mirror to her. Tell her: *This is what you really look like.*

I waited while the echoes in my ears faded and the normal sound of human talk came back. Sober or not, everyone sounded slightly high. Talked faster than usual, hand gestures urgent. They'd remember this display for a long time, talk about it, compare future events against its standard.

Morgan had got what he wanted.

I looked at the two still figures beside me. So had I. Stephen was dead. She wasn't. She'd live to pay for what she'd done. The obscenity she'd called business, and now the knowledge she'd killed the partner who'd been almost inseparable from her. I was petty enough to hope it would hurt. Badly.

On the marina the chatter and laughter began to fade. Visitors drifted off, parties went down below to continue in greater comfort. Ashore, the crowd had thinned but there was still dancing and music. I waited.

It didn't take long. The same people who'd boarded earlier strolled past, looked up at me, waved. I waved back and they came on board as though they were just another group of revellers dropping in on friends.

They took in the scene on the bridge.

"Both dead?" That was the woman.

"Only him. She shot him. I used the syringe on her. She's been out since the end of the fireworks."

A finger against Amanda's neck. "Out cold. She'll survive." For now. The security guards exchanged glances. The woman nodded at whatever unspoken ideas they'd exchanged. Or perhaps she'd had orders through some augment I couldn't detect. "Best if we just shift the boat out of here in a couple hours, when it's gone a bit quieter. Keep her doped up – and tied up – and deal with the scene ashore. You want to come?"

Thought about it. Didn't see any point. Shook my head.

"No. I think I've seen enough for tonight. If Morgan wants to talk, tell him I'll be around in the morning. Not early. Thanks for the garbage detail."

"No problem. We heard what these have done." Looked down at them with no feeling at all in her eyes. "Scum." It seemed to be the consensus.

I took the little silver pin out of my jacket and left *The Happy Family.*

79

I was bone tired. Didn't want to go looking for anyone. Didn't feel like celebrating. You can't celebrate the end of something so unspeakable it should never have happened. Just be relieved it's over. That it won't go on happening while everyone gets on with their lives, unaware of what's being done in the next street, the next room.

Something else will take its place.

Of course. I just hoped I could be one of the unaware for a little while.

Thought for a moment of Amanda. I didn't begin to understand anything about her except her vanity. Couldn't imagine what allowed her to create something out of nightmares and use it just to accumulate credit. *All wickedness is but little to the wickedness of a woman.*

I went home to the *Pig*. Cherry could look for me there.

It wasn't Cherry who found me. It was Byron. He would have known the moment I took off his transmitter. For some reason decided to retrieve it in person. It could have waited.

"You could have waited," I told him as I opened the deck house door.

"For what?"

I held out the pin. "This."

He shook his head. "Keep it. You might need it again one day."

"That's not why you came?"

"No." He saw me waiting, said with careful patience as though it should have been obvious, "You keep the best wine around, and I've had a long day."

Something, the beginning of the return of feeling, made me want to smile. "Sit down. I've still got a few good bottles left. After that we're down to the vinegar."

"I won't stay that long."

I poured. For a moment we sat without talking, enjoying the taste of something untainted by emotions such as greed or vanity or pride. Just grapes and sunshine.

"You got it all?" I asked.

"Of course. You should have checked out that locker. She nearly killed you." An analysis of my handling of the scene, not concern for my safety.

"I know." If the boat hadn't been moving slightly, if she hadn't been off-balance. I didn't care. Wouldn't have been able to care if I'd been dead; since I wasn't, it didn't matter either.

He nodded. Irrelevant data.

After a while, he asked. "You thought any more about working with me?"

I had. "I can't see we'll agree on handling anything. Or on what's important. If I want to poke my nose into something with no profit, you're going to stop me. If you want to make it all look neat and tie up every loose end, I'm going to get pissed off by the details. I'm not interested in the sort of scam that shows up as scrambled data or whitewashed transactions. You don't like people."

"We both know our minds work differently. Barely share a common function." He lifted his glass, drank. "You could just have said no."

"But I'm not going to. I'm going to say yes." I don't know when I'd made the decision. Hadn't made it, really. Woke up knowing this fitted me. "I hated what happened here today. Hated discovering what was going on and just how vile someone can be, how inhuman. But I liked stopping it. I like knowing I'm responsible for whatever happens to her. That a few people are a bit safer. And –" I took a drink because this was the bit I didn't like admitting, even to myself – "I got a kick out of the risk."

He shuddered. "Must be the sort of thing that makes you live like you do." He gestured at his surroundings. "I suspect one of us is an alien: trouble is I can't decide which."

I looked at the level in the bottle. It might account for that uncharacteristic flight of fancy.

"You're right. Have another drink."

He did, and I did. I thought Millie must have heard, or been told, something and decided to keep Cherry away. I was glad. When I saw Byron off the boat we were both still sober because the weight of what had happened made anything else impossible, but the emotion was a lot further off.

Went to sleep in the deck-house in a bunk made up with freshly laundered sheets and blankets which had been aired and folded. My niece had her good qualities. I decided I could bear to have her around for a few days yet.

80

There was a message on my screen when I surfaced.

"No one answered your door. Saw you were asleep and didn't trust your boat not to dump us if we tried to board. Come and have caf in the mall when you surface." Millie's voice.

I wondered how hard they'd tried to get in. I hadn't even thought about giving Cherry a pass. She could have found herself swimming if she'd tried too hard. Millie probably knew enough to warn her off. Good. I rolled over and shut my eyes again.

Didn't work. Too many memories of last night. Too many loose ends which even I knew had to be tied. Find out what Morgan planned. See whether he was still willing to pay me after his obvious suicide turned into wholesale murder. Update the other girls.

And then there was Cherry.

I liked her. She'd come through OK. But I'd end up worse than my mother if she had to live here. This was my territory; guests were one thing, live-in company something I'd need to think really hard about. But I didn't have to think at all to know thirteen-year-old girls didn't even make it to the list. She was poised between child and adult, probably about to discover just what it was like to make all her own decisions – which meant rejecting what anyone else suggested – and she didn't care about sailing. We'd kill each other.

But she couldn't go back to the Community.

Caf. I crawled out of the bunk. Went below. Showered. Remembered she really had done the chores. A point in her favour. I'd keep her for a week. Hell, I'd pay her to come in once a week, but that didn't solve the problem that threatened to make my head ache.

When I went out on deck, I couldn't help noticing the gap on the marina where *The Happy Family* had moored. I hadn't even heard them take her away. She was now probably in the shed alongside the *Felicity*. Uneasy neighbours.

I needed to finish last night's business before I faced Cherry. Called Morgan. Was told by a drone voice that he was in the boat sheds. Would see me there.

He was looking up at the hull of *The Happy Family*.

"That's a boat that deserves to be re-named," I said.

He looked across at me, back at the boat. "I don't want to have it in my Port any longer than I must. I'm going to hand her and her owner over to the public authorities. This is one crime that can be dealt with by them, and I think she'll like public gaol even less than a Family facility." He couldn't bring himself to speak Amanda's name.

"What about publicity for the Port when it's reported?" I asked.

"Should be containable. And, this once, I don't much care. As long as that woman spends the rest of her life in the most uncomfortable prison there is, I'll be satisfied."

And a little Family influence should ensure that.

"It may not be a long life, in those circumstances."

"I don't mind." Neither did I. He turned to look at me. "This wasn't quite what I expected when I asked you to look into a suicide." I shrugged in a 'what can you do about it?' sort of way. "You took a lot of chances. Did something that made a difference. You should be proud."

I thought about that. Apart from astonishment at a

Family member saying something like that to me, I didn't feel much. "Difficult to be proud when it touches something that disgusting."

"True." He turned back to contemplate the cruiser. "I've passed the credit to your account. Any repairs to your barge are compliments of the yard."

I stared. Managed to mutter thanks. Decided that I'd spent enough time with aristos. Needed something more down to earth.

81

The mall was clean and tidy but had a sort of morning-after look to it. Not exactly hung over, just unfocused. It wasn't busy. Most of last night's revellers were either still asleep or had drifted away altogether. Back to their real lives. Away from Morgan's fantasy – which was probably going to be every bit as successful as he'd planned.

I thought about my credit account. Decided I could afford a chart. Was headed in that direction when I saw Cherry staring through the window of one of the fashion outlets. Not wistful. Critical. Couldn't make up my mind what that meant.

"Hi, Cherry. Millie look after you OK?"

"Humility! You're awake! Weren't the fireworks mag? You didn't miss them, did you?"

"No. I saw them. Had a great view."

She looked hard at me, older than her years for a moment. "And you sorted out the people behind what was happening to those girls." Not a question.

She might be too young for the truth, but she'd lived with it anyway. Knowledge like that doesn't go away. She deserved to know how it ended. "Yes. One of them's dead – shot by the other one. She's in custody."

Thought about it. "Good. Hope she's hurting." Suddenly she hugged me. I don't do hugs, don't often get that close, and it startled me. Moved me, too, so that I found myself hugging her back and felt my eyes prickle. "I'm glad you're OK," she muttered into my jacket.

"So am I." I held her away slightly so that I could look into her face, let her know I meant what I was saying.

"I'm also glad you're safe. And that you came here, and I found you."

Complications about where she was going to live were less important than that truth.

"Isn't that nice? Now what about that bloody caf?" You can always rely on Millie to rescue you from an emotional situation.

"Good point. Lead me to it."

She led, I followed, with Cherry bouncing alongside us, re-living the fireworks and the evening spent with Millie. She'd had a good time. And I guessed I was deep in Millie's debt.

The caf was hot and strong and black and I needed it. Felt the kinks and tension of the past week begin to ease. Realised that I could get on with my life, complications and all. Get the *Pig* hauled and repaired. Go sailing.

Talk about crime with Byron. But not for while yet.

"So how much of last night do I want to know about?" Millie demanded.

"Not much. The baddies are dead or in Vinci care. No one spoiled Morgan's party, which was a great success."

"You're telling me." More than a hint of smugness. "Fireworks were really great: the perfect end. Won't get a chance to set that up again any time soon, but the calls are stacking up. Business," she decided, "is looking good. Very good."

"So it should. You've done a great job and I hope you're charging Morgan a really painful amount of credit."

"Agonising," she confirmed. Put her cup down and settled back in her chair. "Which leaves just one little item to be settled."

"What's that?" Did I care?

"What you charging for your niece?"

"*What?*"

Cherry was looking smug. Millie grinned. "You're the nearest thing to a guardian she's got round here, aren't you?"

"Yes." I was really cautious this time. "So?"

"So I told you I was looking for an apprentice and might take on someone younger this time."

"Millie. She's thirteen and has no idea at all about what goes where in this world." She also didn't know much about the way Millie's life worked.

"So she's not been influenced or had time to get into bad habits. I'm serious, Humility." I looked hard, realised she was. Started listening properly. "I know she's still a child…"

"I'm not!"

"Shut up, Cherry." Unison from both of us.

"But she's got the eye. She's a natural. She's obviously also too independent, a pain in the neck, and probably heterosexual. But we can work round those details – and a couple of them might change."

"Why would they? All except the last describe you, and you haven't changed. Are you sure about this? And what about her education? Where would she live?"

"I've got all the education I…" We both looked at her. She shut up.

"Details. She'll need training and a place, I know that. But she wants this. We talked about it last night. She can always run away to you again if she has to, but this will suit us both. And *don't* tell me you think she wants to live on your barge."

I looked at Cherry. Leaning forward in her seat. Eager. Uncertain. Both hands clutching each other. Excitement not quite suppressed. "This is really what you want?"

"*Yes.*" It was a breath as much as a word. Her life's breath. It mattered that much.

And it got me off the hook. That's why I was worried. Did I want this for Cherry because it gave me an excuse to be selfish? I looked at her again. She'd never glowed at the idea of living on board the *Pig*.

I nodded. "Seems like I'll have to look out for a replacement cabin girl and cleaner, then. If this is what you want, Cherry, go for it. It's your choice."

I discovered it was possible to have a celebration in a half-empty mall with nothing more intoxicating than caf and hot chocolate and assorted pastries. On the whole, it felt good. Peculiar, but good.

Epilogue

I stood in the small white room. Byron was there. So was Morgan. I'd told Cherry not to come, but she was there too with Millie beside her. At the back, keeping well clear of anyone who looked like Family, was Sal. None of us had said anything to her about the fact that Ardco's yard had gone up in flames two nights ago. Jennifer had brought someone with her, a girl I recognised.

The man at the front spoke about innocence. He spoke of the kindness of people, of love triumphant over suffering. He spoke about rest and peace and the end of pain.

Then he gave some unseen signal and the small box slid slowly away through the screen which showed a holo of green fields and blue skies.

I didn't know her name. But a promise is a promise.

More action-packed crime novels from Crème de la Crime

Personal Protection
Tracey Shellito

ISBN: 0-9547634-5-9

Lapdancers at Blackpool's top erotic nightspot are being targeted, but the local police don't seem to care.

Randall McGonnigal, five foot five of packed muscle and a bodyguard, cares a lot. She's determined to track down the pervert who raped Tori, her exotic dancer lover.

Randall soon unearths murky secrets from the club's membership list – but she has to beat off attackers outside the club, and it becomes plain that she's getting too close. As she battles with her own dark side as well as the suspects who emerge from the woodwork, she lays her life on the line to protect the woman she loves – but will it be enough?

Dead Old
Maureen Carter

ISBN: 0-9547634-6-7

Blood-spattered daffodils stuffed in a dead woman's mouth: random violence by a callous gang - or hatred and revenge?

West Midlands Police think Sophia Carrington's murder is the latest attack by teen yobs – but Detective Sergeant Bev Morriss won't accept it.

To her the bizarre bouquet is a chilling message which will point straight to the killer – but Bev's reputation has hit rock bottom and no one is listening. Even Oz, her lover, has doubts.

The glamorous new boss buries Bev in paperwork and insults, and Birmingham's most gritty detective rebels.

Then the killer decides Bev's family is next…

Another gritty mystery for Bev Morris, Carter's hard-nosed female detective.

No Help for the Dying Adrian Magson

ISBN: 0-9547634-7-5

Everyone thought Katie Pyle died ten years ago – but her newly murdered body has just been found.

Katie's baffling disappearance was Riley Gavin's first assignment as an investigative journalist, so Riley has to find out where had the girl been all those years, why she vanished, and what drove her away from a loving family?

More dead runaways make Riley realise there is more to it than drugs.

Who is behind The Church of Flowing Light? Why has a former colleague of Riley's also vanished? And why is Riley being watched? Riley and former military cop Frank Palmer follow the trail into the London subways and the highest levels of society.

The second fast-moving adventure in Magson's popular Gavin/Palmer series..

A Kind of Puritan

Penny Deacon

ISBN: 0-9547634-1-6

Jon was nobody – no money, no influence. So who killed him and dropped him in the river?

Bodies are bad for business, so when one is dredged up the Midway Port developers want it buried. Deep. But Humility found the body and she's not going to let it go – not until she knows who killed the guy everyone said was harmless.

She's a low-tech woman in a hi-tech world and no one wants to give her any answers. But with her best friend's job on the line, a series of 'accidents' at the Port, and the battered barge she calls home threatened with seizure, she's not going to give up.

The mystery leads her to parts of the city where people kill for the cost of a meal and it's dangerous to get involved. When she has to seek help from the local crime boss she knows his price is likely to be high.

It's a world where she's not sure anyone is who they claim to be, and one death leads to another… and the next one could be hers!

Praise for *A Kind of Puritan*:

A subtle and clever thriller...
   – The Daily Mail

This novel manages to unnerve yet thrill, keeping a tight storyline with crisp descriptions and frightening visions of 2040… It's impossible to read a book of this standard without once thinking 'what if?' This is a great first title release.
   – Macavity's Mail Order

A bracing new entry in the genre ... a fascinating new author with a hip, noir voice.
   – Mystery Lovers

An amazing style coupled with an original plot. I look forward to her next.
   – Natasha Boyce, Ottakar's Yeovil

No Peace for the Wicked

Adrian Magson

ISBN: 0-9547634-2-4

Old gangsters never die – they simply get rubbed out. But who is ordering the hits? And why?

Hard-nosed female investigative reporter Riley Gavin is tasked to find out. Her assignment follows a bloody trail from a south coast seafront to the Costa Del Crime – and sparks off a chain of murders.

Riley and ex-military cop Frank Palmer uncover a web of vendettas, double-crosses and hatred in an underworld at war with itself for control of a faltering criminal empire.

The story soon gets too personal as Riley dodges bullets, attack dogs and psychotic thugs – and suddenly facing a *deadline* takes on a whole new meaning…

Praise for *No Peace for the Wicked*:

A real page turner… a slick, accomplished writer who can plot neatly and keep a story moving…
- Sharon Wheeler, Reviewing the Evidence website

…a hugely enjoyable roller-coaster of a thriller… adrenalin and heart-racing action… highly charged and explosive end…
  Macavity's Mail Order

A hard-hitting debut…
  Mystery Lovers

If It Bleeds
Bernie Crosthwaite

ISBN: 0-9547634-3-2

There's only one rule in newspapers: if it bleeds, it leads.

Press photographer Jude Baxendale is despatched a grisly but routine job: snapping a young woman's body in a local park. But the murdered girl is her own son's girlfriend. Nothing in her life will be the same again.

Who stabbed and mutilated Lara – and why? Who hated her enough to dump her body in full public gaze? Jude and reporter Matt Dryden begin to unravel the layers of the girl's complex past. But nothing about Lara was as it seemed…

Finding the truth will risk Jude's job, health and sanity, and place her squarely in the killer's sights.

Some deadly truths are best left uncovered.

Praise for *If It Bleeds*:

A cracking debut novel… small-town atmosphere is uncannily accurate…
the writing's slick, the plotting's tidy and Jude is a refreshingly sparky heroine.
 - Sharon Wheeler, Reviewing the Evidence website

A Certain Malice
Felicity Young

ISBN: 0-9547634-4-0

Glenroyd Ladies' College has a reputation to protect – and a charred corpse in the grounds. Who wanted the caretaker silenced? And why did they set fire to his body?

Senior Sergeant Cam Fraser has just returned to the sleepy Australian town of his youth following the death of his wife and son in a fire. The burnt body brings back ghosts and grief.

Everyone in the community has something to hide: the two young teachers who seem very close; the waspish headmistress desperate to prevent a scandal; Cliff, who runs the local volunteer fire service and has dangerous friends.

Cam is close to the truth when fire rips through the evidence. He is already in more danger than he could imagine.

Praise for *A Certain Malice*:

a beautifully written book… Felicity draws you into the life in Australia… you may not want to leave.
- Natasha Boyce, Ottakar's Yeovil

a pleasant read with engaging characters
- Russell James, Shotsmag

Working Girls   Maureen Carter

ISBN: 0-9547634-0-8

Dumped in a park with her throat slashed, schoolgirl prostitute
Michelle Lucas died in agony and terror.

Detective Sergeant Bev Morriss of West Midlands Police thought
she was hardened, but Michelle's broken body fills her with cold
fury.

This case is the one that will push her to the edge, as she struggles
to infiltrate the jungle of hookers, pimps and violent johns in
Birmingham's vice-land. But no one will break the wall of silence.

When a second victim dies, Bev knows time is running out. To win
the trust of the working girls she has to take the most dangerous
gamble of her life – out on the streets.

Praise for *Working Girls*:

*Working Girls is dark and gritty… Carter's writing has energy and bounce…
an exciting debut novel, both for Carter and new British publishing house
Creme de la Crime.*

   - Sharon Wheeler, Reviewing the Evidence website

*Fans of TV from the Bill to Prime Suspect and the racier elements of chick-
lit will love Maureen Carter's work. Imagine Bridget Jones meets Cracker…
gritty, pacy, realistic and… televisual. When's the TV adaptation going to
hit our screens?*

   - Gary Hudson from the West Midlands writing on the Amazon
   website

*A hard-hitting debut ... fast moving with a well realised character in
Detective Sergeant Bev Morriss. I'll look forward to her next appearance.*

   - Mystery Lovers